"I can't leave. I'm needed here,"

Claudia stated clearly.

Jonathon couldn't decide which disturbed him the most. The intent, almost fervent look in her eyes, or the impassioned timbre of her voice. Both were so eerie they gave him the creeps. He came to the conclusion that she was either a nut or one hell of an actress. He didn't find either option reassuring.

"Are you always so dramatic, Ms. Peppermill?"

"Claudia," she corrected. "And I suppose that did sound dramatic. Please, forgive me. Sometimes I get a little carried away."

"Why are you needed here?"

"I don't know yet."

"When will you know?"

"When it's time."

"That's encouraging."

Claudia grinned wryly at his dry tone. "You think I'm crazy."

"The thought has crossed my mind."

Dear Reader,

The New Year is starting off splendidly here at Silhouette Intimate Moments. Take our American Hero, for instance. Riley Cooper, in Marilyn Pappano's *No Retreat,* is a soldier with a soft side. When his first love walks back into his life, troublemaking son in tow, it's surrender time for this tough guy.

Laurey Bright, long a favorite with readers of the Silhouette Special Edition line, makes her first Intimate Moments novel a winner. In *Summers Past* you'll find passion, betrayal and one all-important question: Who *is* little Carley's father? Allyson Ryan's *Secrets of Magnolia House* takes a few spooky detours along the road to romance; I think you'll enjoy the ride. *Two for the Road* is the first of Mary Anne Wilson's new "Sister, Sister" duo; look for *Two Against the World,* coming soon. Joanna Marks lights up the night with *Heat of the Moment,* and Justine Davis checks in with *Race Against Time,* a tale full of secrets, crackerjack suspense and irresistible desire. In short—I don't think you'll want to miss a single one of this month's books.

As the year goes on, look for books by more of your favorite authors. Kathleen Eagle, Doreen Roberts, Paula Detmer Riggs and Marilyn Pappano are only a few of the great writers who'll be coming your way in Silhouette Intimate Moments. And then there's our Tenth Anniversary celebration in May! Be sure to join us for all the fun.

Leslie Wainger
Senior Editor and Editorial Coordinator

SECRETS OF MAGNOLIA HOUSE

Allyson Ryan

Published by Silhouette Books New York

America's Publisher of Contemporary Romance

SILHOUETTE BOOKS
300 East 42nd St., New York, N.Y. 10017

SECRETS OF MAGNOLIA HOUSE

Copyright © 1993 by Linda Kichline

ISBN: 0-373-07471-9

First Silhouette Books printing January 1993

Printed in the U.S.A.

ALLYSON RYAN

loves reading, people-watching and traveling. Starting in Colorado and working her way across the country, she finally settled in Pennsylvania with her husband and their four beloved cats. She attributes seventeen years of marital bliss to her husband's uncanny ability to remember their anniversary—one day after the eldest cat's birthday.

To Isolde Carlsen:
The best writing friend I
could have

Prologue

Claudia Peppermill bolted upright in bed, her breathing harsh and her ears ringing with the silent echo of a scream. Though her body was drenched in sweat, she felt chilled and her teeth chattered uncontrollably. She glanced frantically around her bedroom to reassure herself that the menacing shadow in her dream wasn't real—that it wasn't hovering in some dark corner ready to spring out at her. Terror was replaced by relief when her search proved that she was alone.

As she tried to pull the disturbing dream into focus, she raked a hand through her tangled hair in agitation. Had it simply been a nightmare, or was it a precognitive vision? She shivered at the thought of the shadow being real. It had been so malevolent.

Forcing herself to lie down, Claudia closed her eyes and concentrated on the dream. All her mind would give her were hazy images of a magnolia grove in full bloom. Even in this ethereal state, it was beautiful with its stately trees; their leaves a dark, shiny green and their white blossoms larger than her hand. As she meditated on the image, she visualized herself walking through the grove. The exercise worked so well that Claudia could actually smell the heady, intoxicating fragrance of the flowers and hear the harmonious buzzing of bees. Nothing could be wrong here, she assured herself. The grove held nothing but an overwhelming sense of peace.

But as her mental stroll brought her to the edge of the trees, the feeling of danger returned. *The threat wasn't in the grove, but in whatever lay beyond it!* She tried to step out of the trees, only to be met by an impenetrable force of resistance. She tried to project her mind beyond the barrier, only to find herself engulfed in cold shadow. At that moment Claudia knew that she hadn't had a nightmare. The shadow was real, and it was so vicious that her mind recoiled from it in horror.

Her teeth began to chatter again, and she curled into a fetal ball, hugging the covers tightly to her chest. All her life she'd been clairvoyant, but this was the first time she'd experienced such a frightening vision. She also knew why the shadow was so terrifying. She couldn't tell if it was physical or metaphysical; a person or a symbol. Normally her dream visions were crystal-clear.

Claudia had no idea what time she'd awakened nor how long she lay waiting for daybreak. But the moment the first ray of sunshine peeked through her window, she tossed back the covers and leaped out of bed. She had to find the magnolia grove before it was too late. The shadow was stalking someone, and if they were to survive, they needed her help.

Chapter 1

He was just there. Claudia hadn't heard him approach nor had she sensed his presence. As had been her habit since she'd moved into the guest house at Magnolia—an old southern plantation on the Mississippi River—she'd been sitting in the porch swing doing her morning meditation. When she'd opened her eyes, she'd found herself gazing at a man so handsome he took her breath away.

At first, she thought he was an illusion. But as her gaze roamed over his face, she realized that his strong, almost hawkish features were too well defined to be anything but real. His tawny hair was fashioned in the devil-may-care style of the Old South. His hazel eyes were more a honey-gold than brown, and his lips were moodily sensual. One flick of her eyes over his body—clad in navy slacks and a light blue shirt—confirmed that his shoulders were wide, while the remainder of his physique was narrow and lean.

By the time Claudia completed her assessment, she recognized him as her landlady's grandson, Jonathon Jackson Tanner, III. He populated a good number of the family photographs that filled the antebellum mansion. The pictures hadn't done him justice.

As she continued to regard him, she was intrigued by the fact that she wasn't receiving any mental emanations from him. That was a first for her. If nothing else, she should be picking up on his emotions. Since she wasn't, she supposed that was how he'd managed to sneak up on her. It also made her wary of him. She still had no idea who she was supposed to help here or where the threat was coming from. That meant she had to be suspicious of everything and everyone.

"Good morning, Mr. Tanner," she said. "We weren't expecting you until this evening."

Jonathon blinked at the woman's words, too startled for a moment to reply. When his grandmother, Adelaide, had told him she'd moved a "psychic" into the guest house rather than a full-time housekeeper as they'd agreed, he'd been convinced she'd set herself up for one of the oldest con games around. Since the legacy of Magnolia had passed on to him at his father's death, and with it the responsibility for his grandmother, he'd immediately come to the rescue. To his chagrin, trying to keep the octogenarian out of trouble was becoming the norm rather than the exception.

"How did you know my name?" he asked warily.

Claudia shrugged. "Adelaide has a million pictures of you in the house, and she's shown me every one of them. I particularly like the one of you on the bearskin rug."

"Someday I'm going to burn that damn picture," Jonathon muttered. Of all the photographs taken of him over the years, his grandmother had to have an absurd fondness for the one of him as a naked infant lying on a bearskin rug.

Claudia laughed knowingly. "You'd break Adelaide's heart if you did that, and you'd never do anything to break her heart."

"And how do you know that?" he countered.

"Because I only have to listen to Adelaide to know that you're extremely close."

For someone who claimed to be clairvoyant, she wasn't exhibiting much ability in that area. "You foresaw my arrival?"

"Not you specifically, but someone from the family."

"I see." Jonathon tucked his hands into his pockets and studied the woman. Considering her occupation—if being a con woman was an occupation—he'd expected Claudia Peppermill to be flamboyant. Instead she looked demure, almost shy. She was also extraordinarily beautiful, with black hair that tumbled halfway down her back and emphasized her huge, gray-blue eyes. Her cheeks and lips were a soft, red wine color that enhanced her creamy complexion. The pale yellow sundress that fell loosely around her slender body made her look fragile.

Jonathon sensed that the image was deceptive—there was nothing fragile about her—and as he met her direct gaze, he felt a strange sense of familiarity, almost as if he knew her. But that was absurd. Claudia Peppermill was the type of woman a man would remember meeting, even if it had only been in passing. As his gaze flicked over her again, he was caught by a sudden sensual tug of interest. He excused the unbidden response as normal. Even if she was a crook, she was a beautiful woman. Any healthy man would get a charge out of looking at her.

"You sound skeptical about my prediction, Mr. Tanner. Don't you believe in clairvoyance?" she asked. The tolerant amusement in her voice pricked at Jonathon's temper, but he quickly capped it. Anger would only put him at a disadvantage, and he was determined to maintain the upper hand in this meeting.

"Let's just say that I'm reserving judgment, Ms. Peppermill."

"Claudia," she corrected. "May I call you Jonathon?"

Jonathon would have preferred that they *not* be on a first-name basis, but he couldn't think of a polite way to refuse. If he insulted her, his grandmother would be furious, and when she was in a temper, she refused to listen to logic. That meant he was going to have to be very careful in the way he went about ousting Claudia Peppermill from the guest house.

"Feel free to call me Jonathon," he said magnanimously. "My grandmother isn't home. Do you know where she is?"

"When I told her to expect company, she hurried off to the grocery store. She should be back shortly."

"Can't you use your clairvoyance to give me a more specific time?"

Claudia pushed her foot against the porch floor, making the swing sway gently. His voice had been neutral when he'd asked the question, but his expression clearly stated that he didn't believe in her abilities. She wasn't affronted. She was accustomed to the doubting Thomases of the world and had long ago given up trying to convince them that they were wrong.

"Sorry, but my powers don't work that way."

"How do they work?"

"I receive mental vibrations," she told him.

"I see. These mental . . . vibrations, they're just there?"

"Sometimes they are, and sometimes I have to talk to a person awhile before they start coming."

"Are you getting any of these vibrations about me?"

"No."

"Too bad. I'd like a glimpse into my future, so I guess I'll have to talk with you until they start coming. How much do you charge?"

He'd delivered the question so smoothly that Claudia almost missed the underlying sarcasm in his voice. When it registered, she automatically became guarded. She also made a concerted effort to connect with his mind, but still there was nothing. She was fascinated by the aberration.

"I don't charge a set fee for a reading," she finally answered. "My clients give me what they feel the session is worth."

"So, if I consult with you, I'll only have to pay you what I think the session is worth?"

"That's right."

"And if I think it's worth nothing?"

"Then you pay nothing."

"That sounds like a haphazard way to conduct a business."

"I'm not a business, Jonathon. I'm a clairvoyant."

"A clairvoyant who makes her living giving readings."

"Right again."

"How many readings have you given my grand-mother?"

Again, the question was delivered so smoothly Claudia almost missed the sarcasm. That was what this game of twenty questions was all about. He thought she was after his grandmother's money!

She supposed she should be offended, but it wasn't the first time she'd been accused of illicit activities, and she doubted it would be the last. Besides, she was also sure that Jonathon's concern for his grandmother was based on love. She couldn't get angry with him for that. Love had been a rare commodity in her life and she valued it highly.

"I haven't given Adelaide any readings."

"I thought you predicted my arrival."

"I did, but that wasn't a reading. It was a courtesy to a friend. You know as well as I do that Adelaide doesn't like to be surprised."

"Do I detect a bit of censure?"

"A bit," Claudia agreed. "But I'm sure that the moment Adelaide realizes it's you who's come to visit, you'll be forgiven. She's forever telling me that you're her favorite grandson."

Jonathon climbed the stairs, leaned against one of the posts supporting the porch roof and crossed his arms over his chest, eyeing Claudia consideringly. If she was a fraud, she was certainly a composed one. He supposed that shouldn't be surprising. A nervous con artist wouldn't stay in business for long.

"What brought you to Magnolia?" he asked.

"A Help Wanted ad in the newspaper."

Claudia increased the swing's speed and thought about her answer. The morning after she'd dreamed about the shadow, she'd seen the advertisement and known that it was the magnolia grove she was seeking. Though the ad had specifically sought a full-time housekeeper, she'd called the number anyway. The moment she'd heard Adelaide's voice, she'd adored her. Apparently the feeling was mutual.

Claudia had admitted to Adelaide that she wasn't much of a housekeeper but would be willing to help. Adelaide had stated that she already had a satisfactory housekeeper who came in twice a week. She'd then explained that she had only run the ad to appease her grandson, who was worried about her living alone. What she really needed, she'd confided, was some companionship, and if Claudia didn't mind listening to an old woman reminisce about the past, the guest house was hers.

Claudia had moved in four days ago and had been waiting for the menacing shadow of her dreams to resurface. Hopefully that would happen soon, because she couldn't afford to remain away from her clients for more than a few weeks. As it was, she'd had to dip into her meager savings to pay the rent here—

"Magnolia is fairly remote," Jonathon said, interrupting her musings. "Isn't it difficult for you to see your clients?"

"Let's get to the point, Jonathon," Claudia said, growing tired of his game, particularly when his question came so close to her own thoughts. It left her with the perturbing feeling that he was reading her mind, which, of course, was impossible. If he was psychically gifted, she'd be able to connect with him. "You're here because you think I'm after Adelaide's money."

"Are you after her money?"

"No."

"Of course, I'm supposed to believe you."

"If you do, you're foolish, and I know you're not a fool. I also know that in your place, I'd suspect me. I wish I could give you proof of my integrity, but I'm afraid I can't."

"You could prove it by moving," he suggested.

Claudia's gaze wandered to the magnificent grove of magnolia trees that was as old as the mansion and gave the plantation its name. The grove was centered in the circular drive and blocked the sight of the mansion from the road. As she switched her gaze to the mansion, she knew she'd never forget her first glimpse of Magnolia.

It had gleamed as white as the magnolia blossoms in the grove. Wide, sweeping stairs, which led to French oak doors framed with panes of stained glass, were centered between four majestic Doric columns that rose two stories and supported a pitched roof. A large octagonal cupola topped the roof on the right, giving the impression of a castle turret tower. The floor-to-ceiling jib windows were framed with black shutters. Wide galleries circled the house on both the entry level and second floor, with the Ionic columns on the lower gallery supporting the upper gallery.

The grandeur of the mansion was breathtaking, but even as Claudia had marveled at it, she'd also felt the brooding aura surrounding it. Perhaps it was whimsy, but she'd sensed that the mansion itself knew that trouble was coming.

She returned her attention to Jonathon. "I can't move."

"You mean you *won't* move," he rebutted.

"I mean I *can't* move," she reiterated. "I'm needed here."

Jonathon couldn't decide which disturbed him the most. The intent, almost fervent look in her eyes, or the impassioned timbre in her voice. Both were so eerie they gave him the creeps. He came to the conclusion that she was either a nut or one hell of an actress. He didn't find either option reassuring.

"Are you always so dramatic, Ms. Peppermill?"

"Claudia," she corrected with an abashed duck of her head. "And I suppose that did sound dramatic. Please, forgive me. Sometimes I get a little carried away."

"That's an understatement," he muttered under his breath. In a normal tone, he said, "Why are you needed here?"

"I don't know yet."

"When will you know?"

"When it's time."

"That's encouraging."

Claudia grinned wryly at his dry tone. "You think I'm crazy."

"The thought has crossed my mind."

"I'm sure it has."

Her comment didn't require an answer. Jonathon frowned when he realized that she'd not only taken over the conversation, she'd brought it to a dead end. He hadn't had anyone outmaneuver him so adeptly in years!

He arched a brow when Claudia suddenly said, "Oh, dear. Adelaide bought a chocolate pie for dinner, and it's going to fall off the back seat. I hope you like chocolate mush."

"Was that supposed to be an example of your psychic powers?"

"Maybe. At least it'll be easy to check out."

"Mmm," Jonathon remarked noncommittally. "How long have you been psychic?"

"All my life."

"You must have had an interesting childhood."

"You might say that." Claudia didn't like talking about her childhood because it filled her with such conflicting feelings. She decided to change the subject. "How long are you going to be here?"

As long as it takes to get rid of you, Jonathon answered inwardly, thankful that he'd had the foresight to turn the day-to-day operation of his business over to his senior vice-president, Allen Gregory, while he rescued his grandmother. Experience had taught him that that could take days. "You predicted my arrival, but you don't know how long I'll be staying?"

"The image wasn't that clear."

"Is that normal?"

"No." Again she tried to connect with his mind, disconcerted when she still failed. "But then, nothing about you seems normal. May I touch you?"

"Touch me?" he repeated, taken aback by the unexpected question.

She laughed softly at his dubious expression. "It won't hurt, Jonathon. I promise."

Jonathon wasn't sure why her bizarre request made him uneasy, but gut instinct was telling him to give her an unequivocal no. His common sense, however, insisted that if he refused, it would be the same as saying he believed in her clairvoyance. And he wasn't about to lend credence to her claim.

"I suppose we could shake hands."

He tensed when Claudia rose to her feet and walked toward him, her gaze locked with his. When she reached him and held out her hand, Jonathon had to force himself to accept it. But the moment their hands connected, he was hit with a surge of energy unlike anything he'd ever felt before. It was as if he'd stuck his finger in an electrical socket. Appalled by his physical response to her touch, his heart began to pound. His body began to tremble. He became achingly aware that he was fully aroused.

What in hell was happening to him? He *never* lost control of his libido. To make the situation even more demeaning, Claudia Peppermill was most likely a crook! He kept telling himself to pull away from her, but no matter how hard he tried, he couldn't remove his hand from hers.

Claudia was just as shocked by Jonathon's touch as he was because she was immediately filled with a chilling sense of danger that made her blood run cold. Before she could latch onto the source of the threat, however, she was hit with the familiar free-floating sensation. It was as if a spiritual part of herself was separating from her body. Everything around her became hazy, undefined, and she caught her breath as the vibrations settled into a distinct form. Finally she was connecting with him, but the scenes flowing through her mind made her knees go weak and her throat go dry. She was receiving crystal-clear visions of Jonathon making love with a woman, but it wasn't the lovemaking that startled her. It was the fact that the woman in those images was her!

Claudia kept telling herself to break contact with him immediately, but it was as if she'd lost all free will. She was as mesmerized by the vision as she was captive of it.

She could feel Jonathon's warm breath and the rasp of his beard as he showered her naked body with kisses that spread a pleasurable ache from her breasts to her womb. Her hands caressed his body, which was such a contrast of rough and smooth textures that he overloaded her senses. He was whispering tantalizingly erotic words in her ear as he grabbed her hand and dragged it to his erection, which was hard, bold and pulsating with life. He groaned at her touch, and she was filled with a throbbing ache in response that had her gripping his shoulders and whimpering with need. He stroked his hands up and down her inner thighs as he urged them apart, and then he lowered himself be-

*tween them. She moaned an unintelligible plea as she
felt the teasing brush of his manhood against her
womanhood.*

But when he flexed his hips to enter her, Claudia's self-
protective instincts began to blare. She jerked her hand
from Jonathon's to end the vision before it could reach its
natural conclusion. Though the loss of contact stopped the
images, it didn't alleviate the burning ache inside her.

She wrapped her arms around her middle and stared at
him, in bewilderment. She'd never had a vision so vivid she
could feel it, and she was *never* a participant. So what
happened?

Before she could think the matter through, Jonathon
demanded, ''Just what kind of parlor trick was that?''

His voice was low and deadly, and chased a shiver of fear
up Claudia's spine. She caught her bottom lip between her
teeth as she regarded him apprehensively. The moment
she'd broken away from his touch, she'd also lost contact
with him, but she suddenly recalled that chilling sense of
danger that had washed over her when she'd first taken his
hand. Was he capable of violence? But if he was a physical
threat to her, how could she have seen herself making love
with him?

A surreptitious glance toward him assured her he was
waiting for an answer. She didn't know what to say, because she wasn't sure what he was asking. Was it possible
he'd shared that erotic vision?

Absolutely not! her common sense declared. But Claudia wasn't reassured, because she again tried to connect
with Jonathon's mind and failed. She no longer found the
aberration fascinating. It scared the daylights out of her.

''Well?'' Jonathon rasped when Claudia didn't respond
to his question.

''Why would you think I was playing some kind of parlor game? Did something happen when you shook my
hand?''

He opened his mouth to tell her that she knew perfectly
well that something had happened, but snapped it closed.
Admitting to that bolt of energy would give her the perfect

platform for declaring that something psychic had occurred between them. Since he had no proof that it was a trick, he'd sound ridiculous if he argued with her. Damn it all to hell! The woman had outmaneuvered him again.

He scowled as he tried to figure out how to get out of this mess without giving her the upper hand. Just when he came to the conclusion that she'd won this round, she pivoted her head toward the main house and said, "Adelaide's almost home."

Jonathon automatically followed her gaze and noted that you couldn't even see the front of Magnolia from the guest house, let alone the drive. He tilted his head, listening intently for the sound of a car. All he could hear was the soft chatter of insects and the cawing of birds. Several minutes passed before he finally heard a car's engine. A moment later his grandmother's Cadillac sedan came around the side of the house. It certainly wasn't the strangest event that had occurred between Claudia and him, but for some odd reason it made the hair on the back of his neck bristle.

Thankfully, his common sense surfaced before he could succumb to any paranormal explanations. Either his grandmother had told Claudia when to expect her, or she'd simply deduced the amount of time it would take her to make the trip. The conclusions were so simple that he unknowingly sighed in relief.

When his grandmother waved, he waved back. Then he glanced toward Claudia and his eyes narrowed. She was standing no more than two feet away from him and should have been awash in sunlight, just as he was. Instead she was cloaked in a shadow so dark he could barely see her. This time, every hair on his head bristled. What in the hell . . .

He blinked when Claudia said, "Jonathon? What's wrong?"

In that brief closing and opening of his eyelids, the shadow was gone. Sunlight once again surrounded her. He raked his hand through his hair, deciding that the woman was even more dangerous than he'd thought. Somehow she was managing to play tricks with his mind. First it had been that damn bolt of energy. Then that weird shadow. If she could have such an effect on him, what was she doing to his grandmother, who didn't have a levelheaded bone in her body?

Just the thought was enough to strengthen his resolve. He had to get Claudia away from Magnolia as soon as possible. The trick would be convincing his grandmother that her boarder was unsatisfactory. He knew from experience that the old woman made a career out of contrariness. One indelicate move on his part, and she'd not only give Claudia a life-long lease but probably free rent for the next ninety-nine years.

"Nothing's wrong," he said when he realized Claudia was eyeing him in puzzlement. "I'd better go help Gran with the groceries."

Claudia frowned as she watched Jonathon hurry down the steps and jog toward Adelaide's car. For a moment he'd had such an odd look on his face that she'd wondered if he'd become ill. It was evident that he hadn't, so why had he been looking at her so strangely?

Nothing about the man was *usual*, she finally concluded, so trying to figure him out would be a waste of time. The decision to make herself scarce during his visit was a sudden, fierce one. Her self-preservation instincts were clamoring. Just because she'd seen herself making love with him didn't mean that the event was a *fait accompli*. She had an eighty percent accuracy rate when it came to her predictions, which was actually quite impressive. In this instance, however, she was going to make sure that this particular vision was consigned to her twenty percent margin for error. She was here on a life-saving mission, not to have an affair, and she didn't need her clairvoyance to recognize that that was all she'd be able to have with such a doubting Thomas as Mr. Jonathon Jackson Tanner, III.

As she walked back into the guest house and closed the door firmly behind her, a part of her couldn't help wonder if she was going to spend the rest of her life feeling so unbearably lonely.

Chapter 2

Jonathon glared at his grandmother. They'd just finished lunch, and she was sitting across the table from him eating a small bowl of chocolate mush. Claudia had been right. The pie had fallen off the back seat, and though he loved chocolate pie in any way, shape or form, he couldn't bring himself to eat any. He was having a difficult time persuading himself that Claudia's prediction had been coincidence, which infuriated him.

"Is something wrong, Jonathon?" his grandmother asked.

He knew she was being purposely obtuse. She was also being particularly stubborn and totally unreasonable about Claudia Peppermill. They'd been arguing the issue all morning, and he hadn't made any headway.

He narrowed his eyes and studied her, trying to figure out what it would take to reach her. Her white hair was perfectly coifed in the soft Gibson girl hairstyle she'd been wearing for fifty years. Her face was relatively unlined, and her blue eyes were bright and alert. She could easily pass for a woman twenty years her junior, both in mind and body. So why was she refusing to acknowledge the obvious drawbacks to her soothsayer boarder?

"Why are you playing games with me, Gran?" he asked, frowning darkly.

She dabbed at her lips with her napkin. "I'm not playing games, and don't scowl like that. You'll get terrible wrinkles."

"If you don't stop getting into trouble, I won't live long enough to get any more wrinkles than I already have," he muttered aggrievedly.

"If I didn't get into trouble, who'd spice up your life? And I keep telling you that Claudia isn't trouble. She's a dear, sweet girl."

"Come on, Gran," he drawled derisively. "That dear, sweet girl claims to be a clairvoyant! If she isn't out to con you, then she has a few loose marbles. For all you know, she may be violent."

"Gracious, you do have a wild imagination, Jonathon. Claudia doesn't have a violent bone in her body, and even if she did, she'd never harm me."

"And how do you know that?" he demanded in frustration. "Have you had experience with insane people?"

"Of course, dear. As you well know, your great-uncle Hubert was nuttier than your Aunt Virginia's fruitcake, and Virginia has a heavy hand with the nuts."

"Great-uncle Hubert wasn't crazy, Gran. He suffered a head injury when he fell off his horse."

"Well, he certainly seemed crazy. And we do have a long line of crazy people in the family. Why, the stories I could tell you—"

"You can tell me some other time," he interrupted, knowing that if he didn't, she'd launch into a long-winded narrative. "And I'll concede that Ms. Peppermill may not be crazy, but the purpose of renting the guest house was to hire a full-time housekeeper. She is *not* a housekeeper."

"The purpose of renting the guest house was so that you wouldn't worry about me living alone," she corrected. "Mrs. Massey is a satisfactory housekeeper, and I don't want to let her go. Claudia moving in allows us both to have what we want."

"Gran—" he began, but Adelaide cut him off.

"Jonathon I will not discuss this any further. Help me clear the table. It's time for my afternoon nap."

Jonathon recognized that this was his grandmother's way of telling him they were engaged in a power struggle. What she had yet to realize was that he had every intention of winning. He adored her and would do anything for her, except give in on the issue of letting Claudia Peppermill stay at Magnolia. Even if he were to allow that the woman might have psychic powers, his meeting with her had been too unsettling for him to trust her.

He wanted to ask his grandmother if she'd experienced any odd events in Claudia's presence, but bit off the query just in time. Gran would want specifics. Since he couldn't explain what had happened, he'd just be handing her ammunition to prove her point. Besides, there were some things in life a man didn't discuss with his grandmother. Sexual arousal headed the list, even if it was brought on by trickery. He also recognized that she'd use the revelation to start matchmaking. After burying his wife three years before, Jonathon had vowed to never marry again. Unfortunately, Gran refused to accept his decision, and if a woman walked, talked and breathed, his grandmother considered her fair game.

A short time later Adelaide went upstairs to take her nap. Normally Jonathon wouldn't have minded entertaining himself, but today he was restless. He tried watching an old movie on the television in the sitting room, but Claudia Peppermill's image kept superimposing itself on the screen. Finally he acknowledged that he had to deal with his physical reaction to her touch.

He switched off the television and began to pace. He barely noticed the antique Victorian furniture, it's accompanying bric-a-brac, or the dour portraits of his great-great-grandparents, Evelina and Charles Tanner, who peered down at him from their spot over the black marble mantelpiece. He reassured himself that his response to Claudia was normal. After all, she *was* a beautiful woman. But it wasn't her beauty that had affected him. It had been that damn surge of energy.

How had she done it? Was it some type of hypnosis? That was the most logical explanation, because it also accounted for the shadow that had engulfed her. To think that Claudia might have hypnotized him without him knowing it was untenable, but if she had, what was he going to do about it? Convince his grandmother to throw her out, of course, but considering her stubbornness on the point, that could take days. Who knew what other mischief Claudia would be up to in the meantime?

With a muffled curse, he headed for the library. Maybe a good book would keep him occupied until his grandmother's nap was over and they could resume the battle.

When he entered the library, he paused to absorb its essence. It smelled of leather, a century and a half of wood smoke and a musty odor that he'd always equated with books. He surveyed the floor-to-ceiling bookcases that covered three walls. Many of the books were collector's editions, and it occurred to him that Claudia wouldn't have to blatantly rob his grandmother. She could make a fortune by simply helping herself to a handful of books or some of the smaller antiques cluttering the house.

It wouldn't be the first time that had happened. Two years ago he'd caught Billy Joe Jordan, who'd been the caretaker at Magnolia, stealing small antiques. If he didn't want history repeating itself, it would behoove him to hire someone to catalogue and appraise everything in the house. He'd wanted to do that after the incident with Billy Joe, but his grandmother had adamantly refused because she didn't want strangers pawing through her things. This time he'd insist.

Knowing he'd be doing something positive released some of the tension that had plagued him all morning, and he began to peruse the bookshelves. When he spied a slim volume with the word Journal stenciled across its spine, he reached for it out of curiosity.

He opened the heavy, red velvet curtains and carried the book to one of the deep, leather chairs, where he examined his find. The cracked leather binding suggested the journal was old. When he opened it, the brittle, yellowed pages and the date, January 1, 1860, confirmed it. The handwriting was faded and written in a flowery calligraphy. It took him awhile to decipher it, but then he read.

It is difficult to believe another year has passed. Come April, my Charles and I will celebrate twenty-six years of marriage. Come June, my beautiful Magnolia will be twenty years old. I promised my Charles that we would visit the Kendalls in Charleston this May. I fear now that I will disappoint him. I cannot be gone from Magnolia when the trees come into bloom. I will suggest instead that the Kendalls come to Magnolia for a visit.

Jonathon gave a dazed shake of his head when he finished the passage. Charles was his great-great-grandfather, which meant the journal had been written by his great-great-grandmother, Evelina, for whom Magnolia had been built. This was Magnolia's history as witnessed by one of his own ancestors! Eagerly, he turned the page.

Her next several entries were about household events and witty commentaries on *les affaires des couers* among the local gentry that made him chuckle. By modern standards the flirtations were harmless. In 1860, they were the stuff that duels were made of. Then, halfway through the journal, the tone began to change.

June 21, 1860. Summer has come, but it is not only the heat that afflicts me this year. Mr. Butler arrived today with the news that should Mr. Lincoln be elected President, the South will secede from the Union. He declares that our own State of Mississippi will be one of the first. I am fearful of this news. My Charles tells me not to fret. But how can I not when even as I write my husband and sons sit with Mr. Butler in the library and speak heartily of war? I pray that Mr. Lin-

coln will not be elected President. I pray that this
fretful issue of Abolitionism is resolved.

Again, the journal reverted to household matters and
gossip, but at the end of November, the tone again
changed.

November 26, 1860. The worst has happened. My
Charles returned today from a visit with Mr. Butler
and confirmed the news that I have refused to believe.
Mr. Lincoln has been elected President. The cry has
gone out for the South to unite and form a Confeder-
acy. War is coming. It is inevitable. I have seen it in my
dreams. I am prostrate with fear.

Jonathon scanned the next several entries until he
reached a particular one that caught his eye.

December 23, 1860. My Charles received a message
from Mr. Butler today confirming that South Carolina indeed seceded from the Union on December
twentieth. All the joy has been taken from the holi-
days, and not even Pastor Eames can console me. Already my Charles and our sons are preparing for war.
Who will protect my dearest daughters and me once
they are gone? Who will protect my beautiful Magnolia?

The journal continued along in the same vein.

December 25, 1860. I have told my Charles how I fear
for our safety should he and our sons desert us for war.
As a special gift for me on this holy occasion, he has
announced that he will build a secret room for us to
hide in. This gift has made my heart lighter, though it
is still sorely oppressed. Instead of a secret room I
would wish for the continued peace we have enjoyed

at Magnolia these long years past. I would be petulant if I told my Charles this, so I will hold my tongue and be grateful for his gift.

He scanned several more pages, which contained an account of the remainder of Christmas Day, and then still again reverted to discussions about household events and gossip. Finally, the last entry.

December 31, 1860. I have come to despise Mr. Butler. Today he sent news that it is only a matter of days before our wonderful State of Mississippi becomes the second state to secede from the Union. I am so distraught that my Charles has declared that work on the secret room will begin on the morrow. He has promised me that he will remain at Magnolia until it is completed. I pray that it takes months to build. I pray that my Charles does not go to war. I pray, because my dreams say that if he goes he will never return to Magnolia. How will I survive without my Charles? Tomorrow we must welcome another new year. I fear that I will only be able to greet it with tears.

Jonathon closed the book, feeling stunned. Had the room been built? As a child he'd fantasized about a secret room at Magnolia. Although he'd spent hours exploring the mansion in search of one, he'd never really believed in its existence. Now he had proof that one did exist. But where in the world was it located? He crossed to the bookshelves in search of another journal, hoping it would provide the answer, but if there were more such diaries, they weren't in the library.

Where *was* the secret room? Did his grandmother know about it? He glanced at his watch to determine how long before she awakened from her nap. He was surprised to note that two hours had passed. She should be up by now. Grabbing the journal, he went looking for her.

"Hi, Gran," he said when he walked into the kitchen and found her sitting at the table and watching the coffee-maker. He dropped a kiss to her powdered cheek. "You know, if you had a full-time housekeeper, you wouldn't have to sit and watch the coffee brew. It would be ready for you when you came downstairs."

Adelaide released a long-suffering sigh as he settled across the table from her. "Jonathon, don't start in on me again."

"I'm not starting in on you. I'm merely making an observation. You've had live-in servants all your life. Why are you so determined to be alone now?"

"Not alone, Jonathon. Independent. I'm eighty years old, and this is the first time in my life that I can do what I want when I want without worrying about someone else. A live-in servant is a responsibility. Waiting ten minutes for the coffee to brew is a small disadvantage when compared to that obligation."

"But don't you get lonely?"

"I did until Claudia moved in. She's the perfect neighbor. She's willing to visit when I want company, but she isn't offended if I prefer to be alone. Ah, the coffee is finally ready."

"I'll get it," Jonathon said, the realization of just how difficult ousting her pesky boarder was going to be making him grimace inwardly. It was going to be more difficult than he'd thought. He wasn't just dealing with obstinacy here.

In some ways he understood what she was saying. She'd grown up in an era where a woman went from being daughter to wife to mother to grandmother. Never once had she strayed from the path of tradition, but at some point she must have wondered what she could have accomplished if she had.

"Do you have any regrets about your life, Gran?" he inquired curiously as he carried their coffee to the table.

"Of course not," she answered so quickly that he knew it was the truth.

"Then why this sudden bid for independence?"

"It's not sudden, Jonathon. As I said, this is the first time the opportunity has presented itself. Right now, I'm happy to be alone. Tomorrow I may wake up and decide that I want a houseful of servants again."

He grinned. "In other words, you're going through a stage."

She chuckled wryly. "You make it sound as if I'm going through my second childhood, which I probably am. So indulge me, okay?"

Jonathon's first impulse was to tell her that he'd be happy to indulge her if she got rid of Claudia Peppermill. Gut instinct, however, told him to maintain his peace. Now that he understood her motivation, he'd find a way to persuade her to see things his way.

"Gran, have you ever heard of a secret room at Magnolia?"

"A secret room?" she repeated in surprise. "Why would you ask me something like that?"

He slid the journal toward her. "I found this in the library. It's Evelina Tanner's diary for the year 1860, which was the year that Abraham LIncoln was elected president and South Carolina seceded from the Union. She knew conflict was inevitable and was worried about her and her daughters' saftey if great-great-grandfather Tanner and their sons went off to war. He agreed to build a secret room for them to hide in."

Adelaide opened the journal and thumbed through it carefully. "You said you found this in the library?" When he nodded, she said, "I've never seen it before. How did it get in the library?"

"I assume that it's been there all along."

"No. I've read nearly every book in the library, and I would have run across it long before now. I wonder how it got in there?"

"I don't know how it got in there. What I *am* interested in is the secret room. Are you sure that Gramps never mentioned it?"

"Positive. A secret room wouldn't be something I'd forget. Maybe it was never completed."

"I'm sure it was. Great-great-grandfather Tanner promised Evelina that he wouldn't go to war until it was finished, and he was killed at Shiloh. You know as well as I do that a Tanner never breaks a promise."

"You're right," Adelaide stated thoughtfully. "If he'd made her a promise, he would have upheld it. It's odd, though, that your grandfather didn't know about it."

"Maybe he did and just didn't tell you."

Adelaide shook her head. "Jonathon told me everything, and even if he hadn't there would have been no reason for him to hide a secret room from me."

"Then it must no longer exist," he replied with disappointment. He'd been excited about the secret room, and it had been a long time since he'd been excited about anything. "After the war was over, they probably decided that it was no longer needed and turned it into a closet or a pantry."

"I doubt that Jonathon. Times were very troubled following the war. They would have kept it as a precautionary measure. If they built it, then it's still here. All we have to do is find it."

Jonathon glanced around the kitchen. Though it was modernized with the most up-to-date appliances, it was still a reflection of an era long past. There was an old marble fireplace that, though no longer in use, was still functional. Antique lace curtains hung at the windows. The mahogany claw-footed table they sat at was nearly as old as the mansion and had been as lovingly cared for. The kitchen was half the size of his apartment in Natchez, and it was the smallest room in the mansion.

"Considering the size of this place, that will be quite an undertaking," he remarked. "The entrance isn't obvious, or someone would have stumbled across it by now. That means that we'll have to carefully inspect every room."

"There might be an easier way to find it," Adelaide ventured.

Jonathon leaned toward her in anticipation. "I'm all for easy. What do you have in mind?"

"We could ask Claudia about it. She is a clairvoyant. Maybe she can touch the journal and tell us where it's at."

"No way!" He sat back in his chair and glared at her. "I told you she's either a crook or a nut, and I'm betting on the former. If she is a crook, I'm not going to give her the run of the house so she can case the place."

"Jonathon, that's ludicrous! What's more, I don't think you're worried about Claudia being a crook. I think you're afraid she'll prove that she's exactly what she says she is. Then you'll have to admit that you're wrong, and you're like every other male Tanner I've ever known. You despise being wrong."

"Now, that *is* ludicrous!" he exploded, angered by her charge. "If she can prove to me that she's a clairvoyant, then more power to her."

"I'm glad to hear you say that," Adelaide stated with a satisfied smile. "That means you can run over to the guest house and ask Claudia to join us. We'll show her the journal and see what she has to say about it."

Jonathon couldn't decide whether to laugh or groan. He, the president and chairman of the board of Tanner Transportation, Inc.—a multimillion-dollar transportation and storage conglomerate—had just been bested by his eighty-year-old grandmother! *Damn!* Why hadn't he seen what she was doing? He opened his mouth to refuse to do her bidding, but clamped it shut. He'd let himself be painted into a corner, and there was no graceful way out.

He rose and headed out the back door, barely refraining from slamming it behind him. First Claudia Peppermill had manipulated him, and now his grandmother was doing it. It wasn't proving to be a very auspicious day.

Claudia tried to put the visions of lovemaking with Adelaide's handsome grandson out of her mind, but by late afternoon, she knew it was an impossibility. She had to acknowledge them, because they had been accompanied by that awful, chilling sense of danger. She was going to have to spend time with him to learn the source of the danger.

Her self-protective instincts were vehemently opposed to that option, but she'd come here because someone's life was in jeopardy. If Jonathon held the key, she had to deal with him.

And what about those erotic visions? a nagging inner voice taunted.

She shrugged the question aside. She would keep those visions from coming true by simply saying no.

Despite her resolve, she couldn't shake the feeling that her life was about to be set on a course where she'd have no control. A foreboding that drove her out of the guest house and into the magnolia grove, where she found it easier to relax.

Many of the trees were so tall they seemed to stretch to the sky. Their breadth was so wide and their limbs so low to the ground that the grove would have been impenetrable if some enterprising gardener hadn't trimmed the branches to create walking paths through the trees. As Claudia entered it, for the first time she felt as if she were lost in a maze. But she knew that each path meandered its way to the center, where a bench sat beneath the bows of one magnificent tree.

As she reached the center, she settled on the bench and felt her tension begin to ease. It was as if the grove maintained the true essence of the plantation—a reflection of the peace and harmony that should exist here. So what had happened to disturb Magnolia's tranquility? Even more important, who was in danger here?

It was logical to conclude that Adelaide was at risk. After all, she was the only person who lived at Magnolia. Though Claudia's connection with Adelaide was weak, it was strong enough to reassure her that there was no imminent danger in Adelaide's future. Of course, she had no way of knowing just how far into the future her reading went. It could be as short as a few hours or longer than a year.

She leaned her head back and gazed at the flowering branches overhead, wishing that Adelaide would let her do a formal reading. But the few times she'd broached the subject, Adelaide had refused. She claimed she was too old to look into the future. Claudia would never explore Adelaide's mind without her permission, and even if she did, she probably wouldn't discover anything significant without Adelaide's cooperation. For now, she'd have to be satisfied with the brief flashes she received whenever she was around the older woman and hope that that would be enough to protect her if the need arose.

"Communing with nature?" a familiar baritone drawled.

Startled, Claudia swung around on the bench and spied Jonathon standing on the path directly across from the one she'd taken. He'd sneaked up on her again, and the fact that he had, rattled her. She'd convinced herself that her inability to connect with him earlier had been nothing more than a fluke.

Why couldn't she connect with him? she wondered as her gaze automatically flicked over him. He'd changed into a maroon, body-hugging, T-shirt that accentuated the breadth of his chest, and a pair of worn denims, whose intimate fit left little to the imagination. Unfortunately she didn't need her imagination to fill in the gaps. Touching him this morning had made her more acquainted with his body than she cared to be.

She blushed as the memory of what he looked like—felt like—naked and aroused flooded through her mind. The image was so graphic she could describe him right down to the small mole on his left hip and the scar on his shin. Her fingertips tingled with the sensory recollection of the myriad textures of his skin and the pulsating heat of his throbbing erection. She had to clear her throat to find her voice. "Good afternoon. Out for a walk?"

"No. Gran would like you to come to the house. I was on my way to get you when I saw you come into the grove," he said in a formal tone that Claudia suspected he used with his business clients.

She eyed him curiously, trying to determine his mood. But before she could, a magnolia blossom fluttered to the grounds in front of him. He picked it up and, cradling it on his open palm, caressed its satiny white petals with the fingers of his other hand. Claudia watched him, mesmerized. She knew exactly how that touch felt. In the vision, he'd caressed her inner thighs just as delicately.

She was snapped away from the fantasy when he suddenly tossed the flower to the ground and returned his gaze to her. His expression was neutral, but the tense set of his shoulders and the tilt of his chin indicated he was angry. *Very* angry, she intuited, and she cursed the fact that she couldn't read him. Frustration rose within her. Was he the source of the danger she'd felt when she'd taken his hand? Was he capable of violence?

Suddenly the grove no longer seemed peaceful. It took on the same dark, brooding quality that Jonathon projected as he regarded her with an unnerving stare.

"Is something wrong with Adelaide?" she asked, needing to break the intensity of the moment.

His voice was still formal when he said, "She's fine. She has something she wants to show you. Will you come to the house?"

"Of course." When she joined him on the path and they began walking toward the mansion, she asked, "What does Adelaide want to show me?"

"A book."

"What kind of a book?"

"You're the clairvoyant. Why don't you tell me?" he jeered.

Claudia arched a brow. There was no doubt he was angry. "Are you always this grumpy in the afternoon, or do you reserve your surliness for clairvoyants?"

She knew she shouldn't taunt him, but was unable to help herself. Besides, there was every possibility that if she goaded him, she'd gain access to his thoughts. And she desperately needed to connect with him. It was the only way she could determine if he could be trusted.

"What do you think?"

"I think you're angry with me. Would you mind telling me why?"

He stopped abruptly and turned to face her, his expression hostile. "You're right. I am angry. You don't belong here, and I'm going to do my damnedest to get rid of you. I'm also warning you that if you do anything to hurt my grandmother—and I mean *anything*—you'll answer to me. Have you got that?"

Claudia told herself not to lose control. He was only trying to protect his grandmother. But he was standing there looking so piously self-righteous that she lost her temper anyway. All her life she'd had to deal with irrational prejudice toward her gift. She'd learned to accept it, but it didn't make the sting of unjustified condemnation any less painful.

"You know, Jonathon, people like you amaze me," she told him, unable to keep the bitterness out of her voice. "You don't know me or anything about me, but because I claim to be a clairvoyant, I'm automatically untrustworthy. If I told you that the only brush I've had with the law was a parking ticket when I was seventeen, you'd say it's only because I haven't been caught. After all, everyone knows that clairvoyants are fakes and crooks.

"Well, I'll admit that there are many people in my profession who are fakes and crooks," she went on in an angry rush. "But there are just as many unsavory people in the business world. I haven't asked you to prove your integrity because you're a businessman, and I resent being accused of having criminal intentions because I'm clairvoyant. If you want to indulge yourself in unfounded bigotry toward me, that's fine. You can, however, do so in silence. Have *you* got *that?*"

Instead of answering, Jonathon stared at her, feeling both thoroughly chastised and absolutely intrigued. It had been a long time since a woman had stood up to him. For that matter, it had been a long time since a man had had the courage to put him in his place. And she was right. He was condemning her on nothing more than her claim of clairvoyance. Though he despised the term, she had every right to call him a bigot.

It didn't change his feelings toward her, though. He still didn't trust her, but Lord, she was stunning, particularly with anger heightening the natural color in her cheeks and turning her gray-blue eyes stormy with challenge. Her lips were pursed in a disapproving line that beseeched him to soften them with a kiss.

He wasn't surprised by the sudden flash of desire that swept through him. Indeed, he was relieved by it, because it wasn't some trick she was playing on him. It was honest and real. And that, he recognized, made it ultimately more dangerous.

He took a step back from her, jammed his hands into his pockets and drawled laconically, "I hear you loud and clear, Claudia. Now, shall we go? Gran's waiting."

"Yeah," Claudia mumbled when she met his eyes. What she saw reflected in their depths made her senses careen. It was the awakening of desire, and something utterly wanton stirred inside her in response.

She quickly turned away from him, refusing to even contemplate the matter. What she had to concentrate on was the shadow, and the faster she determined what danger it represented, the faster she could go home. And at the moment home had never sounded more appealing, especially when she approached Magnolia. If it had presented an ominous feeling before, it felt almost sinister today. She tried to attribute it to the fact that clouds had scudded across the sky, blocking the sun and casting the mansion in darkness.

As she recalled the dream-vision that had brought her here, she shuddered. If Jonathon hadn't been dogging her steps, she'd have headed for the guest house and called Adelaide on the telephone. Instinct told her that once she stepped through the doors of Magnolia today, her life would never be the same again.

When she entered the kitchen, Adelaide rushed across the room, enveloping her in a welcoming hug. "Thank you for coming over, Claudia. Isn't it exciting about the secret room?"

"Secret room?" Claudia repeated in bewilderment.

"Yes. The secret room in Evelina's journal. Didn't Jonathon tell you about it?"

"No. He said you wanted to show me a book."

"Good heavens, Jonathon. You could have at least enlightened the girl."

He gave an unrepentant shrug and sank into a chair at the table. "This is your party, Gran."

"So it is, and don't you forget it," she declared. Then, to Claudia, "Jonathon found Evelina's journal, and she says there's a secret room at Magnolia."

"Who's Evelina?" Claudia asked in confusion.

"My great-great-grandmother," Jonathon supplied. "My great-great-grandfather built Magnolia for her. It appears that he also built her a secret room at the beginning of the Civil War. Unfortunately her journal doesn't tell us where it is. Gran thinks you can save us the trouble of having to search for it."

"Me?" Claudia questioned doubtfully.

"Yes, you," Adelaide said, grabbing a book off the table. "Just touch the journal, Claudia, and see if you pick up anything."

"Adelaide, my abilities don't lie in that area," Claudia demurred as she eyed the book distrustfully. It was clearly old, and though she didn't know why, she felt threatened by it. "I don't have telepathic communication through objects, and I have never had a vision about the past."

"Now, that's a convenient excuse," Jonathon drawled.

"Jonathon, don't be rude," Adelaide scolded. "Just touch it, Claudia. If nothing happens then nothing happens, but I have a feeling that something will."

Claudia had the same feeling, and some inner alarm was warning her to get as far away from the book as possible. Normally she listened to her inner alarms, but this time she happened to glance up at Jonathon. There was a cynical gleam in his eyes, which was reflected in the mocking curve of his mouth. It was clear that he considered this a test. It was also evident that he expected her to fail it.

Her pride surfaced. Though she was sure she was destined for failure—her abilities really didn't lie in this area—she wasn't going to fulfill his expectations without at least trying to prove him wrong. She took the book from Adelaide.

The moment she did, she was hit with a wave of terror so powerful she swayed on her feet. The air around her grew so heavy she couldn't breathe. Images began flashing through her mind with such speed that they were no more than vague impressions. But there was one pervading presence throughout them all. The shadow, and it was even more vicious than it had been before.

She threw the book to the floor and leaped back, gazing at it in abject horror and gasping for breath.

"Claudia, what is it?" Adelaide asked in alarm.

Claudia glanced up at the sound of Adelaide's voice, but her face was blurred. Indeed, everything in the room was blurred, and no matter how hard she tried, she couldn't catch her breath.

"You must forget the secret room!" she exclaimed harshly, and then she fled from the mansion before the evil she'd sensed could suffocate her.

Chapter 3

After looking everywhere else he could think of, Jonathon found Claudia sitting beneath an ancient oak tree on the bank of the Mississippi River. Normally he would have found the sight of her seated beneath that huge old tree, whose misshapen limbs were bent low to the ground and dripping with Spanish moss, artistically touching. But with her dismaying reaction to the journal so fresh in his mind, it was rather unnerving to see the tree hovering over her. Almost as unnerving as it had been seeing her cloaked in that dark shadow this morning.

Though he wanted to believe the scene in the kitchen had been an act, he knew that not even the finest actress could have faked the pallor or the clammy sweat that had sprung up on her brow. He could still hear her strangled gasps for breath, which had been so tortured his own chest had begun to ache. But the most disturbing thing of all had been the absolute terror he'd seen in her eyes.

He walked toward her, uncertain as to what approach to take. He was sure she'd claim to have had a psychic experience. He was just as sure a psychiatrist would have another name for it. He decided to play it by ear and hope to God he wasn't in over his head.

Claudia started when Jonathon appeared at her side. Intent on reconciling what had happened when she'd touched the journal, she hadn't heard his footsteps. Then again, she thought grimly, she would have sensed him without having to rely on her hearing, if she could connect with him.

When he sat down beside her, she regarded him warily. She'd retained enough of those high-speed images to know that Jonathon was intrinsically linked with the shadow. What she couldn't determine was if he represented the danger, was the catalyst to the danger, or was in danger himself. Any way she looked at it, though, the best way she could see to avoid disaster was to persuade him to leave Magnolia until she could figure out what was going on.

"Are you all right?" he asked, picking up a small, smooth stone and throwing it at the river. It skipped three times across the placid surface of the muddy brown water before sinking.

"I'm fine," she answered, rubbing her hands against her upper arms. It was a fruitless effort to assuage the bone-deep chill that had engulfed her when she'd touched the journal.

As she watched a branch of the tree sway in front of her, trailing Spanish moss in the water, she wondered why she'd fled to this haunting spot on the river. It didn't give her the solace she would have found in the magnolia grove. But perhaps that was exactly why she'd subconsciously chosen to come here. The grove would have allayed her fears and dulled the threatening manifestation of the shadow. Here, facing the wide expanse of the river that seemed so slow and peaceful but whose annual flooding wreaked havoc from St. Louis to New Orleans, she was able to retain the sense of terror. Her instincts told her that to forget the shadow's malevolence for even a moment, to let down her guard, could prove devastatingly destructive.

Jonathon drew up a knee and rested his forearm against it as he asked, "Would you like to talk about what happened at the house?"

His voice was soft and mollifying, which told her he thought she was nuts. Frustration surfaced, but she forced herself to remain calm. Any overt show of emotion would only convince him that he was right.

She took the offensive by asking, "Do you believe in intuition, Jonathon?"

He hesitated, as if trying to decide if it was a trick question. Finally he said, "Sure."

Claudia nodded. "I know you don't believe in clairvoyance, but if you did, you'd understand that it's like a heightened intuitive state. Right now my intuition is telling me that your presence at Magnolia is dangerous."

"Why is my presence dangerous?" he inquired in an indulgent tone one might use with an overwrought child.

"I don't know." She shifted so she could face him. "Do you always know why you intuit something, or do you just feel and react?"

He flashed her a wry smile. "About an hour ago I caught hell from you for doing just that. You accused me of being a bigot."

Claudia gave an impatient wave of her hand. "That was different."

"Was it?" When she didn't respond, he asked, "What happened at the house, Claudia?"

Claudia considered telling him about the shadow, but decided against it. If she started talking about a nebulous, threatening entity, he'd probably pack her bags and drive her to the nearest mental health facility.

"I sensed terrible danger," she said. "Somehow that danger involves you and the secret room."

"I see." He picked up another stone and skipped it across the water. "I don't want you to take this wrong, but I told you my great-great-grandfather built the secret room at the beginning of the Civil War. A secret room implies fear of the war. War implies danger. Isn't it possible that you subconsciously reacted to those implications when you found out I wanted to search for the room?"

Lord, he sounded like a psychiatrist! And she should know. Her parents had dragged her to plenty of them during the first twelve years of her life.

"There was nothing subconscious about my reaction," she denied quietly but firmly. "There is danger surrounding that secret room. You have to stay away from it. You have to get away from Magnolia. If you don't, something terrible is going to happen.''

He was silent for a long time before saying, ''Okay, Claudia. Let's say you're right. But if I leave, how long am I supposed to stay away? A week? A month? A year? I can't do that. I own Magnolia. I'm responsible for it. Someday I'm going to make my home here.''

''If you insist on staying, then promise me you won't look for the secret room,'' she implored.

He shook his head. ''I can't promise you that, because I have every intention of looking for it.''

''Why?'' she demanded, giving way to her frustration.

''Because it's part of Magnolia. Now that I know it exists, I have to find it.''

''Even if it could be dangerous?''

''Even if it could be dangerous.''

Claudia knew when she was faced with a losing battle, and she returned her attention to the river. The fact that he didn't believe in her abilities was maddening. If he did believe, all of this would be so simple. She could tell him what she felt and what she saw. She could advise him and work with him, so they could discover the source of the danger and neutralize it.

Unless he is the danger, her conscience reminded. *He was in the visions with the shadow, so you can't dismiss him completely.*

She raked a hand through her hair at the thought. God, she'd give anything to be able to read him at this moment! She needed to clear him or condemn him. Until she knew what role he played in this drama, she couldn't determine if he was friend or foe.

''Will you let me help you look for the secret room?'' She might not be able to clarify Jonathon's role in any of this, but she knew without a doubt that the danger revolved around the secret room.

Jonathon's jaw tightened reflexively at Claudia's request. After that disturbing scene in the kitchen, he had to say no. Firmly he told himself that it wasn't out of any strange urge to protect her. She could still be a crook, and if she was, it was best not to give her the run of the house.

But then again, if she was a crook, he would need to keep an eye on her. Despite his better judgment, he heard himself ask, "Are you sure you're up to it?"

"Yes," Claudia said with a relieved sigh. "I was caught unaware before. Now that I know what to expect, I'll be fine."

He looked at her askance, but only said, "Then you're welcome to help. We'll start first thing in the morning."

"I'll be there."

He rose to his feet. "Well, I'd better go tell Gran that you're all right. Would you like to walk back with me?"

Claudia shook her head. "I'm going to stay here awhile."

Jonathon felt oddly averse to leaving her alone, but wasn't certain why. Perhaps it was because she looked so small sitting beside the river that looked as if it stretched a half mile from bank to bank.

He could also sense her lingering distress, and he was hit with an unexpected urge to brush his hand against her hair in an effort to soothe her. But before he could act on the impulse, he recalled that strange bolt of energy when he'd touched her this morning.

He tucked his hands into his pockets, and said, "I guess I'll see you in the morning."

Claudia glanced up at him with an absent smile. "Yes. Have a good evening, Jonathon."

"You, too." Unable to think of anything else to say, he walked away.

Claudia shifted beneath the tree so she could watch his progress across the wide, grassy field that separated Magnolia from the river. When he reached the path at the back of the mansion, she shivered. The mansion seemed to loom above him, and then he faded into its shadows. It left her with the eerie feeling that Magnolia had somehow absorbed him.

She turned back to gaze at the river fretfully. If she could only recall those terrifying images she'd received from the journal in detail, she might be able to come up with some answers. And why had she received those images in the first place? She'd never received telepathic communication through an object. *Never!* So why had it happened this time?

When night began to fall, she climbed to her feet and headed for the guest house. Tomorrow the search for the secret room would begin. Tonight she'd have to prepare herself, because when she walked back into the mansion, she had to be ready for anything. As she walked across the field, she wondered why, out of the half dozen psychically gifted people in the region, she'd been the one chosen for this mission.

Some of her friends would claim it was karma. Others would claim that she'd just happened to be tuned in to the same channel as the person in danger. As she reached the path and regarded Magnolia, she concluded that she pre-ferred the latter explanation. To even consider that her destiny might be tied to that beautiful, brooding mansion was enough to give her the creeps.

As Jonathon hurried downstairs, he couldn't remember when he'd last been so excited. He felt like a kid getting ready to set out on an adventure.

"Good morning, Gran," he announced cheerfully when he entered the kitchen. She was standing at the sink, and he crossed the room, snatched her off her feet and spun her around in a circle.

"Good gracious, Jonathon! Whatever has gotten into you?" Adelaide sputtered, raising a hand to smooth her hair when he dropped her back to her feet.

"High adventure," he answered, helping himself to the coffee. He leaned a hip against the counter and grinned. "Don't tell me you aren't excited about looking for the se-cret room."

"I'd feel a whole lot better if Claudia didn't think the room was dangerous," Adelaide remarked with a worried frown.

"Don't start in on that again," he grumbled, cursing himself for relating Claudia's fears. "That room probably hasn't seen the light of day in more than a hundred years. What could possibly be dangerous about it?"

"I have no idea, but if Claudia says it's dangerous, then I believe her."

Jonathon gave a disgruntled shake of his head. He considered arguing with her, but then decided that he wasn't going to let her destroy his good mood. If she and Claudia wanted to stand around predicting doom, let them. When he found the room, they'd see it was all nonsense.

He set his mug on the counter and said, "Sit down and take a load off your feet. I'll cook you my famous omelet for breakfast."

"Oh, no you won't!" Adelaide exclaimed determinedly. She picked up his mug and handed it to him. "The last time you cooked me your famous omelet, it took me all day to clean up the kitchen."

"Well, if you had a full-time housekeeper, you wouldn't have to worry about my mess," Jonathon observed smugly.

"You know, Jonathon, you're just like your grandfather. He didn't know when to let go of a bone, either. But I'll let you in on a secret that it took him thirty years to learn. The more you harp at me, the more I dig in my heels."

"Well, in that case don't, under any circumstances, get a full-time housekeeper. After all, I wouldn't want you to enjoy your twilight years in leisure," he joked.

"Twilight years?" she repeated with a snort of disgust. "Let me tell you something, young man. I may be old but I'm not in decline. Now, get out of my way so I can fix breakfast. Claudia will be here any second. I called and asked her to join us."

As if on cue, there was a knock at the door. Jonathon again set his mug aside and went to answer it. The polite greeting on his lips died when he pulled it open. Claudia was wearing a yellow T-shirt and a pair of denims that, unlike her loose-fitting sundress, displayed her figure to perfection. The last time he'd seen curves like hers had been when he'd idly flipped through a *Playboy* that had been abandoned on an airplane!

He didn't realize he was staring until she nervously rubbed her hand against her thigh and said, "I thought jeans would be the appropriate attire for looking for a secret room."

"You were right," he responded gruffly as his gaze strayed to shapely legs while he gestured her inside. The sensual tug was back, and he frowned in aggravation. "Please, come in. Gran is being a spoilsport and refusing to let me make my famous omelet."

"I'm not being a spoilsport," Adelaide corrected as Claudia entered. "I'm refusing in self-defense. You're the only person I know who can use every dish in the house just to scramble half a dozen eggs."

"You just have no regard for culinary genius," he declared.

Adelaide chuckled. "Good morning, Claudia. I'm glad you could join us. Just ignore my grandson, and for heaven's sake, if he ever offers to cook you his famous omelet, refuse! You'll spend the next ten years cleaning up the kitchen."

"The rule at my house has always been that if you dirty it, you clean it," Claudia said as she quickly took a seat at the table, which had already been set for breakfast. The way Jonathon was staring at her made her feel distinctly uneasy. He'd spoken to her with formal politeness, but there was something almost contemptuous in his expression. He was probably regretting having agreed to let her help in the search.

She started when he said, "Would you like some coffee, Claudia?"

"Uh, no, thanks. I'll wait for breakfast."

He dropped into a chair across from her and continued to stare intently at her, a strange heated light in the honey-gold depth of his eyes making her breath catch. Finding his scrutiny unsettling, she glanced toward Adelaide. "What can I do to help, Adelaide?"

"Keep Jonathon out of my hair. He's as big a pest now as he was when he was a boy."

"That's 'bigger' pest, Gran," he responded without glancing away from Claudia. "I've grown a few inches since my boyhood."

"You've gotten more smart-mouthed, too. Now leave me alone and entertain Claudia."

"That's an interesting prospect," he murmured deeply as he leaned back in his chair and folded his arms over his chest. "Tell me, Claudia. How does a man go about entertaining a psychic?"

Claudia eyed him warily. She sensed that he was baiting her, but she couldn't figure out what he was after. She again made a concerted effort to connect with him and was baffled when she failed. Why couldn't she receive *something,* even if it was nothing more than a single emotion?

"I prefer the term clairvoyant," she said. "Psychic is a generalized term that covers all forms of extrasensory perception phenomena. It's like the word doctor, and, like doctors, most psychics are specialized. My specialty, so to speak, is clairvoyance."

"In that case, I'll rephrase the question. How does a man go about entertaining a clairvoyant?"

"He'd entertain her the same way he'd entertain any other woman." Too late, she bit back the words, realizing what kind of an opening she'd inadvertently given him. But he remained silent, though his eyes had deepened to darkest honey, mesmerizing her.

His gaze slowly slipped from her face to her breasts, and she was horrified to feel her nipples tighten against the fabric of her bra. She cursed the telltale blush that flew into her cheeks as he returned his gaze to her face and smiled at her with unabashed arrogance. He knew exactly the effect he had on her!

Adelaide, apparently oblivious to the undercurrent between them, said, "I still can't get over this secret room business. It's the most exciting thing that's happened around here in a long time."

"Does the journal give any hint as to where the room's located?" Claudia asked, leaping at the chance to change the conversation.

"No," Jonathon replied. "I suspect that it's either in the basement or on this floor. Both would provide easy access to the outside, which would be critical if they had to hide for any length of time. Remember, they didn't have canned goods or refrigeration in those days, so they'd have needed to replenish their food and water supplies."

"It's in the basement," Claudia said with a certainty that startled even her.

Jonathon eyed her with wary speculation. "Why the basement?"

"The room is dark and very damp," she said slowly though she didn't know where the information was coming from. It was probably a recessed memory from her visions the day before.

"You see it?" Adelaide questioned excitedly.

Claudia shook her head. "It's more of an impression."

"Maybe if you touched the journal again, it would be clearer," Adelaide suggested as she placed a plate of toast on the table.

"Gran, I don't think that's a good idea," Jonathon warned.

"Afraid I'll go off the deep end again?" Claudia asked ruefully. Before he could answer, she assured, "I won't. As I said yesterday, now that I know what to expect, I'll be fine."

"Jonathon, get the journal," Adelaide ordered.

"Gran—" he began, but stopped himself in time. A lifetime of having proper manners pounded into him wouldn't allow him to defy her in front of a guest. Reluctantly he headed for the library.

"Are you sure you want to do this?" he asked Claudia when he returned. All too readily he recalled her reaction to the journal yesterday. He had no desire to witness a repeat performance and, quite frankly, he was worried about her health. He was well-trained in first aid, but he didn't know how to deal with a person who couldn't breathe. What if she couldn't catch her breath this time? What if she . . .

"I'll be fine," Claudia said, interrupting his worried thoughts as she extended her hand.

He searched her face, looking for some sign of distress that would allow him to deny her request. She met his gaze head on, her expression calm, almost serene. Hesitantly he handed the book over and braced himself, expecting her to go into hysterics.

"Well?" Adelaide prodded when Claudia didn't speak.

"Nothing," she said with a heavy sigh as she placed the journal on the table. "But it isn't surprising. As I said before, I've never had telepathic communication through objects."

"Except for yesterday," Jonathon remarked dryly, wondering if he'd been wrong about her not being able to fake her previous reaction. After all, showmanship was an integral part of the fortune-teller's act, and it seemed damned suspicious that she'd gone off the deep end yesterday but nothing had happened today.

Claudia glanced toward him in surprise. Was he admitting that he believed in her clairvoyance? His mocking smile assured her he wasn't. She had no idea why that hurt, but it did. She shrugged off the feeling, reminding herself that she was here on a life-saving mission. What Jonathon thought about her didn't matter. "Except for yesterday," she agreed.

"What exactly did you see yesterday?" Adelaide inquired as she went back to the stove and began dishing up bacon and scrambled eggs.

"I didn't really *see* anything," Claudia hedged. "It was more like a series of rapid impressions and an overwhelming sense of danger."

"Then, how can you be sure that the secret room is dangerous?" Adelaide asked.

"I'm not sure that the room itself is dangerous. It is, however, the focus of the danger."

"I see." Adelaide returned to the table with the food, handed the platter to Claudia, and then sat down. "How serious is this danger? Is it life-threatening?"

"Just stop it!" Jonathon ordered impatiently, deciding that enough was enough. "It's an old room. The only danger it might present would be architectural, but I doubt it. Magnolia is built solid. Now, I don't want to hear any more of this ridiculous melodrama from either of you. Understand?"

"Of course, dear," Adelaide murmured with a benign smile that clearly indicated she was pacifying him.

It pricked at his temper, but he quickly curbed it. He was not going to let her goad him into an argument. He grabbed a piece of toast and smothered it with honey. The silence at the table grew more noticeable with each passing second, and he released an exasperated sigh. Whoever had claimed that silence was golden had never known his grandmother.

He glanced up, muttering, "I'm sorry. I shouldn't have snapped, but all this talk about danger isn't logical. We're talking about a damn *room,* for pity's sake."

"Claudia said that it may not be the room that's dangerous," Adelaide reminded.

Jonathon tossed his toast on to his plate and slumped back in his chair in defeat. He might as well talk this out with them. Nothing they said would change his mind, but maybe they'd finally drop the subject.

"Okay, Claudia," he said. "What are we dealing with? A ghost?"

"Oh, what a delightful idea!" Adelaide exclaimed. "Is it a ghost, Claudia?"

"No," Claudia quickly denied.

Jonathon's lips lifted in a taunting smile. "What's the matter, Claudia? Don't you believe in ghosts?"

"I've never had an experience with a ghost, so I neither believe nor disbelieve," Claudia answered, recognizing that he was purposely heckling her. She wasn't going to take the bait.

"Well, if it isn't a ghost, then what is it?" Adelaide questioned.

"I don't know for sure. It could be a person or perhaps an object. My impressions are too vague to tell for certain."

"If they're too vague, then why are you so sure that there's danger surrounding the secret room?" Jonathon asked immediately.

"The feeling of danger is unquestionably clear," Claudia responded carefully. It was also crystal clear, from Jonathon's attitude, that he was only being tolerant. She doubted he'd take her seriously, but if she handled this discussion right, he might be more careful.

"Is it life-threatening?" Adelaide again asked.

Noting Jonathon's darkening expression, Claudia evaded with, "It might be."

"So what we have is a clear *feeling* of danger from an *obscure* source that *may* be life-threatening," Jonathon summarized.

"Yes," Claudia agreed.

He leaned forward and propped his forearms on the table. "Just for the sake of argument, let's say I believe you. Can you honestly say that the danger will go away if we don't look for the secret room?"

"I'm fairly sure it will," she again evaded.

He nodded, then asked, "How often are your... predictions right?"

Claudia wanted to dodge that question. Instinctively she knew that Jonathon would be an odds player. And she had a feeling that her odds would encourage rather than discourage him.

Lie! an inner voice urged, but no matter how much she wanted to, she couldn't bring herself to do so. "I'm right about eighty percent of the time."

"So there's a twenty percent chance that you're wrong." When she nodded, he asked, "If you were in my place, what would you do?"

"Look for the secret room," she answered miserably, knowing that by doing so, the die had been cast. There was no backing out for any of them now, and soon the danger the shadow represented would no longer be nebulous. It would be a frightening reality.

Claudia shuddered as she followed Jonathon into the basement. It was everything she'd felt about the secret room—cold, dank and dark—assuring her that this was indeed where the room was located. The dim light overhead only cast enough light to give the nearby piles of clutter eerie, shadowy shapes. Because of the darkness, she couldn't get a fix on the length or the width of the room. Rationally she knew it couldn't be any longer or wider than the house itself, but her inability to see the walls gave her the irrational feeling that it stretched into eternity.

She shuddered again, thinking of the horror movies she used to watch as a kid. This was exactly the moment when a monster would leap out of the shadows and grab you. Only this time, it wouldn't be make-believe.

"Good Lord, maybe we should begin upstairs," Jonathon stated when he reached the bottom step. He shined his flashlight into the corners, where the dim bulb didn't reach. "I'd forgotten how much junk is down here."

"Well, if nothing else, this search will give you a good excuse to do some housecleaning," Claudia remarked with false cheer.

"Don't let Gran hear you say that. She doesn't believe in throwing anything away. She says that one man's junk is another man's record of history."

"I don't know if it's such a good idea to let her come down here, anyway," Claudia stated in concern. "It's terribly dark, and though I know she'd deny it, her eyesight isn't very good."

"If you think you can stop her from helping with the search, you don't know my grandmother very well," Jonathon responded as he headed for a particularly dark corner, irritated that Claudia's concern mirrored his own. It intimated that she cared for his grandmother, and he was still convinced she was using her. He also knew his grandmother well enough to know that, hazardous or not, she'd insist on joining in on the search. The only way he'd be able to stop her would be to hog-tie her, and she'd still probably find a way to get down here. "If stubborn had to be known by another name, it would be hers."

Like grandmother, like grandson, Claudia thought, grimacing as she watched him bat cobwebs out of his way without any hesitation. While they'd finished breakfast, he'd laid out his plans for the search. They'd begin in the basement, and if they didn't find the secret room there, they'd move upward a floor at a time. Then he'd detailed which rooms upstairs he felt would be the most likely to conceal a secret room. It was then that Claudia recognized that if he'd already put that much thought into the project, nothing she could say would stop him.

After breakfast Jonathon had offered to clean up the kitchen, but Adelaide had demurred, saying she'd load the dishwasher, change her clothes and join them later. Jonathon, eager to begin the search hadn't argued, and Adelaide had insisted that Claudia go with him to "keep him out of trouble."

As if she—or anyone else for that matter—could, Claudia thought ruefully. In the past half hour, she'd begun to realize that once his mind was made up Jonathon was an irresistible force.

"There's more than one way to light a room," he announced, returning from the corner with two large lanterns. "The test, of course, will be to see if the batteries are still good."

He set the lanterns on the floor beneath the ceiling light and squatted beside them. As Claudia watched him, she found herself noting the way an errant lock of hair fell across his broad forehead. The way his brows drew together in concentration. The way his T-shirt stretched across his shoulders. When she found her gaze wandering to the denim stretched across his hips, however, she quickly turned away. She was *not* going to let her thoughts wander down that path.

She surveyed the room, taking note of the piles of furniture and boxes. There were shelves cluttered with canning jars and tools, and those were just the recognizable paraphernalia. A meticulous inspection of the basement was going to be a mammoth undertaking. Perhaps the sheer immensity of the project would be enough to make Jonathon's enthusiasm wane.

"This search may take forever," she said as he finished turning on the lanterns, which only underscored the clutter.

Hands braced on thighs, he looked around. "We'll take it an inch at a time, and before you know it, we'll have covered a yard."

"Do you approach everything so optimistically?"

He shrugged as he stood. "I can stand here and let myself be overwhelmed by the big picture, or I can concentrate on one corner at a time."

"Have you ever been overwhelmed?" Claudia asked. She
couldn't imagine him facing anything he couldn't handle.
He looked too capable.

"Not by anything within my control," he answered, an
unexpectedly serious note in his voice. Then he shook his
head, as if warding off some unwanted memory. "Well,
should we start on my right or your left?" This time it was
his tone that was falsely cheerful.

"Since we're facing each other, isn't that the same direction?" Claudia replied, wishing again that she could pick
up on his emotions. When he'd gotten so intense a moment ago, she could have sworn she'd seen a flash of pain
in his eyes, but she wasn't positive. She was so accustomed
to dealing with people on a mental level that her skills in
interpreting emotion without her sixth sense were almost
nil.

He flashed her a quick grin. "I can see that I'm going to
have to get up early to fool you."

Claudia shrugged self-consciously. "Well, as my mother
would say, she may have given birth to a freak, but not a
fool."

Jonathon's eyes darkened, focusing in on her face
searchingly. "Your mother calls you a freak?"

"Why is that so surprising? You think I'm either crazy
or a crook."

"That's different," he said with a frown. "I'm not your
mother."

Realizing he was truly disturbed by her revelation, Claudia relented. "My parents love me, but they've never
known how to deal with me. We've agreed to live and let
live, and now that we have, we get along fine. So, you see,
it isn't as bad as it sounds."

Jonathon stared at her, disconcerted. He couldn't imagine what it would be like to have your mother consider you
a freak. The Tanner clan had many faults, but a lack of
motherly devotion wasn't one of them. Indeed, in the case
of his aunt Virginia, she was so fiercely overprotective of

her son, Steven, that it was almost an obsession. Thankfully Steven's wife, Ruth, was a malleable, shy woman who didn't mind being bulldozed by her mother-in-law on a regular basis.

As had happened at the river yesterday afternoon, he was suddenly hit with the unexpected urge to reach out to Claudia in comfort, followed by a fierce stab of anger at her parents. They'd hurt her. No matter how lightly she spoke of it, he instinctively knew she'd never gotten over it. The urge to step forward and take her into his arms grew stronger, alarming him. It disturbed him far more than the strange bolt of energy he'd experienced with this woman ever could, because Jonathon knew what it meant. When a woman began to draw on a man's protective instincts, it could only lead to trouble. And the day his wife had died, he'd promised himself that he'd never let himself in for that kind of trouble again.

Thankfully, Adelaide chose that moment to come down the stairs saying, "Good heavens, Jonathon. You were ranting and raving about getting to work down here, so why are you standing around twiddling your thumbs?"

"We were just waiting for you, Gran. We didn't want you to miss out on any of the fun," he mumbled as he swung away from Claudia and grabbed a lantern off the floor. As he carried it to a far corner, he made himself a promise. Until he had proof of just what Claudia was, he wouldn't apply any more labels to her. He was also going to stay the hell away from her.

Chapter 4

Claudia kept telling herself that she should go home. It was growing dark, but the redwood chaise she was reclining in was so comfortable that she couldn't summon up the energy to move.

She glanced toward Adelaide and Jonathon. Both looked as lethargic as she felt. After spending an uneventful day in the basement, they'd thrown together some sandwiches and a salad and eaten dinner on the back gallery. Adelaide was in the recliner next to her. Jonathon was sitting in a chair with his feet propped up on the porch railing, his hands folded over his stomach and his eyes closed.

As Claudia regarded him, she was bemused by the easy friendship he'd shown her throughout the day. He'd been kind, courteous, and hadn't once made a jab at her clairvoyance. That didn't mean she was deluding herself. She knew he hadn't changed his mind about her. If anything, she suspected he was just being nice because her comment about her mother had made him feel sorry for her. But even that, she found mind-boggling.

She couldn't recall anyone ever feeling sorry for her—at least not literally. Her family had never been able to come to grips with her clairvoyance and in fact, still kept her at arm's length. She'd had some psychiatrists and a few paranormal specialists show her some sympathy over the years, but those had all been on a strictly professional level. Even her friends didn't feel sorry for her. Those who had psychic abilities themselves empathized; those who didn't simply accepted her.

She was pulled away from her thoughts by a sudden influx of vibrations. They weren't strong enough to be visionary, but they were powerful enough to make her sit up and take notice. "Someone's coming, Adelaide."

"Really?" Adelaide questioned in surprise. "Who?"

Claudia shrugged. "All I can tell you is that it's a man."

"Why, Gran, have you got a suitor you haven't told me about?" Jonathon teased.

Adelaide shot him a look of pure annoyance. "If I did have a suitor, you can be sure I wouldn't tell you. You'd probably run him off."

"Damn right, I would," Jonathon responded only half joking as he dropped his feet to the porch. "Especially after your little escapade with Mr. McKenzie."

"My little escapade with Mr. McKenzie was nothing more than a harmless flirtation," she said with a sniff.

"Sure, Gran. It was so harmless, his wife came looking for you with a shotgun."

"You're exaggerating, Jonathon, as usual. It was a pistol, and it wasn't even loaded."

"You were involved with a married man?" Claudia blurted out in disbelief.

Adelaide gave her a brilliant smile. "Of course not, dear. As I said, it was a harmless flirtation. Why, Mr. McKenzie and I never shared more than a cup of tea and some stimulating conversation together. I'm afraid, however, that his wife is the jealous sort. It really is too bad, because I did so enjoy my little tête-à-têtes with him. Oh, you were right, Claudia," she continued when the sound of a car floated through the air to them. "Someone *is* coming."

"What the hell is Uncle Richard doing here?" Jonathon demanded, leaping to his feet when the car came around the side of the mansion. He despised his uncle, who was, as far as Jonathon was concerned, a greedy narcissistic bastard.

He'd been bilking Gran out of money for years, and when Jonathon had finally put a stop to it, his uncle had blatantly started stealing from her.

"I would say that he's come to visit me," Adelaide answered as she also stood.

"Uncle Richard doesn't come to visit, Gran, and you know it. What in hell is he up to this time?"

"He's not up to anything, Jonathon, and I don't know why you're always so quick to think the worst of him."

"Maybe it's because I've never seen anything but his worst side," he snapped. "Tell me what's going on, Gran."

"Nothing's going on!" she exclaimed in exasperation. "He's just interested in the secret room. He wants to take a look at the journal, and—"

"How in hell does he know about the journal?" Jonathon demanded.

"I told him about it, of course," Gran answered blithely. "He's very excited about the secret room, and he wants to see the journal—"

"Absolutely not!" Jonathon declared adamantly.

"Jonathon, stop being so difficult," Adelaide ordered as she started down the stairs. "And be nice. We have a guest, remember?"

Claudia gulped and wished she could disappear when Jonathon shot her a glowering look. When he turned his attention back to Adelaide and the man she was greeting at the bottom of the stairs, she looked around to see if there was a way to leave unnoticed.

Before she could determine if there was, Adelaide returned on the arm of her son, whom Claudia figured to be in his late fifties. His hair was the same silvery-white color as his mother's, but his eyes were such a pale blue they were almost opaque. When they flicked over Claudia in a cool appraisal, she barely suppressed a shiver—they gave her the creeps.

"Claudia, this is Richard," Adelaide said. "Richard, this is Claudia Peppermill, the dear, sweet girl I've been telling you about."

"Hello, Mr. Tanner," Claudia stated as she quickly climbed to her feet and extended her hand. "It's nice to meet you."

He ignored her hand. "You don't look like a psychic."

"What's a psychic supposed to look like, Uncle Richard?" Jonathon questioned in a soft silky drawl that made Claudia even more uneasy. She had no idea what Jonathon was feeling, but if it was anything like the hostility Richard was projecting as he turned those weird eyes on him, she'd be surprised if there wasn't some bloodshed soon.

"If you don't know that, Jonathon, then it just goes to prove what I've contended all along. You aren't as smart as you think you are."

"I'm smart enough to see through you, Uncle Richard. What are you doing here?"

"I came to see Mother. I'd also like to take a look at this journal you've found."

"What interest could you possibly have in an old journal? Are you stealing rare books now?" Jonathon asked, barely concealed contempt in his voice as he crossed his arms over his chest and glared at Richard.

"Why, you arrogant son of a—"

"Now, boys, stop it!" Adelaide interrupted hastily. "We have a guest, and I expect the both of you to remember it. And you stop talking to Richard as if he's a crook, Jonathon. He says he wasn't involved with Billy Joe, and I believe him."

"Come on, Gran," Jonathon muttered derisively. "Billy Joe was stealing antiques from the house. Uncle Richard sells antiques. I may not have proof that they were in collusion, but we both know that they were."

"I don't know any such thing," Adelaide declared angrily. "What I do know is that Richard is my son and your uncle. We're *family*, Jonathon, and you don't treat a member of the family like a criminal! Now, come along, Richard. We'll go inside and visit."

"I don't think so, Mother," Richard stated angrily, disengaging her hand from his arm. "I don't stay where I'm not wanted, and it's obvious that Jonathon doesn't want me anywhere near Magnolia. We'll get together sometime next week for lunch.''

"But, Richard!" Adelaide objected as he started down the stairs.

"Next week, Mother," he repeated, jerking open his car door and climbing inside.

"Now look what you've done!" Adelaide railed at her grandson as Richard spun his car around and shot down the drive way. "You've made him feel as if he's not welcome here."

"As far as I'm concerned, he's not," Jonathon responded tersely.

"Well, this is still my home, Jonathon Jackson Tanner the Third, and if you ever treat Richard like that again, I'll ... I'll ... Oh! I don't know what I'll do, but you better believe that you'll be sorry!"

Jonathon muttered a curse when she marched into the house and slammed the door behind her. He scowled, furious with himself for upsetting her. But damn it, he was right about his uncle, and if he knew Richard, the only reason he was interested in the journal was because he was hoping to cash in on it in some way. The Mississippi River would turn to solid ice before Jonathon would let him anywhere near it.

Claudia shifted uncomfortably from one foot to the other while again trying to decide if she could slip away unnoticed. She'd been able to pick up enough from Adelaide and Richard to understand this was an old argument between the three of them. She'd also picked up enough to know that regardless of Adelaide's claims to the contrary, she wasn't convinced that her son wasn't involved with this Billy Joe person. But motherly love prohibited her from admitting it, even to herself.

As far as Richard went, though, Claudia hadn't been able to pick up anything that would confirm or deny his guilt, which she found odd. She would have thought he'd respond either with feelings of innocence or guilt when being accused of thievery by a member of his own family. She was also bemused by his refusal to shake her hand. At first she'd thought he was just being rude, but then she'd realized that he was afraid to touch her. What she hadn't been able to discern was why.

She studied Jonathon covertly, wondering if she should enlighten him about Adelaide's ambivalent feelings regarding Richard's innocence. Grandmother and grandson had such a good relationship that she hated to see them arguing over something they might actually agree on. He looked so unapproachable, however, that she decided to hold her peace. She concluded that slipping away unobtrusively was impossible, so she began gathering the dishes.

She glanced up in surprise when Jonathon suddenly said, "I can take care of the dishes, Claudia."

She gave him a tentative smile. "I'm sure you can, but if I help, you'll be done in half the time, right?"

"You don't have to offer twice."

As he joined her, he said, "I'm sorry you had to witness that little spat."

Good heavens, if that was a little spat, she wouldn't want to see a big one! "You don't need to apologize, Jonathon. All families have their arguments. It goes with the territory."

"Yeah, well, unfortunately, my uncle Richard also goes with the territory." He gave a disgusted shake of his head. "Why is she so blind when it comes to him? Why can't she see him for what he really is?"

Claudia lifted the dishes she'd gathered, recognizing that Jonathon was talking to himself, not her. Her common sense told her to leave the situation alone, but then again, she might be able to help by enlightening Jonathon about Adelaide's feelings. "He's her son, Jonathon. If she admits that he's done something wrong, then she'll feel as if she's failed him in some way."

"That's absurd!" Jonathon lifted the remainder of the dishes and headed for the door. He held it open for Claudia.

She entered the kitchen, saying, "It's not absurd, Jonathon. It's human nature."

"Well, her human nature needs some fine-tuning," he grumbled. "If it hadn't been for my father, Uncle Richard would have bankrupted Gran years ago. She's given him enough money to pay off the national debt! Now it's up to me to keep him in line, and believe me, it's a full-time job, particularly when he has no qualms about stealing from her. And I mean that literally. If I could prove that he'd been working with Billy Joe, I know that Gran would finally see the light.''

''Who's Billy Joe?'' Claudia asked, curious.

Jonathon's jaw tightened as he placed his dishes in the sink and turned to open the dishwasher. ''He was the caretaker here a couple of years ago. When he applied for the job, my instincts told me he was trouble. But he'd grown up with Aunt Virginia, and she felt sorry for him. She talked me into hiring him.''

''She must be very persuasive if she talked you into going against your instincts,'' Claudia noted.

''I can tell you haven't met Aunt Virginia,'' he stated dryly. ''She yammers at you until you'll do anything to shut her up. Anyway, it looked as if Billy Joe was going to work out. He was doing a passable job at keeping the place up, but then I caught him stealing some small antiques from the house.''

''And you think your uncle was involved?'' Claudia asked as she began to rinse dishes and hand them to him to load into the dishwasher.

''I don't think it, *I know it,*'' Jonathon answered. ''The trouble is, before I could get the truth out of Billy Joe, he disappeared. That was two years ago, and no one's seen him since.''

''So without Billy Joe, all you have are unconfirmed suspicions against your uncle.''

''Now you sound like Gran,'' he grumbled.

''Well, try to look at this situation from Adelaide's standpoint. Richard is her son and she loves him. Even if she suspects he's guilty, she won't admit it without proof. When you argue with her, you only force her into defending him. Maybe if you stop forcing her into a defensive posture she'll start seeing him for what he really is.''

''I doubt that. I'm not kidding. She really is blind when it comes to my uncle.''

"Don't underestimate Adelaide, Jonathon. She's a lot more perceptive than you think she is. She just needs some room to reach her own conclusions about Richard, and she'll reach the right ones."

"I wish I could believe that. It would sure make life easier around here."

"Well, you'll never know if it'll work unless you give it a try," Claudia responded as she handed him the last dish. Now that she'd given him something to think about, it was time to change the subject. "Are you disappointed that you didn't find the secret room today?"

"No. I figure it will take days, perhaps even weeks before we locate it," he answered as he closed the dishwasher and leaned a hip against the counter.

"Can you afford that much time off work?" she asked casually thinking that that might be the solution to her dilemma. If Jonathon had to go back to work, it might give her a chance to figure out why there was danger surrounding the secret room.

"I'll have to visit the office every now and then, but my staff's one of the best in the country. They can take care of just about anything that comes up."

Well, so much for that solution, she thought in resignation. "Adelaide said you're in transportation. What kind of transportation?"

"A little of everything," he replied. "Tanner Transportation started out as a steamboat shipping line in Natchez during the early eighteen hundreds. My great-great-grandfather had gotten tired of paying out profits to export his cotton and decided not only to save himself some money, but to earn some extra on the side. We're still involved in some minor shipping along the river. The majority of our business, however, deals with everything from express trucking deliveries to moving and storage companies. Eventually I plan to restore Magnolia to a working plantation, and when I do, I hope to also expand the shipping end of the business. I'd like to see both the plantation and the company returned to a facsimile of their original purposes."

Claudia gave an amazed shake of her head. "It must be wonderful to be tied to so much history."

He tilted his head, as though considering her remark. "I think obsessed is a better word. You witnessed that today. We'd have gotten a lot more work done if Gran hadn't had to reminisce over every piece of junk we ran across."

"As I recall, you did a little reminiscing of your own," Claudia accused with a smile.

"So I did," he agreed, surprising her with a smile of his own. "I'm amazed you stuck it out. We must have been damn boring."

"I thought you were rather sweet," she murmured, feeling oddly breathless beneath the impact of his smile. He should smile more often, she concluded, ignoring the urge to reach out and trace the curve of his lips with her fingertips. Though he looked far from old, the smile made him look younger, more carefree. The laugh lines etched at the corners of his eyes and his mouth told her that he'd once smiled a lot. She couldn't help wondering what had happened to take his laughter away.

"Lord, don't let it get around that I've been doing something sweet," he drawled. "I'd never be able to hold my head up in polite society again."

She eyed him speculatively. "Somehow, I don't think that would bother you. I get the impression that you don't care what polite society—or impolite society for that matter—thinks about you. In fact, I'd be willing to bet that you sometimes go out of your way to shock people."

Jonathon was uncomfortable with her insight into his personality. She was right. He didn't really care what people thought, and he did like to give them a bit of a shock every now and then. It got the adrenaline going, and he periodically needed that rush to kick him out of the despondent moods he'd been prone to since his wife's death. "What have you been doing? A little crystal ball reading on the side?"

He hadn't meant the words to come as a gibe, but he realized they had when Claudia said stiffly, "I don't read crystal balls, and it's time I said good night."

"I'm sorry, Claudia. I didn't mean that the way it sounded."

He'd deliberately avoided touching her all day, but when she started to step around him, he automatically reached for her. The moment his hand wrapped around her upper arm, he recognized his mistake. That strange bolt of energy was back, and this time it was twice as strong. It hit him in the gut with the force of a blow and erupted into a brilliant flare of desire.

He kept telling himself to jerk his hand away, but instead he found himself drawing her toward him. Her eyes were wide and puzzled as she stared up at him. He would also swear that he could see a reflection of his desire in their depths, and that made him ache with need.

This is no more than pure chemistry, he told himself as he raised his free hand and touched her hair. It was soft and thick and curled around his fingers, as if yearning for his touch. As he cupped the back of her head and tilted her face up to his, her lips trembled, and then parted softly. It was an invitation he couldn't resist, and he lowered his head, telling himself he was crazy to kiss her. But then again, there were times when a little insanity was good for the soul.

When Jonathon grabbed Claudia's arm, her mind was instantly flooded with visions of lovemaking. They were so erotic that she was too stunned to speak or move, and though she kept telling herself to pull away from him, she couldn't find the strength to do so, because the visions had her enthralled. . . .

This time she was showering his body with kisses. His shoulders and biceps were like silk over steel. His chest was a tantalizing mixture of crisp hair and smooth skin. Wherever her lips touched, he grew hot. Wherever her hands trailed, he grew hard. As her lips travelled down his taut abdomen, he tangled his fingers in her hair. When she moved even lower, he whispered her name in fevered response. But even as she moved to accommodate his request, he rolled, pulling her beneath him. This time she was whispering his name as

*she parted her thighs in urgent invitation, her lips
clinging to his as he pressed against her, seeking entrance.*

The vision was shattered as Jonathon's lips brushed
against hers lightly. It was in direct contrast to the heavy,
drugging kiss he'd been delivering in that steamy world of
visionary erotica, making this one all the more real and ultimately more seductive.

When Jonathon unexpectedly jerked away from her, she
was again too stunned to move or speak. She blinked
against the haze clouding her eyes, and then wished she
hadn't when her gaze collided with his hostile one. He was
furious, she realized as she watched him clench and un-
clench his fists at his sides. It was only then that she recalled that for one brief second, before the visions had
overridden all other thought, she'd felt that chilling sense
of danger. Why hadn't she had the presence of mind to
latch onto it and seek out its source?

She took a cautious step backward, and then another
when he demanded in a low, accusatory rasp, "How do you
do it?"

She eyed him in wary confusion. "Do what?"

"Damn it, Claudia, don't play games with me!" he
railed. "I'm talking about the energy. Just tell me how you
do it. Better yet, tell me *why* you're doing it!"

She stared at him, perplexed. "Jonathon, I honestly
don't know what you're talking about. Maybe if you tell me
about this 'energy', I can explain it."

Jonathon cursed. She was standing there looking so innocent that he wanted to shake her. He tucked his hands
into his back pockets to make sure he didn't act on the impulse. He'd barely been able to hold onto enough sanity to
pull away from that blasted kiss that still had him throbbing. If he touched her again, he might not be able to stop
until he'd dragged her to bed and eased his sexual frustration.

What was this inexplicable hold she had over him—this
mysterious force of energy that made him react with no

more thought than a rutting animal? Even as a teenager he'd had more control over his libido!

"Claudia, I promise I won't get angry if you'll just tell me the truth," he stated with forced patience.

"You're already angry," she pointed out. "And I am telling you the truth. I don't know what you're talking about."

Jonathon glowered, he could tell that she wasn't lying. But that was impossible, because if *she* wasn't responsible for it then where was the energy coming from?

"Nothing happened when I touched you?" he asked suspiciously.

"No."

Her answer had been too swift, and Jonathon eyed her narrowly. She was lying now. He could see it in her eyes. That confused him—if she was that transparent, then her earlier innocence couldn't have been an act.

A part of him was urging him to push the issue, while another was telling him to back off. He opted for the latter. His emotions were in too much of an uproar to guarantee maintaining any semblance of control over them. And every instinct he had was shouting that it was imperative he be in control whenever he dealt with Claudia. Meaning that, from this moment on, he couldn't allow himself to even brush against her accidentally. It was when he touched her that he lost control.

"I think we're both tired and need to call it a night," he said carefully.

"Yes," Claudia murmured, understanding only that he wasn't going to tell her about the mysterious energy. Despite her curiosity, she was relieved. She'd never been a particularly brave person, and his anger frightened her. Since she had no way of confirming if her alarm was justified, she wanted to get out of there. "Good night, Jonathon."

When she'd gone, Jonathon closed his eyes and massaged the bridge of his nose with his thumb and forefinger. He was getting a headache, and he had a feeling it was going to be a humdinger.

But the ache in his head was probably going to be nothing compared to the ache in his groin. *He shouldn't have kissed her.* Hell, he shouldn't have touched her. He'd suspected what would happen.

He cursed inwardly as he opened his eyes. He'd been so sure that she was causing that damnable energy phenomenon, but now he wasn't so certain. Where was it coming from?

The obvious answer was that it was a simple case of physical attraction. But even as he offered himself the excuse, he dismissed it. There was nothing simple about what was going on here. The question was, did he try to find out where the energy was coming from, or did he run like hell?

Three days later Claudia was finishing up the section of the basement wall Jonathon had assigned her to examine. She was concentrating so hard on the project that it took her a moment to recognize the familiar free-floating sensation coming over her. She froze, her world suddenly wavering into hazy, indistinct patterns, and she held her breath as she waited for the vibrations to intensify into a clear, prescient form. Was the shadow finally making its reappearance? Heavens, she hoped so, because Jonathon's dour presence was getting on her nerves. If something didn't happen soon, she might be forced to leave Magnolia just to protect her sanity.

Soon, however, she realized that it wasn't the shadow, and she gasped disbelievingly, *"Merlin?"*

"What?" Jonathon murmured absently from across the room.

Claudia spun toward him, smiling widely. "I can't believe it. Merlin's coming! I'm sorry, but I have to go."

With that she ran across the room and up the stairs, not bothering to respond when Jonathon called after her, "Who's Merlin?"

She chuckled when she heard Adelaide say, "Why, Jonathon, he's a wizard. Surely you remember the story of King Arthur."

She didn't hear Jonathon's answer, but she could imagine his response. She raced out the back door and to the front of the mansion, arriving just in time to see Merlin's bright red sports car turn into the drive. Evidently he saw her at the same time, because he honked. Claudia waved exuberantly, and when he pulled to a stop in front of her and climbed out, she was in his arms in an instant.

"Oh, God, Merlin! When I realized you were coming, I couldn't believe it! How in the world did you know I was here?"

He laughed as he gave her a rambunctious hug and then pushed her back so he could see her. He arched a brow and let out a low whistle as his gaze traveled from the top of her head to her sneakered feet, and then reversed the journey.

His blue eyes were twinkling with devilry when they returned to her face. "I always said you were the best looking broad I've ever seen in a pair of jeans. I'm glad you decided to greet me in style rather than in one of those shapeless dresses you usually wear." He tugged playfully at the sleeve of her T-shirt, which was smudged with dirt. "I didn't realize, however, that slovenly was *haute couture* for the country, or I would have stopped off at a mud puddle. As far as finding you, that was easy. I threw myself on the mercy of your landlady."

Claudia grinned. "In other words, you charmed the socks off her. You're as incorrigible as ever, and for your information, I'm dirty because—"

"She's been helping us clean the basement," Jonathon tersely completed from behind her.

Claudia glanced over her shoulder at him, not only startled by his presence, but bewildered by his stormy expression and the obvious fact he wanted to keep their search a secret. "Yes. I've been helping clean the basement," she said slowly, "Merlin, this is Jonathon Tanner, my landlady's grandson. Jonathon, this is Merlin York, a very close friend of mine."

"Pleased to meet you," Merlin said, extending his hand.

"The same," Jonathon returned, accepting it while sizing up Merlin York. He was around Claudia's age, his lean, wiry frame an inch or two shorter than Jonathon's own six-foot-two. He was handsome in a dark-haired, pretty-boy kind of way, Jonathon supposed. He also had a devilish glint in his blue eyes that Jonathon instinctively disliked. He couldn't help wondering just how *close* Merlin's and Claudia's friendship was.

"And who is this beautiful vision?" Merlin asked flirtatiously when Adelaide joined them.

"Oh my, what a charmer," Adelaide said with a chuckle. "I'm Adelaide Tanner, and you are...?"

"Merlin York," he answered with a flourishing bow.

"You have a very unusual name," she noted.

"That's because I'm a very unusual man."

"Don't tell me," Jonathon stated dryly. "You're another clairvoyant."

"Good heavens, no!" Merlin said, aghast. "I wouldn't wish that curse on my worst enemy." He glanced toward Claudia and smiled sheepishly. "No offense, dear heart, but it's the truth."

"None taken," Claudia assured. "I wouldn't wish it on my worst enemy, either."

Merlin returned his attention to Jonathon and Adelaide, "I'm just a navy pilot."

"He's not *just* a navy pilot," Claudia corrected. "He's a Top Gun."

"Oh my, how exciting!" Adelaide proclaimed. "I saw the movie three times. Is life as a Top Gun really that exciting?"

Merlin laughed. "It's not quite so dramatic, and, alas, there's no Kelly McGillis in my life. Of course, that would change if Claudia would agree to run away with me."

Claudia chuckled and shook her head. "Don't let him fool you, Adelaide. The reason there's no Kelly McGillis in his life is because he's a confirmed playboy who falls in and out of love faster than he can say his own name."

"I take offense at that!" Merlin objected, clasping his hand to his chest melodramatically. "I have *never* fallen out of love with you."

"Nor I with you," Claudia said with a grin. "How long can you stay?"

He dropped his arm around her shoulders and gave them a squeeze. "Just overnight."

"But that won't give us any time to catch up!" Claudia objected. "Can't you stay longer?"

"Sorry, but I'm on my way to a conference in Atlanta, and as it is I had to do some fast talking to get an extra day so I could even see you. We have tonight, Claudia. That's better than nothing, right?"

"Right," Claudia agreed in resignation. "Since the clock is running, we'd better get our visit started. I'm staying in the guest house. Just drive your car around the side of the mansion and you'll see it. I'll meet you there."

"Gotcha. Mr. Tanner, it was nice meeting you," he said, nodding toward Jonathon. Then he caught Adelaide's hand and pressed a kiss to its back. "And you, my fair lady, have captured my heart."

"Oh, go on with you," Adelaide ordered with an amused laugh.

My sentiments exactly, Jonathon thought sullenly when Merlin laughed and headed for his car. *In fact, the further away from Magnolia, the better.*

"Jonathon?" Claudia said.

He swiveled his head toward her and snapped, "What?"

Claudia's eyes widened in surprise at the fierce frown that marred his brow. "I just wanted to say that I won't say anything to Merlin about the secret room."

"And I'm supposed to take your word for that?" he retorted.

"Well, it's either that or bug my house," she shot back, cut deeply by the question. Though he'd been about as friendly as a bear with a sore paw since their kiss in the kitchen, she'd still believed they'd made some progress during the past few days. Apparently she was wrong. "And if that's what it takes to prove to you that I'm not a liar, then go ahead and do it."

With that she stalked away, and Jonathon glared after her retreating back.

"You know, Jonathon," Adelaide murmured, "jealousy doesn't become you."

"What is that supposed to mean?" he demanded as he switched his glare to her.

She smiled up at him sweetly. "It means exactly what you think it means."

"I am not jealous of Claudia!"

His grandmother shook her head wisely. "You can lie to me if you want, Jonathon but don't lie to yourself. You're starting to like Claudia."

"What does that have to do with anything? I like a lot of women."

"Yes, but there's like, and then there's *like*. I'm not so old that I don't know the difference."

"Gran, you're making something out of nothing," he muttered.

"Whatever you say, dear. Since Claudia will be tied up with Merlin, we might as well call it a day. I'm going upstairs to bathe and change."

As Jonathon followed her into the mansion, he told himself that she was wrong. He wasn't jealous of Claudia. If he was feeling irritated, it was because he didn't like all these strangers hanging around Magnolia. It didn't have a thing to do with the fact that he was trying to guess where Merlin York was going to spend the night in the one-bedroom guest house.

Chapter 5

"I'm telling you, Merlin, the man drives me nuts!" Claudia railed, picking up on the conversation they'd been having before she'd taken a shower and changed. She plopped down onto the sofa and drew one leg beneath her. "What do I have to do to prove to him, that I'm not a liar, a nut, or a crook? Sign my name in blood?"

Merlin shook his head as he took a seat on the other end of the sofa, "Why are you letting him get to you, Claudia? You've dealt with the Jonathon Tanners of the world for years, and you know you can't change their minds."

"He's different," Claudia murmured, raking a hand through her damp hair. "I can't read him, Merlin. I can't even pick up on his emotions. The only time I get anything from him is when I touch him, and—"

She stopped abruptly when she realized that she was about to confess the erotic images she'd gotten of her and Jonathon. She blushed and ducked her head when Merlin eyed her questioningly. They'd been best friends since first grade, but she couldn't bring herself to discuss *that* with him.

"What is it, Claudia?" he asked, reaching over to catch her hand. "I'm Merlin, remember? You can tell me anything."

"I can't tell you about this," Claudia mumbled. "It's too—embarrassing."

"Embarrassing?" he repeated quizzically. Then, "Oh, damn, Claudia, you aren't sleeping with the man!"

Claudia's head shot up at his appalled tone. "Of course, not."

"Thank God." He collapsed against the cushions behind him. "If you were, I'd have to punch him out, and Tanner looks he as if he could beat the daylights out of me with both hands tied behind his back."

"What do you mean, you'd have to punch him out?" Claudia demanded, incensed. "I'm twenty-seven years old. If I want to sleep with a man, then I'll sleep with him, and no one, not even you, will have anything to say about it!"

"Get real, Claudia," Merlin admonished. "You may be twenty-seven chronologically, but when it comes to men, you're prepubescent. If you want to sow your oats, start out with some nice, shy guy who's as naive as you are. Tanner is a barracuda. He'll chew you up and spit you out before you even know what's hit you."

"Well, thank you for the vote of confidence," Claudia said, miffed.

Merlin smiled wryly. "Claudia, I'm not picking on you. I'm just telling it like it is. Tanner is major league. Mess with him and you'll get hurt."

"That may be true, but it's still my decision to make."

"What are you trying to tell me? That you plan on going to bed with him?"

"Never!" Claudia exclaimed with conviction.

"Then why are we having this discussion?"

She shrugged helplessly. "Because when I touch him, I *see* myself making love with him.... That's never happened to me before. But I could never make love with a man who not only distrusts me, but I can't link with mentally."

"Link with mentally?" Merlin scoffed. "Claudia, we're talking about sex, and believe me, you don't need a mind link to get the job done."

"I hate this discussion," Claudia said as she drew her legs up. She wrapped her arms around them and rested her forehead on her knees. "Do you know what the worst part about all this is? I've always fantasized about being romantically involved with a man I couldn't read. You don't know what it's like to have a man show up at your door with flowers or candy or some other equally romantic gift, only to start receiving messages that he's trying to figure out how long it will take to get you into bed.

"I'm not blaming those guys," she continued with a heavy sigh. "I know that part of the dating game is physical attraction, and I suppose I should feel complimented that men find me attractive. And most of the guys I've dated really do like me. It's just that when you pick up on a man's libidinous emotions, it's all so...unromantic. But now that I've met a man I *can't* read, I couldn't feel more helpless if I'd suddenly been struck blind, especially when I see *him* tumbling me into bed! It's scary, Merlin. Really scary, and it's happening when I need my powers the most. What am I going to do?"

"If you're asking for my advice, I say pack your bags and go home," Merlin stated pragmatically.

"I can't leave," Claudia said, raising her head and frowning at him. "I already explained that I came to Magnolia because someone is in danger. If they're going to survive, they need my help."

"So, now we're back to this shadow of yours." He settled more deeply into the cushions and frowned at her in concern. "If what it represents is as dangerous as you think, what makes you so sure you can stop whatever's going to happen?"

She gave a helpless shrug. "I just know I can."

"And what if you're wrong? What if you're placing yourself in danger? Have you considered that you may be on a kamikaze mission?"

"No," Claudia answered honestly. "But even if I am, I can't walk away any more than you could walk away from your squadron if you were faced with imminent danger."

"You have a point, but the difference between you and me is that I'm trained for danger. You're flying blind."

"Yes, but clairvoyance doesn't come with a training manual or a team of instructors. I fly blind most of the time."

"Again, you've got a point, but most of the time you're guaranteed a soft landing. This one doesn't look that promising."

"You're worried about me," she said softly.

"I always worry about you. You're so . . ."

"Alone," she finished for him.

"Damn it, Claudia don't read my mind!"

"I'm not reading your mind, and you know it. I'm just picking up on all those strong vibes you're generating." She gave him an impish grin. "But since you've mentioned it, I've always wanted to take a stroll through that convoluted brain of yours. How about inviting me in?"

He gave her a mock look of horror. "No way, Claudia. You might find out that I'm just as much a sex maniac as those jerks you've been dating. Even worse, you might see a wife and kids in my future. Do you have any idea what a trauma like that would do to my overinflated ego? Why I might actually have to grow up and become responsible and respectable!"

"Oh, perish the thought!" Claudia exclaimed, bursting into laughter. When she regained control, she smiled at him lovingly. "I'm glad you're here. I needed a good laugh with the best friend a woman could have."

He reached over to catch her hand, his expression suddenly serious. "I wish I could stay and help you with this shadow business, Claudia. I'm going to be worried sick about you."

"Cheer up, Merlin. I haven't had any visions of imminent disaster in my future."

"Come on, Claudia, don't try to pacify me," he chided. "I know that you rarely have any insight into your own future, and I suppose that's a blessing. It would be boring if you always knew what to expect. But in this case, I'd prefer that you were bored as hell so I didn't have to worry about you."

"Hey, Jonathon Tanner, major league barracuda, will be here. What more could a clairvoyant ask for?" she teased, inwardly wondering if the major league barracuda wasn't the problem in the first place. She wished she could tell Merlin about the possibility that Jonathon was the source of the danger, but she couldn't bring herself to do so. Merlin was already concerned enough about her. It wouldn't be fair to compound his anxiety when there was nothing he could do to help.

"A chastity belt!" Merlin declared sardonically. "I swear, Claudia, if he lays a hand on you—"

"It will be because I let him," Claudia interrupted firmly. "Now, let's stop talking about me. I want to hear all about you."

Merlin's look clearly said he wanted to pursue the topic of Jonathon, but he relented and said, "All right. We'll talk about me."

As Jonathon settled into one of the redwood chaises on the gallery he told himself that he wasn't spying on Claudia. He was just taking the opportunity to enjoy the balmy night air, a liberty that would be impossible once summer arrived in a few weeks with its unrelenting heat and humidity. The fact that this section of the gallery was the only place in the mansion that provided an unrestricted view of the guest house was just a coincidence.

"Should I get you the binoculars?" Adelaide asked as she stepped outside.

"Why would I want the binoculars?" Jonathon responded innocently.

"Oh, I don't know. Maybe you'd like to do some stargazing."

"It's overcast, Gran."

"So it is." She sat down in the chaise next to his. "Mind if I join you?"

"It appears that you already have."

"You're awfully grumpy tonight."

"Maybe that's because a sledgehammer has more subtlety than you."

She chuckled. "What can I say? My heart's in the right place."

"Well, your heart may be in the right place, but your nose is going to get tweaked if you keep sticking it in where it doesn't belong."

"Why, Jonathon Jackson Tanner the Third. I never thought I'd see the day when you'd threaten your poor, helpless grandmother."

"Gran, you're as rich as Croesus and about as helpless as a full-grown gorilla. You're also a pain in the neck."

"That's what grandmother's are for, dear."

"Thanks for clearing that up."

"You're quite welcome. So, have you seen anything juicy going on at Claudia's?"

"I am not going to dignify that question with an answer."

"That means you haven't, though why you'd think you would is beyond me. Any fool can see that there's nothing going on between Claudia and that nice Mr. York."

"Are you insinuating that I'm a fool!"

"I'm not insinuating anything. I'm merely making an observation."

"I think I've just been insulted."

She chuckled again. "Well, if the insult fits . . ."

He couldn't help it. He laughed despite himself. "I don't know why I put up with you."

"You do it for the same reason I put up with you. You love me."

"Yeah, I do."

She was silent for several minutes before she said, "Jonathon...Katie's been gone for three years. I know this may sound harsh, but you're a young man and life does go on. You shouldn't feel guilty about being attracted to Claudia."

"Now, how did I know you were going to say something like that?" he muttered dryly.

"Maybe because you're thinking it, too?"

"You're way off base there." He paused before asking quickly, "Has anything strange ever happened to you when you've touched Claudia?"

"Strange?" she repeated curiously. "In what way?"

Jonathon shrugged, trying his best to appear casual. He cleared his throat. "A feeling of energy. Like sticking your finger in an electrical socket."

"Good heavens, no. Has something like that happened to you?"

"Yes."

"Hmm. What does Claudia say about it?"

"I haven't told her."

"Why not?"

"Because I think it's a damn trick she's playing on me, and I'm not about to give her the satisfaction by acknowledging it."

Adelaide released an exasperated sigh. "Why do you have this absurd prejudice against clairvoyants?"

"It's not prejudice. It's common sense."

"It's prejudice, Jonathon. What I don't understand is why. If you read up on the subject, you'll discover that clairvoyance is more common that you think. There is even some evidence that small children have frequent clairvoyant experiences. They'll say something like, 'Grandma's going to call,' and a few minutes later she does. Parents dismiss it as coincidence, when it may not be coincidence at all. Just think what might happen if we helped children develop that potential."

"You're looking at it from the standpoint of all the good things that could come from E.S.P. skills. But what about the bad things, Gran?" he rebutted. "How do you think a kid will feel when he looks at someone he loves and knows that they're going to die, and there's nothing he can do to stop it?"

"Gracious, Jonathon, you sound like the voice of experience talking. Has something like that happened to you? Have you predicted someone's death?"

"No!" he exclaimed angrily. "And I'm sick and tired of talking about all this mumbo jumbo, so before we get into a fight, let's change the subject."

"You don't have to bite my head off. All you have to do is ask," she said with an offended sniff.

"I'm sorry," he muttered, deciding that he'd been saying those two words so frequently lately that he should have them tattooed on his forehead to save himself some time. "I shouldn't have snapped at you. Tell me what Aunt Virginia had to say when she called this evening."

Thankfully his grandmother immediately launched into a monologue that required nothing more than a grunt from him every now and then. It allowed him to shut everything out while he tried to chase away the ghosts. He'd blatantly lied to her, and that was a first for him. Even as a child, he'd always felt compelled to tell her the truth. But how could he tell her that he'd dreamed of the deaths of his grandfather, his father, and Katie? How could he explain that there was a part of him—albeit an irrational part—that felt his dreams had actually caused their deaths? He knew that it was a ridiculous notion, but knowing that didn't chase away the guilt.

He closed his eyes against the barrage of emotions that were brought on as much by anger at his inability to stop the dreams he'd had in the past from coming true as they were by the pain of loss. It was why he no longer allowed himself to have any dreams, and it was why he wouldn't—*couldn't*—accept Claudia's clairvoyance. If he did, he feared that the anger, the pain, and ultimately the guilt, would destroy him.

Claudia blinked back tears as she walked Merlin to his car. They'd talked until long past midnight, but there was still so much she wanted to tell him—so much she wanted to hear about him. She was glad he'd come, but she almost wished he hadn't. His visit only underscored her loneliness.

"Hey, no tears!" Merlin ordered as he caught her chin and raised her face to his.

"You know I always cry when you leave."

"Well, I wish you wouldn't, it makes me feel awful."

"Sorry."

"You could say that with a little more conviction."

"*Sorry!*"

"That's better." He wrapped his arms around her and gave her a crushing hug. "I'll be back in six months. In the meantime, I want you to be careful. If you think you're getting in over your head, pack your bags and go home."

She pulled away and gave him a watery smile. "Hey, I have yet to meet a shadow who can get the best of me."

"I wasn't referring to the shadow," he stated grimly.

She jammed her hands into her pants' pockets and frowned at him. "Stop hovering, Merlin. I'm a big girl, remember? I know all about birth control and safe sex. I can protect myself."

"I know you can protect yourself in that area. The question is, do you know how to protect yourself from a broken heart?"

She shrugged. "With any luck, I won't have to find out."

"Instead of relying on luck, just say no."

"Aye, aye, sir," she said, giving him a smart salute.

He grinned and shook his head. "I adore you, dear heart."

"I adore you, too," she mumbled, again blinking back tears. "Now, get out of here before I start bawling."

"I'm gone!" He climbed into his car and started the engine. Then he rolled down his window and said, "You have my number in Atlanta. If you need me for anything, even if it's just to talk, call."

"I will. Now, go!"

He nodded, backed up the car and turned it around in the drive. He waved once, and then he was gone with a squeal of his tires.

"Show off," Claudia muttered as the tears began to roll down her cheeks in earnest. She wiped at them impatiently. Why was she crying? Merlin's future was free from peril, and, though she had yet to determine why, he'd be back sooner than he planned. She supposed her tears were because Merlin was the only person she could really talk to—the only person who had complete faith in her and her abilities—and now he was gone.

She turned back to the guest house and was startled to see Jonathon standing beside it. Oh, God! Surely he hadn't heard her and Merlin talking about birth control and broken hearts. If he had, she'd die. "How long have you been standing there?"

"I just arrived." He was staring at her so intently that she began to shift nervously from one foot to the other. What was he thinking? For that matter, what was he doing here? At this time of morning, he was usually in the basement.

"Are you okay?" he asked.

"Yes. I always cry when I have to say good bye," she explained, resisting the urge to wipe at her cheeks again. No wonder he was staring at her. She probably looked a fright! "I guess I'm overly sentimental."

He nodded, unconvinced but deciding to drop the topic. Leaning a shoulder against the house, he asked, "How long have you and Merlin known each other?"

"Since first grade. We took one look at each other and recognized a fellow tortured soul. It was instant friendship."

"Why was he a tortured soul?"

"Merlin stuttered. The other kids picked on him unmercifully. Thankfully he outgrew the problem by fourth grade, but it took a long time for his scars to heal."

"And what about your scars? Have they ever healed?"

"Who said I had scars?" she parried.

"You called yourself a tortured soul, Claudia. Scars are implied."

"Most of them have healed."

"Have there been other clairvoyants in your family?"

"If there were, they were well-kept secrets."

"So, you're a first. How do you account for that?"

"I don't, and what's more, I don't even try. I am what I am. Nothing is going to change that."

"Does it ever frighten you?"

She was perplexed by the question. It almost sounded as if he was beginning to believe in her abilities, but she warned herself not to read too much into the conversation. Knowing Jonathon, this was probably another one of his tests that she was sure to flunk. She considered dodging the question, but decided against it. The more information she gave him about her clairvoyance, the more data he'd have to digest. He still probably wouldn't believe in her abilities, but perhaps he'd be more tolerant.

"I'm not frightened by what I am. I came to grips with that a long time ago. Sometimes I'm frightened by what I see, but usually the fear is because I don't understand the vision. Once I'm able to interpret it, the fear goes away."

"Have you ever predicted death?" he asked, a curiously intent expression in his eyes.

"Where is this line of questioning going?" she questioned suspiciously. He was moving into an area that was filled with emotional land mines.

"Nowhere. I was just curious." He levered himself away from the house. "I'd better go. Gran's probably starting breakfast. Would you like to join us?"

"I had breakfast with Merlin."

"Oh, of course. Are you going to help us in the search today?"

"I'd planned on it."

"Great. I'll see you later."

As he walked away Claudia bit her lip in consternation. Why couldn't she connect with him? She sensed that something significant had just happened between them, but she had no idea what it was. If she'd felt confused by him before, she now felt completely befuddled. It made her wonder how regular people survived in their dealings with each other without going mad.

Claudia was just walking up the gallery steps when a car pulled up beside the mansion. She stopped and glanced toward it uncertainly. She was receiving some strange vibrations. They seemed to be from an emotion that was similar to anger, but was somehow different. She was still trying to define it when a woman climbed out of the car.

Claudia recognized her from the photographs in the mansion. It was Adelaide's daughter, Virginia. She was an exact replica of Adelaide, except she was taller and sturdier, and her hair hadn't gone completely white yet.

"You must be Claudia!" Virginia stated brightly as she joined Claudia on the steps. "Mother has told me so much about you, and I've been dying to meet you. I've never met

a clairvoyant before, though I did once go to a fortune-teller
at a carnival when I was a girl. You're much prettier than
she was. Younger, too, and you have all your teeth! She was
completely toothless, which, quite frankly, appalled me.
But I suppose it added to her mystique. Tell me, what do
you think about this secret room? Isn't it the most intrigu-
ing thing? It's going to make a wonderful chapter in my
book. You did know that I'm writing a history on Magnolia, didn't you? I think it's so important that we document
our personal history. I'm a second grade school teacher,
and though I think it's important that we teach our children about our country's history, it's just as important to
teach them the regional history. I . . .

"Oh, mother, there you are!" she exclaimed as Adelaide stepped onto the porch. "I was just having the most
delightful conversation with Claudia. You're right. She's a
dear. Where's Jonathon? I haven't seen that boy in ages."

"I'm right here, Aunt Virginia," Jonathon announced
as he stepped out the door and stood behind his grandmother. "How are you?"

Claudia gaped at Virginia in amazed disbelief as she
launched into another breath-defying monologue. She'd
never met anyone who could talk so rapidly. My word, the
woman should be an auctioneer! And she taught school to
second graders? The poor kids!

When Virginia finally stopped talking, Claudia was still
gaping at her. She started when Jonathon suddenly said,
"Well, Claudia, what do you say?"

She looked at him in bewilderment—she had no idea
what he'd been talking about. "Um, say about what?"

She would have sworn there was a malicious glint in his
eyes when he asked, "Is Aunt Virginia's book about Magnolia going to be a bestseller?"

She glanced from him to Adelaide's expectant face, and
then to Virginia. Only now, when the woman was finally
silent, did the vibrations resume. Claudia blinked when she
realized that the strange emotion she hadn't been able to
define was animosity, and if she was interpreting the vibes
correctly, they were directed at her. Uncomfortable, she

dismissed them. Virginia probably felt the same as Jonathon—that she was out to bilk Adelaide.

"I'm sorry, Virginia, but I haven't picked up anything on your book."

"Hey, but don't you worry about it, Aunt Virginia," Jonathon said cheerfully. "Claudia's a little slow on the uptake sometimes. All you have to do is sit down and talk to her awhile and the visions will start coming. Isn't that right, Claudia?"

That was definitely a malicious glint in his eye, Claudia decided, glancing back at him. She also decided that he had a mean streak in him. It was the only reason she could think of for him to sic his talkative aunt on her.

"How...interesting," Virginia murmured. "The more you're around a person the more you learn about them. Now, Mother," she continued as she walked toward Adelaide, took her arm and led her into the house, "I've come to look for that old train set of Steven's. I'm sure we stored it up in the attic. He's talking about collecting trains, and I've decided to encourage him. Maybe it will prod him and Ruth into finally starting a family. Have you heard the latest about Emily Harrison? It's absolutely scandalous! But then, Emily is always scandalous, isn't she? Why when we were girls..."

"Well, what do you think of Virginia?" Jonathon asked as her voice trailed off into the house.

"What?" Claudia asked, absently looking up at him. Her thoughts were on Virginia and the flash of acute fear she'd received from the woman just before she'd turned her attention on Adelaide. It had been so sudden and unexpected that it had taken Claudia by surprise.

"I said, what do you think of my aunt?"

"She must make an interesting school teacher."

He grinned knowingly. "The truth is, she's a fabulous school teacher and has won numerous awards. It's only outside the classroom that she becomes a motor-mouth. Gran says it's her way of letting off steam.

"I'm heading down to the basement," he continued. "Do you want to come along, or would you rather hang around and have another talk with Aunt Virginia?"

"I'm coming with you," she answered quickly.

It was the first time she'd heard Jonathon laugh aloud.

Claudia stood at the window and watched the thunderstorm approach across the night sky. Though it was expected that the storm would move through the area quickly, there was a National Weather Service severe thunderstorm and flood warning in effect.

She shivered as the lightning streaks grew larger and brighter, followed by quicker and louder bursts of thunder. The wind was howling as it battered against the guest house, and the lights had been flickering for twenty minutes. She'd already prepared for a power outage by gathering a flashlight, half a dozen candles and a good supply of matches. It wasn't the storm that made her uneasy as much as the possibility of being alone in the dark. If Jonathon hadn't spent the day staring at her as if she were a bug in a jar, she'd race over to Magnolia and beg him and Adelaide to let her wait out the storm with them.

"Grow up, Claudia," she scolded herself as she withdrew from the window and walked to the sofa. "The dark can't hurt you."

But the chastisement did nothing to alleviate her anxiety. As a child, she'd been terrified of the dark. She'd feared that if she couldn't see something familiar while having a vision, she'd get lost and wouldn't be able to find her way back. That fear had been amplified by her parents, who'd refused to believe what was happening to her and wouldn't even allow her the security of a night-light. Thus, she'd developed an intense dislike of the night, remnants of which had carried over into her adulthood.

She cradled the flashlight on her lap and stroked its handle as she forced herself to clear her mind. Meditation was the only thing that could calm her down, and years of practicing had made the process as simple and as natural to her as breathing. Within minutes the encroaching storm was nothing more than a soft grumble on the periphery of her consciousness. She leaned her head back against the cushions, closed her eyes and let her mind wander. It didn't surprise her when it settled on her two most worrisome problems.

The first one, of course, was that she still didn't know what danger the shadow represented. Logic suggested it was the secret room, since it was the only thing significantly different at Magnolia. It was also Jonathon's discovery of its existence that had made the shadow resurface after days of not appearing to her. But was the room the threat or merely the catalyst?

That brought her to the second problem, which was, in a word, Jonathon. Within his mind was the key to everything. She knew that as surely as she knew her own name. If only she could receive more from him than those damnable visions of lovemaking, she could resolve this whole mess. Why couldn't she connect with him? There had to be a reason, so what was it?

Agitation disbursed her peace and broke her concentration. So much for meditating. With a muttered imprecation, she sprang to her feet and began to pace, her emotions as turbulent as the rain that began to pelt against the windows and pummel the roof. Was it possible that she was subconsciously blocking herself from him? At first that seemed absurd, but then she concluded that it might not be so preposterous. She was after all, a twenty-seven-year-old virgin. Perhaps on some subjective level she didn't want to accept that she could be as wanton as those erotic visions claimed she was. But if that were the case, wouldn't she have had to connect with him initially to repress those feelings? And why were the visions so vivid? She didn't see them. She *lived* them, and that had never happened to her before.

She was so immersed in her thoughts that when the lights went out at the same time that the telephone rang, she jumped and let out a startled scream. The darkness immediately closed in on her, and her heart began to flutter in panic when she realized that she'd been so spooked she'd dropped her flashlight. But before her old fears of the dark could take hold, her common sense surfaced. The dark couldn't hurt her, and there were candles and matches next to the telephone.

She had just blundered her way to the end table, where the telephone rested, when her front door flew open and slammed against the wall. She let out another scream as lightning struck the ground outside, followed by a reverberating bellow of thunder. The lightning was gone as swiftly as it had come, but it had lasted long enough to illuminate the shadow that loomed in her doorway.

"No!" Claudia whispered in terror as the enmity of the shadow hit her with such force that it sent her mind spinning into a black, bleak pit where the air was so heavy she couldn't breathe.

Chapter 6

Jonathon was upstairs making sure that all the windows were closed against the storm when his grandmother screamed his name. It was the first time he'd ever heard true fear in her voice, and his blood ran cold as he raced toward the stairs.

Adelaide was waiting at the bottom, wringing her hands together, her face pale and her eyes huge. "Gran, what is it?"

"The library... a prowler!"

"Go upstairs, lock yourself in your bedroom and call the sheriff," Jonathon ordered without hesitation as he descended the stairs two at a time.

"But, Jonathon..."

"Gran, don't argue with me! Just do as I say!"

He didn't wait to see if she obeyed. He ran into the great room, snatched a two-hundred-year-old silver candlestick off the mantel, and then headed for the library. As far as weapons went, it wasn't the greatest, but he knew from firsthand experience that it was capable of giving a person one hell of a headache. His cousin Patricia had beaned him with it when he was twelve, and he'd seen stars for an hour.

His first instinct when he reached the door to the library was to burst inside, but his common sense made him slide to a halt. There was no light showing beneath the door, which meant the light in the hallway would make him a perfect target. Steeling himself, he turned the handle and in one quick continuous motion, tossed open the door and threw himself back against the wall. Then he eased his arm around the doorjamb, switched on the light and charged into the room, hoping that the sudden light would blind the intruder long enough for Jonathon to capture him.

It only took a moment to discern that he was alone in the library. The double doors leading to the gallery stood open, and rain was streaming through them. Books had been pulled from the shelves and were scattered across the antique Turkish carpets. The rolltop desk in the far corner had been ransacked.

He shook his head in furious disbelief. How could someone have done this much damage without being heard? A flash of lightning followed by a deafening boom of thunder gave him his answer. The double-brick walls of the mansion were so thick they were almost soundproof. Any noise that would have carried had been masked by the storm.

"Jonathon are you all right?"

He let out a yelp and spun around. "Damn it, Gran, put that rifle down before you hurt someone! And what in hell are you doing down here? I told you to lock yourself in your room and call the sheriff!"

Adelaide gave a haughty sniff as she shifted the butt of the rifle from her shoulder to the floor. "This is my home, Jonathon. I have to defend it."

He mumbled a curse before declaring, "Gran, you're such a lousy shot you can't hit the side of a barn at point-blank range."

"Well, the prowler doesn't know that. And even if he did he'd be more apt to run at the sight of me with a gun than you with a candlestick. Now, go close the doors before the rain ruins the carpets. I'll keep you covered."

When she hefted the rifle back to her shoulder, Jonathon prayed that she'd forgotten to take off the safety catch and made a mental note to hide every gun in the place at the earliest opportunity. He also determined that it was time he had a security system installed, even if his grandmother was opposed to such "newfangled contraptions."

"Did you call the sheriff?" he asked after he'd closed the doors.

"Of course, I called the sheriff."

"Good. Now put the rifle away and call Claudia. She should be warned that there's a prowler on the grounds."

"Don't be ridiculous, Jonathon. I'll stay here and guard the room while you go fetch her."

"Why do I need to fetch Claudia?" he asked in exasperation. The last thing he wanted to do at this moment was deal with Claudia. He'd been in an emotional uproar ever since he'd seen her crying as she'd watched Merlin York drive away. If he didn't know better, he'd think he was jealous. But that was ridiculous. In order to be jealous, you had to feel something for a woman, and all he felt for Claudia was unadulterated lust. Even worse, he no longer had to touch her to feel the energy—he'd discovered that he had only to be in the same room with her, and it would happen. Which was why he'd been in a state of sexual frustration all day.

Adelaide rolled her eyes skyward. "You have to go get her because there's a prowler on the grounds. You can't leave the poor girl in the guest house unprotected. I'll call her and tell her you're on the way."

"Gran, I'm not going to leave you here alone."

"I'm not alone," she announced as she gave the rifle a fond pat. "Winchester will keep me company."

He glared at the rifle, irritated with the fact that he couldn't dispute her logic. It would be best to bring Claudia to the mansion until the sheriff arrived. "Do me a favor, Gran. Make sure you ask questions first and shoot later. The life you save may be my own."

"Take a flashlight with you," Adelaide said, ignoring his sarcasm as she walked to the telephone and lifted the receiver. "The lights will probably go out any minute, and the guest house isn't hooked up to the emergency generator."

Jonathon walked to the kitchen, his thoughts forbidding. There'd been a damn prowler in the house, and his grandmother thought she was Rambo. Now he was going to have to traipse through the pouring rain to fetch Claudia, who'd probably come up with some crazy psychic explanation for the prowler having been there in the first place. It seemed impossible that less than a week ago his life had been running a smooth and steady course. He grimly wondered if it was legally possible to put your grandmother up for adoption.

As he sloshed his way toward the guest house, he realized that his grandmother's prediction had come true. The lights had gone out and the guest house was shrouded in darkness. Then a prickle of unease began to vibrate at the base of his backbone as he drew nearer and heard the telephone ringing. His grandmother should have reached Claudia by now. When he arrived at the porch and saw that the front door was open, his stomach knotted into a hard ball of fear.

"Claudia?" he yelled as he raced up the steps and through the door, cursing the fact that the flashlight was nothing more than a weak split of light in the room. Between the thunder and the telephone, which was still blaring out its summons, he couldn't hear a thing.

He closed the door and hurried toward the telephone. By now his grandmother was probably in a panic, and he had no idea what he was going to say to her. He let out a gasp of surprise when he rounded the coffee table and the toe of his sneaker connected with something large and soft. He lowered the flashlight beam, and his heart nearly stopped beating. Claudia was curled into a tight fetal ball between the sofa and the coffee table, and though there was apparently nothing wrong with her physically, she was struggling to breathe with the same frightening urgency as the day she'd touched the journal.

He snatched up the telephone receiver even as he dropped to his knees beside her. "Call a doctor, Gran."

"A doctor?" Adelaide echoed weakly. "What's wrong, Jonathon?"

"I don't know! Just call a doctor, and do it now!"

He dropped the receiver back into place, shoved the coffee table away and tentatively touched Claudia's shoulder, "It's Jonathon, Claudia. I'm here now, and everything's okay. Do you understand me, honey? Everything's okay."

She whimpered and curled even tighter into herself. He could feel her terror as acutely as if it were his own, and he wanted to snatch her up into his arms and hold her close.

Fearing that such a rash act might frighten her more, he took off his raincoat and wrapped it around her as he repeated, "Everything's okay, Claudia. It's Jonathon. I'm here, and you're safe. I'm going to pick you up, and then I'm going to take you back to Magnolia. Everything's okay. I promise, honey. It's okay."

Claudia didn't hear his words as much as felt their soothing rhythm. And when she felt the warmth enfolding her, she burrowed into it. She was so desperately cold, and the air in this dreadfully dark place was so heavy she couldn't breathe. She faced the truth. She was going to die.

But even as the panic began to overwhelm her, the warmth was drawing her away from it. The air became lighter, easier to breathe, and she snuggled even closer to the warmth. She was safe here, and instinctively she knew that as long as she stayed close to the warmth, the shadow couldn't hurt her.

Jonathon felt helpless as he paced the length of the sitting room. Sheriff Helton's deputies were busy gathering evidence from the library, which, according to the sheriff, showed no signs of forced entry. When asked, Jonathon had wanted to swear that the doors had been locked, but the truth was, his grandmother was lax about such things. And since he'd had no occasion to use them, he hadn't thought to check them.

He stopped at the arched doorway and stared up the curved cypress staircase that led to the second floor. The sheriff and the doctor were closeted with Claudia in the rose guest room, and the fact that they'd refused to let him sit in on the interrogation irked him to no end. He still had no idea what had happened to her, and his imagination had been running wild. The only reason he hadn't gone completely berserk was that her clothing had been intact and there'd been no apparent bruises on her body. He resumed his pacing.

"Jonathon, would you please sit down and relax? You're making me dizzy," his grandmother grumbled from her seat on the Queen Anne sofa.

"You deserve to be dizzy," he grumbled back. "When are you going to learn to lock your doors? I keep telling you these aren't the good old days when you were safe in your own home. But do you listen to me? No. And because you don't, look what's happened. The library is wrecked and Claudia is lying upstairs suffering from shock!"

"Why, Jonathon, you're really worried about Claudia, aren't you?"

"Of course I'm worried about her," he snapped as he came to a stop and glowered at her.

"Interesting," Adelaide murmured, grinning at him.

Before he could ask just what she meant by that, Sheriff Helton came downstairs. "How's Claudia?"

The sheriff shrugged and switched the toothpick he was chewing from one corner of his mouth to the other. "She's a little shook up, but other than that, she seems fine."

"Well, what did she say happened?" Jonathon demanded tersely.

The sheriff shrugged again. "It appears that she received a visit from your prowler, but the lights had already gone out, so she can't identify him. He probably didn't know she was there, and when he burst in on her, she most likely scared him as much as he scared her. Let's go to the library and see if you can tell if anything's missing."

Jonathon had been dreading this moment, had known it would inevitably come. He was going to look like a fool, and it was his grandmother's fault. "To tell you the truth, Sheriff, we wouldn't know if anything is missing. We don't have a record of what was in there."

Sheriff Helton arched a brow and switched the toothpick again before drawling, "I don't know much about books, son, but some of those in there look like they might be worth something. Far be it for me to tell you what to do, but don't you think it would be a good idea to get some-one to come in and catalogue and appraise them?''

Jonathon cast a meaningful glare over his shoulder at his grandmother, who only gave him a seraphic smile. ''Believe me, Sheriff, I'm going to be doing exactly that.''

He followed the sheriff toward the library. When he stepped into the room, the destruction made his stomach lurch. He glanced toward the desk and frowned. There was something different about the way it had been torn apart, but he couldn't put his finger on it.

''Sheriff, is it okay if I examine the desk?''

''Has it been fingerprinted?'' the sheriff asked one of his men. When the man nodded, he said, ''It's okay, Mr. Tanner.''

Jonathon approached the desk. By the time he reached it, he knew instinctively what was missing. A quick perusal confirmed his suspicion. Evelina's journal was gone.

Claudia frowned in frustration as she preceded Dr. Morris downstairs. According to the doctor and the sheriff, Jonathon had found her suffering from shock and gasping for breath. She didn't have any recollection of the event. Before waking up in Adelaide's guest room, her last memory had been of seeing the shadow standing in the doorway, and even that was hazy. The truth was, she wasn't sure the shadow had even been there. The wind could have blown the door open, the shadow having been nothing more than an extremely powerful vision.

''Claudia, what are you doing down here? You should be up in bed!'' Adelaide exclaimed in concern when Claudia walked into the sitting room.

''I'm fine, Adelaide. Honest. If you don't believe me, ask Dr. Morris.''

''She's fine,'' the sandy-haired doctor concurred. ''And unless you need me for something else, Mrs. Tanner, I'm heading back to town.''

''Of course. Let me see you to the door,'' Adelaide said as she linked her arm through his. ''I can't thank you enough for coming out, Dr. Morris.''

"You know I'll always come if you need me," he said, patting her hand. "It was nice meeting you, Ms. Peppermill, and if you need anything, anything at all, you just give me a call."

"I will, Doctor, and again, thank you."

When they were gone, Claudia wrapped her arms around herself and rubbed at her upper arms in agitation. Magnolia's brooding atmosphere was utterly menacing tonight. Something was terribly wrong here, and until she found out what it was, Magnolia would not be at peace.

But at that moment Claudia wasn't sure if she was capable of restoring peace here. Tonight she'd had a taste of just how vicious the shadow was, and she didn't know if she was emotionally—or psychically, for that matter—equipped to deal with it.

"Claudia? What are you doing down here?" Jonathon demanded as he walked into the sitting room.

She gave him what she hoped was a smile, but felt more like a grimace. "I'm fine, Jonathon. Really."

"Well, you don't look fine. You're as white as a sheet. You'd better go back upstairs and lie down."

Claudia again rubbed at her arms. She couldn't remain at Magnolia much longer. She felt as if its walls were closing in on her. "Actually, I was thinking about going back to the guest house and doing exactly that. I understand the power's been restored."

"You're not going anywhere near the guest house until I've instituted some security measures around here," Jonathon declared flatly.

"Jonathon, are you picking on this poor child?" Adelaide asked as she bustled back into the room. "After all she's been through, you should be ashamed of yourself! Don't let him upset you, Claudia. He just loves the sound of his own voice. It makes him feel masterful."

"I am not picking on Claudia, nor am I trying to feel masterful," Jonathon stated tersely. "I'm attempting to make her listen to reason. She wants to go back to the guest house!"

Adelaide's brow creased in concern as she regarded Claudia. "You can't possibly want to go back there tonight, Claudia. It's too dangerous."

"Sheriff Helton said he'll check out the guest house and secure it, Adelaide. I'll be perfectly safe," Claudia reassured.

Adelaide's worried expression deepened. "I still don't think it's a good idea, Claudia. You suffered a terrible shock tonight, and I know that Dr. Morris says you're all right, but I'd feel better if you were close by so we can keep an eye on you."

"I'll be fine," Claudia reiterated gently but firmly. "I just want to be among my own things. I'm sure you understand."

"Well, of course I understand, and if you're sure that's what you want to do, as soon as the sheriff leaves, Jonathon will walk you home."

"The hell I will!" Jonathon yelled, losing the fragile control he had on his temper. When both Claudia and his grandmother turned to stare at him, he stated adamantly, "No one is leaving this house tonight, do you understand me?"

Claudia's chin tilted up stubbornly, "I am not staying here Jonathon. I'm going home."

Before Jonathon could respond, Adelaide hurriedly interjected, "Of course you're going home, dear."

Jonathon regarded the two of them darkly. "Don't I get any say in this?"

"You're already outvoted, so we'd just be wasting your time if we listened to you," Adelaide answered.

Jonathon opened his mouth to argue, but their determined expressions told him his grandmother was right. He'd just be wasting his breath. "Both of you are nuts," he charged, "and I refuse to take responsibility for either of you!"

With that he stalked off, concluding that he was never going to understand women. After what Claudia had been through, all she was worried about was being among her own things. And even more stupefying, his grandmother, who had seen Claudia's condition when he'd brought her to Magnolia, agreed with her!

It was nearly an hour later when he grudgingly walked Claudia back to the guest house. He still wasn't happy about letting her stay there, but at least she'd agreed to let the sheriff and his men secure it before they left. Besides, he'd had time to think about the break-in, and he'd come to the conclusion that his uncle Richard had been their prowler.

Claudia gave Jonathon a sidelong glance as he walked beside her. She knew he was upset with her. She considered explaining her feelings, but concluded that would only make him more angry. There was no way he was going to believe that the aura around Magnolia was growing more menacing by the moment.

"Jonathon, why do you think the prowler stole Evelina's journal?" The question had been bothering her ever since she'd learned of the journal's disappearance.

"The reason he stole it was because he wasn't a prowler," Jonathon answered tersely, uneasy with the fact that her question was so close to his own thoughts. Was she reading his mind? The possibility caused a hard knot to form in the pit of his stomach.

"What do you mean he wasn't a prowler?"

He glanced toward her and stated grimly, "Our prowler was Uncle Richard."

"Oh, come on, Jonathon! You can't really believe your uncle did this," Claudia objected.

"He did it," Jonathon stated with conviction. "I had the journal locked in the desk, and Sheriff Helton says that the drawer wasn't forced open. That means our prowler knew where the key was located."

"That still doesn't prove your uncle's guilty," Claudia disputed.

"Sure it does. Uncle Richard wanted to see the journal and I wouldn't let him look at it, so he stole it. He tore up the library so it would look as if we'd had a prowler. Then he decided to add a nice touch to the ploy by stopping by the guest house and scaring the daylights out of you."

Claudia considered his theory. From what she'd heard about the man, it did make a crazy sort of sense that if Richard decided to steal the journal, he'd make it look like a robbery. As far as Jonathon's speculation about Richard being the one to have frightened her, she supposed that was possible, too. After all, he'd been afraid to touch her the day they'd met. If he was afraid of her, it might account for the enmity she'd received from the shadow. Just the memory of all that hatred was enough to make her shudder.

"Have you shared your theory with the sheriff?"

He nodded. "He called Uncle Richard's house, and surprise, surprise. He was out, and Aunt Doreen didn't know where he'd gone. He's going to follow up on it in the morning."

"Thanks for walking me over," she said, relieved when they reached the guest house. She was too weary to think about the break-in any more tonight. She was just going to crawl into bed and pull the covers over her head.

"Are you sure you won't change your mind and come back to Magnolia?" Jonathon asked.

"If, as you suspect, your uncle did this, I'm perfectly safe." He frowned as he tucked his hands into his pants' pockets. "Well, will you at least let me come in and check the place out?"

"The sheriff and his men already did that," she pointed out, trying to ignore the warm glow his protective attitude was giving her.

"I know, but I'd feel better if I did it myself."

"I guess I'd feel better, too."

Once they were inside, she was glad she'd acceded to his request. Her earlier terror still lingered in the air, and she shivered when the lights flickered. When they finally returned to the front door, she was reluctant to see him leave.

"Thanks," she said.

"Sure." He stuffed his hands into his pockets again and hunched his shoulders. "I guess we should say good night."

"Yeah, I guess we should . . . I'm going to be all right, Jonathon."

"Are you trying to convince me or yourself?"

She smiled ruefully. "I suppose I'm trying to convince us both."

"You could come back to Magnolia tonight and convince us both tomorrow."

"I can't do that. I need to stay here."

"Fine," he said with resignation. "Lock the door behind me."

"Don't worry. I will."

He nodded, pulled open the door and walked out. When he stepped off the porch, he looked back at her. "Take care of yourself. Gran would never forgive me if anything happened to you."

"I thought you weren't going to take responsibility for either of us."

"Yeah, well, unfortunately, I was born responsible."

"That must be a heavy burden."

"I've got wide shoulders."

As Claudia's eyes involuntarily traced their breadth, she couldn't disagree with that. She also had a very powerful visionary recollection that they were silk over steel, but when a heated yearning stirred within her, she sternly reminded herself that Jonathon was off-limits. "Good night, Jonathon."

"Good night, Claudia. Sweet dreams."

Claudia released a heavy sigh as she closed the door and locked it. If she had dreams about Jonathon, they wouldn't be sweet. They'd be too hot to handle. Confused, she pondered the fact that she could be so distrustful of him and yet so turned on by him at the same time. Wryly, she admitted that if he'd made any effort to pull her into his arms, she'd probably have thrown all her moral principles out the window.

Merlin was right, she concluded as she headed for her bedroom. She was in over her head, and if she had an iota of common sense she'd pack her bags and go home. Apparently, however, her common sense had deserted her, so she reverted to Plan B. As she undressed for bed, she began to practice saying no.

* * *

Claudia had just poured a cup of coffee when she was hit with a rapid series of strong vibrations. She quickly determined that Adelaide was coming to see her, and if she was interpreting the vibes right, her friend was very angry.

She tightened the belt on her robe and finger-combed her tangled hair as she headed for the front door. Hopefully, whatever was wrong wasn't serious. All night long she'd wrestled with dreams of a bleak, dark pit with air so heavy she couldn't breathe. She was feeling too groggy to deal with a crisis.

She'd just reached the door when Adelaide knocked. She pulled it open and said, "Good morning, Adelaide. What's up?"

"I'm moving out," Adelaide announced without preamble.

Claudia remained silent as she let Adelaide's announcement sink in. She also took the time to absorb the thoughts the older woman was projecting. Adelaide was furious with her grandson. He'd hurt her feelings terribly.

"Adelaide, I'm sure that whatever Jonathon said or did to upset you, he didn't mean it," Claudia murmured soothingly.

"Oh, he meant it," Adelaide muttered. "He told me to pack my bags and get out, so that's exactly what I'm doing. Or at least I've packed *a* bag. I'll send for the rest of my things later."

Claudia stared at her in open-mouthed astonishment. "Adelaide, don't be ridiculous! This is your home. Jonathon would never throw you out of it."

"He not only would, he has. I'm going to Virginia's, so if you need me, you can reach me there. And don't you worry about him trying to throw you out," she continued. "I told him that your lease is good for six months. If he even tries to harass you, I'll sue him myself."

"Adelaide, I don't have a lease," Claudia reminded.

She gave a dismissive wave of her hand. "He doesn't know that, and don't you dare tell him. Now, I'd better get on the road. I just wanted to let you know what was going on before I left."

"Why don't you come in and have a cup of tea?" Claudia suggested. "You're upset, and you shouldn't drive when you're upset."

"No, thank you, dear. If I stay, I'm only going to get more upset."

Still concerned, Claudia let herself connect with Adelaide's mind to see if there was any imminent danger in her future. When she reassured herself that there wasn't, she immediately broke the connection. She was dying to know what Adelaide and Jonathon had argued about, but delving into someone's mind without their express permission and foreknowledge was out of the question. She wasn't about to let herself be tempted to explore just a little further to find out.

"All right, Adelaide, I won't insist that you come in, but I want you to call me as soon as you get to Virginia's. I also want you to promise that if you start getting upset again, you'll pull over to the side of the road until you're feeling better."

"I promise," Adelaide said, her eyes suspiciously bright. "You're a sweet girl, Claudia. I'm going to miss you."

"Oh, Adelaide, you'll be back before you know it," Claudia assured her as she gave her a hug. "And don't worry about Jonathon. I'll keep an eye on him."

Adelaide withdrew from her embrace and gave a haughty sniff. "Believe me, the last person I'm going to worry about is that boy."

Claudia merely smiled, the message Adelaide was projecting this time clearly indicated that she was worried about him. As she watched Adelaide walk to her car and drive away, she again wondered what the argument had been about. She supposed she could have asked, but then again, if Adelaide had wanted her to know, she'd have told her.

She switched her gaze to the mansion. Moisture from last night's storm clung to it, making it glitter in the morning sunlight. The mansion seemed brighter and grander than ever, but for Claudia that only made its brooding aura all the more threatening.

It was then she admitted that the real reason she hadn't asked Adelaide about the argument was that if Adelaide had talked it out, she might have decided to stay. Sometime during her restless night, Claudia had come to the understanding that whatever was going to happen at Magnolia would take place in the near future. As long as Adelaide was with her daughter, she should be safe. And since she was, it was time that she, Claudia, made a concerted effort to find out exactly how one Jonathon Jackson Tanner, III was linked to the danger.

Chapter 7

Jonathon sat down in the redwood chaise and cursed inwardly. He couldn't remember ever being in such a foul mood. The worst part was, he was more furious with himself than with his grandmother. How could he have told her to pack her bags and get out, even in the heat of anger? He might legally own Magnolia, but this had been her home for sixty-two years, and it would remain her home until the day she died. He scowled as he acknowledged he was going to have to apologize to her. He also knew that a simple "I'm sorry" wouldn't suffice this time. She was going to make him beg for forgiveness.

"Want some company?" Claudia asked from the bottom of the gallery steps.

Shifting so that he could see her, Jonathon nearly cursed out loud this time as the energy hit him. It was hormones, he told himself severely, mere ordinary chemical attraction. His gaze roamed from the top of her glistening black hair to the tips of her sneakers. A good, old-fashioned tussle between the sheets would solve the problem. Unfortunately he suspected that a good, old-fashioned tussle with Claudia would only create new and more complicated problems. Since he'd always been of the opinion that it was better to deal with the devil you knew, he decided cold showers were the only alternative in this case.

"That depends. Are you here as friend or foe?" he asked as she climbed the steps and walked toward him. He was relieved to see that her color was back, even if she did look as if she hadn't slept well. He suspected that he looked worse. He'd spent most of the night sitting right in this spot and watching the guest house.

"If you're asking if I'm taking sides between you and Adelaide, the answer is no. I have a strict policy of maintaining complete neutrality in family disputes. And even if I didn't have that policy, I couldn't take sides, because I don't know what's going on."

He arched a disbelieving brow. "You mean Gran didn't give you a blow-by-blow account of what a mean, miserly, miserable bully I am?"

"Are you a mean, miserly, miserable bully?" Claudia asked with a teasing grin as she sat on the chaise beside him.

He shrugged. "I'll concede that I was mean to her this morning, and I'm feeling damn miserable about it. That, however, is as far as I'll go."

Claudia nodded. "Well, in case you're wondering, she's at Virginia's. She got there about ten minutes ago, and they're already planning a shopping spree. She asked me to tell you that she's going to buy an entire new wardrobe for her new life, so you can box up all her clothes and give them to charity. However, since she knows that the packing will be an imposition on your time, you're welcome to claim the charitable deduction on your income taxes."

"Oh, God, this is going to be even worse than I thought," he muttered closing his eyes and giving a disgusted shake of his head. "She's not going to make me beg for forgiveness. She's going to make me grovel, and I've never groveled in my life!"

"Well, cheer up Jonathon. I've done a little groveling over the years, and it isn't so bad. In fact, it can be a rather... humbling experience."

He shot her a look of reproach. "You think this is funny, don't you?"

''No. I think your relationship with Adelaide is too special for you to let your pride get in the way. If you have to grovel, then grovel. In the long run, you won't regret it.''

He stared at her for a long moment before saying in a careful monotone, ''Uncle Richard called here this morning, madder than hell. Sheriff Helton had gone to see him, and my uncle claims I'm trying to frame him for last night's break-in. Unfortunately, I hadn't told Gran that I'd alerted the sheriff to the possibility that Richard was behind all of this, and she was furious with me. She started defending him, and I lost it. I told her that if it turned out that he *had* stolen the journal, I was going to cut off his allowance and he could never set foot in Magnolia again. She told me that I didn't have any right to say who could or could not come into her home, and then I really lost it. I told her that I owned Magnolia, and if she didn't like my rules, she could pack her bags and get the hell out.''

''Ouch,'' Claudia said with a grimace. ''No wonder she's going to make you grovel. I'll have to suggest that she also make you crawl across some hot coals.''

He shot her another look of reproach. ''You don't have to rub my nose in it, Claudia. I know I was wrong, and I have every intention of apologizing to her. I'll even grovel if I have to, though it will grate like hell. Uncle Richard is the one who should be groveling.''

''I know you don't like your uncle, but you have no proof that he broke into the house. And when you come right down to it, why would he want to steal the journal?''

He shrugged. ''He probably believes that there's a buried treasure in the secret room, and if he can find it before me, he can steal it. Since the journal is the only proof we have of the room's existence, he wanted to see if he could find a clue that I'd overlooked.''

Claudia raked her hand through her hair. A buried treasure might be the key to the danger surrounding the secret room. Greed did have a way of making people do things they wouldn't normally do. ''Do you think it's possible that there's buried treasure in the secret room?''

''In a house this old anything's possible, but it isn't probable. The Tanners have never been hoarders.''

"But you think that your uncle believes there's a buried treasure?"

He sighed and shook his head. "I don't know that for sure, Claudia. I'm only trying to think the way he does, and the only reason for him to be interested in the room is if he feels he can cash in on it."

"Well, I agree that Richard does look suspicious, but then again, he'd have been taking a terrible risk breaking into the house to steal the journal. If I were him, I wouldn't have staged a break-in that was almost guaranteed to cast suspicion on me. I would have sneaked in in the middle of the night, taken the journal somewhere where I could photocopy it, and then brought it back before you got up. That way, I'd have a copy of the journal to peruse at my leisure, and you'd never even know it."

"Do you do this a lot?" he asked with a wry twist of his lips.

"Do what a lot?" she asked in puzzlement.

"Play devil's advocate."

She shrugged self-consciously. "I've never thought about it, but I suppose I do. Many of my clients aren't really looking for predictions for their future. They're looking for guidance. When they're faced with a difficult decision, they want someone to assure them that they're making the right one."

"And do you always tell them the truth?"

It was a loaded question, and she knew it. She told herself to give him a pat answer, but some elemental part of her insisted that she answer him truthfully. "I'm a clairvoyant, Jonathon, but I'm also a human being. Sometimes it's kinder to withhold the truth."

It wasn't what she said as much as the melancholy tone of her voice that rocked him, to the core. He didn't have to ask what she was talking about, because he knew the answer intuitively—death. As he felt the pain rising, he squashed it down. When the guilt began to gnaw, he thrust it aside. The anger, however, he latched onto as if it were a lifeline, but even that he kept carefully controlled and contained.

"Well, it's time I got to work in the basement," he stated brusquely as he stood. "You don't need to hang around, Claudia. I'm sure you have better things to do."

Claudia was startled by his abrupt dismissal. One moment they'd been sitting here talking as if they were friends, and now he was acting like... She didn't know what he was acting like, but it hurt.

She opened her mouth to say something scathing, but closed it quickly. She'd just lectured him on being more tolerant of his uncle, and it was time she took her own advice. Besides, she couldn't afford to alienate him. Last night she'd had a warning, and it was critical that she determine whether or not she could trust him.

"I don't have anything better to do," she said, getting up, as well. "I came here to work, so put me to work."

Jonathon muttered an imprecation when he answered the knock on the kitchen door and realized his grandmother was going to play hardball. Aunt Virginia's son, Steven, and his wife, Ruth, stood in front of him. He'd rather face his uncle Richard's demonic progeny—his twin cousins, Patrick and Patricia—any day. Golden-haired, blue-eyed Steven always looked like a tortured saint, and mousey Ruth always resembled a child cowering in terror. To speak a harsh word to either of them made you feel like you were kicking a helpless animal.

Steven wrapped his arm around Ruth's shoulder protectively, as though he expected Jonathon to attack her. Jonathon was hit with the absurd urge to yell "Boo" at her. He resisted not only because he knew it would be cruel, but because he also knew that Steven would try to pummel him. Steven might be a mama's boy, but Jonathon had never met a man more devoted to his wife. His entire world revolved around Ruth, and Jonathon had often wondered if Steven's devotion was emotionally healthy.

"Grandmother sent us to get her jewels," Steven announced.

"Then, by all means, come in and get them," Jonathon drawled, standing aside. After they'd entered, he gestured toward Claudia, who was sitting at the table eating her lunch. "I don't believe either of you have met Ms. Pepper-mill. Claudia, this is my aunt's son, Steven, and his wife, Ruth. Steven and Ruth, Claudia Peppermill."

"You're the clairvoyant?" Steven asked.

"Yes," Claudia answered as she regarded the couple cu-riously. Steven was giving off vibrations of excitement, but Ruth was projecting absolute fear. What puzzled Claudia was that if she was interpreting Ruth's emotions correctly, the woman was afraid of her!

"I've been dying to meet you," Steven said. "I'm a sci-ence-fiction writer, and I have a character who has clair-voyant powers. Would you be willing to read my manuscript to see if I've captured the essence of clairvoy-ance?"

"Steven, I'm sure Ms. Peppermill is too busy to read your book," Ruth mumbled, casting an apprehensive look toward Claudia.

"Actually, I'd love to read it," Claudia replied, ignor-ing Jonathon, who was shaking his head vehemently be-hind the couple. "Of course, you realize that I'd only be looking at it from a clairvoyant's standpoint. I don't know anything about writing a book, so I couldn't give you any advice on the story itself."

"Oh, I understand," Steven replied, beaming. "As soon as I get home, I'll make a copy of the manuscript and send it to you. Come on, Ruth, let's go get Grandmother's jew-els. If we hurry, we can get home in time for me to get the manuscript in the mail today."

After the couple left the room, Jonathon sprawled into a chair across the table from Claudia and said, "You're a glutton for punishment, aren't you?"

"Why do you say that?"

"Steven has been writing science fiction since he was eight. A couple of years ago Aunt Virginia harassed me into reading his 'newest' manuscript. I didn't have to read be-yond the first page to know that the book he wrote when he was eight was better, which isn't saying much. Even at the tender age of twelve, I knew that that book was atrocious. I told Aunt Virginia that he should forget about writing and

get a job, instead of living off poor—no, make that *rich*—
Ruth. Aunt Virginia didn't speak to me for six months."

"You really know how to make enemies, don't you?"

He gave her a disgruntled look. "If someone asks for my
honest opinion, I give it to them. It's not my fault if they
don't like what I say."

"Come on, Jonathon," she chided gently. "You know
better than that. Telling someone you don't like what
they've done is one thing. Suggesting a career change is
quite another. You wouldn't be so tactless with your business associates, so why do you behave that way toward your
family?"

"Lord, you're sounding more like Gran by the minute," he grumbled. "What did she do? Give you a crash
course on how to irritate me before she left?"

"If you're irritated, it's probably because you know I'm
right," she surmised.

"If I'm irritated, it's because Gran sent saintly Steven
and pitiful Ruth to fetch her 'jewels.' All her real jewelry is
in the bank vault, and the stuff she has around here isn't
worth enough to pay for a Caribbean cruise. She's doing
this because she knows those two drive me nuts, particularly Ruth. She jumps at the sight of her own shadow, and
she always looks at me as if she thinks I'm an ax murderer.

"And now that Gran's stuck in the knife," he continued, "she'll probably give it a twist by sending my larce-
nous twin cousins, Patrick and Patricia, to fetch her furs,
which consist of a fifty-year-old, moth-eaten mink stole and
a fake rabbit-skin winter coat. Together they aren't worth
seventy-five bucks, but I wouldn't let Patrick and Patricia
walk out of here with them if they were only worth a nickel.
They'd take them to the nearest pawn shop and claim
someone stole the coats out of their car."

"They can't be that bad."

"They're Uncle Richard's kids, so that says it all."

Claudia regarded him thoughtfully. "At the risk of being told to mind my own business, what caused this feud
between you and your uncle?"

"Primogeniture," Jonathon answered grimly.

"Primogeniture?" Claudia echoed in confusion.

Jonathon nodded. "My great-great-grandfather, Charles Tanner—he's the one who built Magnolia and started the family business—was a staunch believer in the eldest son inheriting everything. He was so adamant about it his will states that the business and Magnolia will pass from eldest son to eldest son in perpetuity. His will also states that should the in-perpetuity clause ever be broken, the business and the plantation are to be sold and all monies derived from them given to good works. Uncle Richard resented the hell out of my father for being the firstborn and inheriting everything, and now he resents the hell out of me."

"I can understand why. Primogeniture is archaic!" Claudia exclaimed.

"I agree," he said, surprising her with the sincerity clearly evident behind the two words. "If it was up to me, I'd give Uncle Richard and Aunt Virginia each a third of everything, and then I'd write Uncle Richard and his entire family off. Believe me, it would be cheaper in the long run. But if the in-perpetuity clause is broken, the family loses everything. I don't have a choice but to uphold it."

Claudia shook her head in amazement. "And I thought my family's politics were complicated."

"Well, I guess we all have our burdens to bear. And speaking of burdens, I think I hear our pathetic minions returning from doing their duty. How much do you want to bet that Gran has instructed them to give me a receipt so that, miserly bully that I am, I can't accuse her of stealing her own jewelry?"

Claudia would have laughed, except she suspected he was probably right. She adored Adelaide, but she recognized the perverse streak in her personality. Jonathon had hurt her feelings in the worst possible way. She'd make sure he was adequately tormented before she forgave him, and one of the best ways to do that was to take a jab at his integrity.

While he dealt with Steven, who indeed insisted on giving him a receipt, Claudia concentrated on Ruth, who was becoming more agitated by the minute, the fear she was projecting so intense it was almost palpable. Claudia was intrigued when she realized that Ruth was so panic-stricken because she feared Claudia could read her mind, which, of course, wasn't accurate. She could never pick up on anything Ruth didn't want her to know.

As Jonathon saw them to the door, Claudia couldn't help wondering what an obviously painfully shy woman like Ruth could possibly need to hide. She also found it interesting that three of the Tanners—Richard, Virginia and Ruth—were afraid of her.

Jonathon was restless. He tried to tell himself it was because of his fight with his grandmother, but eventually he had to admit that his agitation had to do with Claudia.

As he paced through the mansion, which seemed empty and lifeless without his grandmother, he faced the truth. He'd never desired a woman the way he desired Claudia. Instinct told him that making love with her would involve explosive, uncontrollable passion. The trouble was, he couldn't determine if his physical response to her was natural, or caused by that strange and maddening energy.

His baser instincts said that it didn't matter why he was attracted to her. He should grab hold of the opportunity to have the time of his life. His scruples, however, kept reminding him that for every action there was a price. Intuition told him that in Claudia's case, the price would be the demand for an emotional investment, and he could never give that to her or any woman. Even with Katie, whom he'd loved to distraction, he'd always kept a part of himself sealed away. And thank God he had, because he didn't think he'd have survived her death otherwise.

But no amount of rationalizing why he should stay away from Claudia would ease the perpetual ache in his groin, and his frustration drove him outside. As he stood on the gallery and stared at the lighted windows of the guest house, he found himself craving to stride across the grounds and knock on the door. He headed for the river before he could succumb to the urge.

When he reached the riverbank, he sat down beneath the same oak where he'd found Claudia the day she'd touched the journal. He gathered a handful of stones, and began skipping them across the water. It was a monotonous activity, but oddly soothing. Soon, he was so relaxed that he was at one with the night. He was attuned to every sound and every movement, and he knew the instant that Claudia arrived. It was only then he acknowledged that he'd unconsciously been willing her to come to him, but he refused to consider the import of that fact. She was here, and for now, that was all that mattered.

Claudia had been reading when she was struck with a sudden sense of urgency. When she wasn't able to figure out what it was, she tried to ignore it. But it kept pulling at her—calling for her. It had been a cry she couldn't ignore, even when she found it urging her out into the night.

Now, as she reached the riverbank and saw Jonathon sitting beneath the old oak, she realized that he had drawn her here. That realization both startled and frightened her. If she couldn't connect with him, then how could he have summoned her?

As she took in their surroundings, the question became even more threatening. Moonlight glistened on the river, making the water look like shimmering black glass. Jonathon himself looked like some dark specter, seated beneath the drooping, misshapen limbs of the gigantic tree. The Spanish moss trailing from its branches took on the appearance of ghostly, grasping fingers as it stirred in the evening breeze.

The entire scene was positively ghoulish, and every self-protective instinct she had was screaming for her to run back to the guest house as fast as she could. But even as she prepared for flight, Jonathon turned toward her, murmuring softly, "Would you like to join me?"

Shivers raced up and down her spine as that oh so familiar yearning stirred at the seductive timbre of his voice. If her self-protective instincts had been screaming before, they were now wailing like banshees. But she could no more ignore Jonathon than a moth could ignore a flame. "Sure."

She walked to the tree. After she sat down, she curled her legs beneath her and adjusted the skirt of her sundress.

When she was done, she glanced at him. He had a strange look on his face. "Is something wrong?"

"No." He studied her sedate neckline and then her full skirt. "I was just thinking that I like you better in jeans. You have a great body, and jeans show it off."

She hurriedly switched her attention to the river. "Yes, well, uh, thanks."

"Have I embarrassed you?"

"Not really. I know I have a good figure. I also know that I have a better mind."

"Ah, yes," he drawled. "Beauty is only skin deep, and all that jazz."

"All that jazz is true, Jonathon," she stated stiffly.

He released a short, humorless laugh. "Good Lord, Claudia. Do you really think I'm that shallow?"

"I don't know." She switched her gaze back to him. "Are you?"

"I'd be lying if I said I didn't get a charge out of a sexy body and a pretty face. It does, however, take more substance than that to turn me on."

She returned her attention to the river. "Now I am embarrassed. If I ask you if I'm more substantial, you'll think I'm fishing for a compliment. You'll also think I'm trying to find out if I turn you on."

"You already know the answer to both those questions, Claudia."

His voice was as warm as a caress and had the same melting effect on her. In self-defense, she said, "I'm not your type, Jonathon."

"And how do you know that?"

"Because we live in two different worlds. You're major league, and I barely qualify for the minors."

"Don't you dream of someday making it into the major league?"

"No," Claudia answered honestly as she again looked at him. "I was born into your world, Jonathon. My parents have money, but I personally prefer being as poor as a church mouse."

"What do you have against money?"

"I don't have anything against money itself. I just don't want the complications that come along with it. When you have money, you have to constantly worry about it. You run from your banker to your accountant to your broker to your lawyer, and then you start all over again. You're always wondering if you're getting the best return on it. If it's invested in the right place. If you're getting all the tax breaks available to you, and who you're going to leave it to. Then there's the biggest worry of all. Is someone trying to steal it from you."

Jonathon winced. "You've made your point, and for what it's worth, I no longer think you're a crook."

"Considering the alternative, I'm not sure if I should be pleased or dismayed," she noted drolly.

"You're not crazy, either."

Claudia stared at him in surprise. "What are you saying, Jonathon? That you finally believe in my clairvoyance?"

"Let's just say that I'm still reserving judgment."

She gave a frustrated shake of her head. "That doesn't make sense. You don't think I'm crazy or a crook, but you don't believe in what I do for a living? Just what *do* you think I am?"

"A very beautiful, intelligent and fascinating woman," he answered slowly in a husky rasp that sent another shiver racing through her. She clasped her hands together in her lap and stared down at them in bewilderment. Was he flirting with her, or toying with her? Both were unnerving prospects.

"Tell me about yourself," he said.

"What do you want to know?"

"I don't know. Did you go to college?"

"No. I barely made it through high school because I couldn't handle being around so many people day in and day out. I can't hold down a normal job for the same reason. Going to the grocery store is a major event for me. I have to build a psychic barrier, or I'm bombarded by so many impressions at such a fast pace that I'm physically ill. But even with the barrier in place, some impressions are so strong that they still seep through. Some of them are up-lifting. Most of them are depressing."

"Then why do you put up with it? Why don't you just shut it off for good?"

"Why don't you ask me to stop breathing?" she asked with a rueful laugh. "I can temper my clairvoyance, Jon-athon, but I can't cut it off completely. It's as essential to my being as my heartbeat."

He stared at her, his eyes filled with what she'd swear was compassion, and she caught her breath when he raised his hand to her face. But when it was just a fraction of an inch away from her cheek, he quickly withdrew it. "I can't be-lieve in what you're telling me, Claudia."

"You mean you won't *let* yourself believe in what I'm telling you," she retorted, not sure if she was angry be-cause of his words or because of his refusal to touch her. Both were a form of rejection, and though she knew she was being foolish, it hurt to have him reject her.

"I'll be the first to admit that I'm an oddity," she con-tinued when he didn't respond. "But you're an intelligent man who's used to digesting the facts. Think of me as a business you want to take over. The books say I'm shaky, but your gut says I'm worth the risk."

Again, his hand hovered near her cheek. When she sensed he was about to move away, she caught his wrist. She should have been prepared for the outcome. But she wasn't prepared, and she was staggered by the power of the erotic visions that engulfed her.

Panicked, she started to pull away, but Jonathon ig-nored her attempt at flight, bringing her hand to his chest. His heart thudded against her palm, its racing cadence matching her own. When his chest heaved, hers heaved with it. When his lips swooped down on hers, she wasn't sure where the visions ended and reality began. All she knew for certain was that he was kissing her with the same wild pas-sion that was raging inside her.

Jonathon felt as if his entire nervous system had gone haywire as he kissed Claudia. Even his skin felt turned on.

He kept trying to blame it on the energy pulsing through him, but he suspected that he'd be this aroused without it.

She was everything he rejected—everything he couldn't afford to believe in. So why did he have this urgent desire to rip her clothes off and bury himself inside her? Why did he have this driving need to lay claim to her? He shuddered when she wrapped her arms around his neck and kissed him passionately, sending the energy into a new burst of activity. When it centered in his groin and Claudia moved against him sinuously, he thought he'd explode.

Claudia was on the verge of her own explosion. When Jonathon's hand slid to her breast, she moaned. When he stroked her nipple with his thumb, desire settled heavily in her womb. Her need was so intense it hurt, yet she'd never experienced anything so pleasurable in her life.

She moved against him restlessly, knowing what she wanted but not knowing how to ask for it. He seemed to understand what she was seeking, slipping his hand beneath her skirt until he reached the juncture of her thighs. Then he stroked her through the satin of her panties until she was writhing against him. She moaned again and clung to him as she rode the wave he'd created within her, until her world burst into a thousand iridescent rainbows.

She was shocked back to sanity when Jonathon began to tug at the waistband of her panties. *Heaven help me, what am I doing?* She'd not only let him kiss her, she'd allowed him to touch her in ways no man had ever touched her before. And if she didn't get away from him right now, he was going to be doing a lot more than touching!

When Claudia gasped, "No!" and began to push frantically against Jonathon's chest, it took him a moment to realize what was happening. When he did, he immediately rolled off her, sat up and raked a shaking hand through his hair. As she bolted into a sitting position beside him, her expression mortified, he sympathized with her, because he was damned mortified himself. If she hadn't pushed him away, he'd have taken her right where they sat! The last time he'd nearly tumbled a woman in the bushes, he'd been nineteen years old.

How did she manage to turn him into a mindless, libidinous zombie? What was it about her that made him lose all control? He didn't have the answers, but he vowed that he'd never lay a hand on her again.

"I am sincerely sorry, Claudia," he told her, fighting to keep his voice neutral. "What just happened between us was... Well, it was inappropriate, and I assure you it will never happen again."

Claudia stared at him incredulously. He was *sincerely* sorry. What had just happened was *inappropriate?* He *assured* her that it would never happen again? My word, he sounded as if he was talking to a disgruntled business client, instead of a woman that he'd just... Well, damn it, she might as well tell it like it was. He'd just brought her to her first sexual climax.

Of course, he didn't know that, and she had no intention of enlightening him. She also wasn't going to let him sit there and talk to her in that uppity businessman's tone, either! she concluded as her temper erupted.

"How dare you sit there and talk to me like you're Lee Iacocca presiding over a board meeting!" she railed. "Just who the hell do you think you are?"

Jonathon could only gape at her in shock. Why was she so mad? He'd just apologized hadn't he? And what did Iacocca have to do with this?

He was still at a loss for words when she scrambled to her feet and glared down at him. "Well, let me tell you something, Mr. High And Mighty Tanner. I don't accept your *sincere* apology, and you're damn right that what happened between us was *inappropriate.* I also *assure* you that if you ever lay a hand on me again, I'll punch you in your pompous nose!" With that, she fled back toward Magnolia.

Jonathon stared after her, his shock and confusion shifting into a low, simmering anger. Where did she get off talking to him like that? She hadn't exactly been an innocent in their little encounter, and she sure as hell hadn't said no until she'd achieved her own satisfaction. He was the one still suffering from unrequited lust!

He rocketed to his feet. If she thought she was going to get away without getting a piece of his mind, she was in for one hell of a surprise!

Chapter 8

Claudia had just reached the porch at the guest house when Jonathon caught up with her. He grabbed her arm and spun her around before she could run up the stairs. However, it wasn't the energy that staggered him this time. It was the utter terror reflected on her face. He had never had anyone stare at him in absolute fear, and when it registered that she was afraid of him, he felt as if his legs had just been kicked out from underneath him.

Some faraway rational part of his brain told him to release his hold on her immediately. But another more elemental part insisted that there was only one sure way to reassure her that he would never physically harm her. He caught the back of her head in his hand and drew her to him slowly.

Claudia couldn't remember ever being so afraid as she gazed up at Jonathon. When she'd seen him running after her, she'd been filled with a panic she couldn't explain. All she'd known was that it was critical that she get into the house before he caught up with her.

But she hadn't made it into the house, and her heart was hammering so hard that she was sure it was going to burst right out of her chest. When he eased her toward him, she recognized the source of her fear. Jonathon was touching her and she wasn't receiving the erotic images. There was only one reason for that to be happening. The visions had been of the future, and the future had arrived.

If she'd been afraid before, she was now terrified. There was no way she could make love with a man she couldn't read and who didn't believe in her abilities. She couldn't possibly make love with a man she didn't trust and might be the very danger she'd come here to fight. So why was she letting him pull her into his arms instead of running away?

Because, heaven help her, she wanted him to make love to her. She wanted to experience what she'd never experienced before, what those erotic visions told her only Jonathon could give her. But even as she made the admission, every moral fiber of her being was telling her that she had to say no.

She was still torn by the inner battle of rational versus explosive sensation when Jonathon molded her body to his and sealed his lips over hers. The moment his tongue teased for entrance into her mouth, she decided to hell with morals. She wasn't foolish enough to believe that making love with Jonathon would last more than one night, but she *needed* him. All her life she'd been a giver—to her clients, to her friends and even to her family—for once she was going to be a taker, allow herself the luxury of feeling like a woman instead of a damn circus freak. If she ended up regretting this in the morning, so be it.

"Make love to me, Jonathon," she whispered as she wrapped her arms around his neck and parted her lips to let him in.

"Oh, God, yes," he rasped as he crushed her to him and plunged his tongue into her mouth.

She'd heard of ravishing kisses, but it was the first time she'd ever experienced one. He explored her with an intimacy that set her to trembling. Just when she was sure she couldn't bear the torment a moment longer, he swept her up into his arms and carried her inside and into her bedroom.

There, he lowered her to her feet, letting her body slide down his, and she gasped as he rocked his pelvis against her, giving her a taste of his arousal. He kissed her again, and when he let her come up for air, she was startled to realize she was wearing nothing but her panties.

She instinctively crossed her arms over her breasts, but he gently pried them away, saying hoarsely, "Don't hide from me. You're beautiful." Then he eased her panties down her hips, lifted her, and laid her on the bed.

Claudia watched him in fascination as he quickly discarded his own clothes. The visions of his body had been vivid, but nothing could compare to the reality of seeing him standing there naked and aroused, muscles rippling and skin gleaming gold in the soft glow of the lamp.

"Do we need to be worried about birth control?" he asked hoarsely as he knelt beside her on the bed.

She shook her head, and then closed her eyes in bliss as his hands began sweeping over her body in long, soothing strokes, while his tongue blazed a hot, wet trail from her neck to her navel, and then reversed the journey. When he stretched out beside her and caught her lips in a steamy kiss, sliding his hand down her abdomen, her world turned inside out. He played with the curls at the juncture of her thighs, and she began to shift restlessly, once again knowing what she wanted but still not sure how to ask for it.

As if sensing her dilemma, he murmured in her ear, "I want to touch you, honey. Is that okay?"

"Yes!" she gasped, and then moaned as his fingers worked their magic. She was hit with a wave of desire so powerful it hurt. She stiffened and tried to escape his touch, but he tossed his leg across her thighs, anchoring her in place.

His hand stilled and he pressed soft, reassuring kisses against her lips. Slowly, she began to relax, and he raised his head and looked at her. He didn't say a word, but his eyes were dark and compelling. He held her trapped in his gaze as his fingers returned to their magic. This time she didn't fight him when the wave of desire hit. Instead she closed her eyes tightly and rode it until it crested, crying out at the exquisite wonder of it.

She was still shuddering from her release when he settled between her thighs. She opened her eyes and found herself trapped in his compelling gaze. This was the part of the visions that had never come to fruition, and she shivered in anticipation as she felt the tip of his manhood slide against her. She grabbed his shoulders, wrapped her legs around his waist, and eagerly arched her hips up to meet him.

"You're so sweet. So beautiful, and so sweet," he murmured as he flexed his hips and entered her swiftly.

Though she was prepared, the sharp pain still caught her off guard, and she released an involuntary cry of distress. Jonathon immediately froze and stared down at her in shock.

"Don't stop!" she ordered pleadingly as she rocked her hips against him. "Please, Jonathon. If you stop, I think I'll die."

"You should have told me," he mumbled even as he began to move inside her, his rhythm increasing in direct proportion to the tension building inside her. "You should have—"

Claudia silenced him with a kiss that deepened as the waves of pleasure began to crash through her. She rode them, and when she reached the top, the tension inside her exploded, leaving her with the exhilarating feeling of having been reborn. She clung to Jonathon joyously as he followed with his own release.

He collapsed against her, and immediately rolled to his side, bringing her with him. "Are you okay?"

"Wonderful," she murmured, rubbing her cheek against his shoulder.

When he didn't respond, she eased her head back so she could see his face. She closed her eyes at his somber expression. Though she knew she was asking the obvious, she said, "What's wrong, Jonathon?"

"You should have told me you were a virgin, Claudia."

"Why? Would it have made a difference?" she asked, sitting up and snatching the covers to her chest.

"Hell, yes, it would have made a difference!" he snapped as he shot out of bed, grabbed his jeans off the floor and pulled them on. Without bothering to zip them, he strode to the window and braced his hands on the windowsill. As he stared out into the darkness, he said, "Tonight was something you should have saved for someone special."

"You are special," she told him softly. "Special in ways that you could never understand."

"Damn it, Claudia!" he railed as he spun around to face her. "I'm not looking for a relationship. I don't want a relationship. I just took your virginity, and I have nothing to offer you in return!"

His words hit Claudia with the force of a blow, but even as the hurt began to surface, she ruthlessly forced it back down. When she'd decided to make love with him, she'd known it was going to be like this, and it was foolish for her to want—or expect—anything more.

She regarded him for a long moment before she said, "I'm twenty-seven years old, and I wanted the experience of making love. When I realized you were willing to give it to me, I jumped at the chance. So as you can see, you didn't take my virginity. I gave it to you, and I did it without expecting—or wanting—anything in return."

"It isn't that simple," he snapped as he raked his hand through his hair.

She sighed in frustration. "Of course it's that simple. I'm not some schoolgirl with stars in her eyes, Jonathon. I'm a grown woman. I can deal with a one-night stand."

Her last statement caused a hard knot to form in Jonathon's stomach, and he turned back around to stare out the window. A one-night stand? She'd been a *virgin,* for pity's sake! When a woman lost her virginity, it should be with a man who cared for her, not one who'd buried his capacity to care with his wife. She also shouldn't be sitting in bed afterward defending her decision, but lying in her lover's arms, being stroked and soothed and cherished for the gift she'd given him. And she sure as hell shouldn't be sitting there calmly discussing one-night stands!

He jumped when Claudia's hand came down on his shoulder. He swiveled his head toward her. She was standing beside him, wrapped in a sheet and looking fragile and vulnerable.

"I'm sorry, Jonathon," she whispered as a tear rolled down her cheek. "If I'd known you were going to beat yourself up like this, I would have never asked you to make love with me.''

"Oh, Claudia," he murmured as he pulled her into his arms, feeling like the biggest heel in the world. As she pressed her face to his chest and he felt the dampness on her cheek, he decided that he might not be able to give her the caring she deserved, but the least he could do was give her the stroking, the soothing and the cherishing.

He swung her up into his arms, carried her back to bed, and set about doing exactly that.

Claudia was standing in the magnolia grove when she felt something summoning her. She walked toward the edge of the trees, and when she stepped out of the grove, she was standing in front of the mansion.

Suddenly the house seemed to shimmer and waver, and she was thrust into a cold, dank and dark world where space didn't exist and time was immeasurable. The air around her began to grow heavy, and she couldn't breathe. Before she could panic, she saw the light overhead. She knew instinctively that all she had to do was close her eyes and open them, and she'd be free.

She closed her eyes, and when she opened them, she was staring at her bedroom ceiling. As the meaning of the vision registered, she turned toward Jonathon in excitement. But the excitement died when she realized he was gone.

As the hurt began to rise, she forced it back down. She'd known that this was the way it would have to be and she'd accepted it. Besides, now that she knew how to find the secret room, her time here was limited. To become any further involved with him would only be asking for trouble.

She tossed back the covers and slowly climbed out of bed, wincing at the soreness of muscles unaccustomed to use. She needed to find Jonathon and tell him what she'd learned. With any luck, they'd find the secret room before the day was over.

* * *

Jonathon sat down at the kitchen table and buried his face in his hands. He was a coward. A damn lily-livered yellowbelly. When he'd awakened in Claudia's bed, he'd been hit with the morning-after guilt. So instead of waiting for her to wake up and making sure she was all right, he'd hightailed it out of there as fast as he could.

He muttered a curse as he leaned back in the chair, deciding that this was all his uncle's fault. If he hadn't stolen the journal, Jonathon would never have had a fight with his grandmother. If he hadn't had a fight with Gran, she wouldn't have left. If she hadn't left, he wouldn't have ended up in Claudia's bed.

But all those events *had* taken place, and rather than face the consequences like a man, he'd run. He'd never been so disgusted with himself, and what made it even worse was the knowledge that if he had it to do over, he'd still run.

He sighed and massaged the bridge of his nose, admitting that the reason he hadn't been able to face Claudia was because she was touching him on an emotional level. The trouble was, he didn't know what emotional chord she was striking. But whatever it was, it was rocking the very foundations of his carefully contained and controlled world. His intuition told him that if he didn't keep his guard up, those foundations were in danger of crumbling, and there was no way he could let that happen.

Unfortunately, keeping his guard up around Claudia was becoming exceedingly difficult. If the attraction to her was nothing more than desire, he was sure he could handle it. But she was also drawing on his protective feelings. On the surface Claudia appeared strong and confident, but he sensed her vulnerability. There was the sad wistfulness to her smile when she'd spoken of her parents. The way she'd cried when Merlin York had driven away. And, heaven help him, the way she'd apologized to him last night for asking him to make love to her.

Yet even more alarming than the desire and the protectiveness was the way she was inserting herself into his life in small ways. Like yesterday when she'd talked with him about his fight with his grandmother. It had felt good having someone to confide in. It had even felt good when she'd chided him about the way he'd criticized Steven's writing. She'd been right. He'd have never dealt with a business associate like that, and he should extend the same courtesy to his family, even if they did drive him nuts. The only excuse he had for his behavior was that he hadn't realized what he was doing until she'd pointed it out. It was the type of thing his wife would have done. It made him yearn for companionship again, and that scared the hell out of him.

Yes, if he had it to do all over again, he'd still have run from her this morning. Of course, he'd eventually have to face her, but at least he'd had this respite to come to grips with his feelings and get them under control.

As Claudia walked over to Magnolia, she told herself that the reality of facing Jonathon wasn't going to be as bad as the anticipation. So they'd made love. It wasn't any big deal. People made love all the time. She and Jonathon were adults, and they'd both made their positions clear last night. He wasn't offering anything and she wasn't asking for anything, so there was no need for her to be nervous.

It would have been easier for her to believe in her pep talk if Jonathon had awakened her before he'd left. A simple goodbye would have assured her that they were returning to the status quo.

When she reached the kitchen door, she forced herself to ring the bell before she lost her nerve. While she waited, she again told herself that this was going to be easy. In fact, it should be easier than ever, because now that they'd made love, she'd no longer be bothered by those crazy erotic visions. She'd be able to concentrate entirely on figuring out what danger the shadow represented. When examined in that light, making love with Jonathon had been the best decision she'd made since coming here.

She almost had herself convinced when the door opened. All it took was one look at him to make all her persuasive arguments fly out the window. Before last night, he'd had to touch her for her to see the visions. Now that she'd made love with him, she had a whole set of memories to torment her. Right now they were doing a darn good job of doing just that, and she admitted that she'd been lying to herself. She didn't want to return to the status quo. She wanted— no, *needed*—something more from Jonathon, though at the moment, she wasn't sure exactly what it was. Tenderness? Caring? *Love?*

The last thought rattled her to the core, and she drew in a deep breath to control the panic rising inside. She was just being sentimental. He'd been her first lover, she was confusing love with lust.

"Hi," she said, nervously shifting from one foot to the other as he regarded her with cool impassivity. Never had she wanted to read him more than at that very moment. Was he, as his expression indicated, feeling nothing at all? The thought was highly distressing, since it would mean that last night had meant nothing to him. She might not be looking for avowals of love, but she'd like to believe that their lovemaking was at least memorable.

"Good morning," he said formally. "I'm sorry it took me so long to get to the door. I was on the phone to the office."

"I'm sorry. I hope I didn't interrupt."

"You didn't."

"I'm glad," she said, deciding that if this was what all morning afters were like, she was never going to make love again. "Look, Jonathon—"

"Claudia, I—" he began at the same time.

They both stopped and stared at each other uncomfortably.

"I'm sorry," he said. "You go first."

"No. You go first," she stated, because she wasn't really sure what she'd started to say. Instinct also told her that she was on the verge of making a fool of herself, and she wasn't about to let that happen. When he looked as if he'd object, she said, "Please, Jonathon. I want you to go first."

He still hesitated, but eventually he said, "I just want to say that... Well, about last night, I... Oh, hell, I don't know what I want to say!"

Claudia hadn't realized she'd been holding her breath until she released it in relief at his obvious frustration. He was feeling as confused about this situation as she was, and because of that, she was finally able to relax.

"There's no need to say anything about last night. We're two adults who enjoyed each other. It was...nice, but now we're facing a new day. It's time for us to move on."

Jonathon grimly concluded that he couldn't have said it better himself, so why was he so irked that she was dismissing last night as if it had been nothing? It had been her first time, for Pete's sake. Hadn't that meant anything to her?

"What?" he said when he realized she'd been speaking and he hadn't been listening.

"I said that I know why we haven't been able to find the secret room. It's because we've been examining walls when we should be looking for a trapdoor. I saw it in a vision."

"You saw it in a *vision?*" When she nodded, he said, "I see. Where is this trapdoor supposed to be?"

"I assume it's in the basement."

"It couldn't possibly be in the basement. The floor is solid brick, and even if it wasn't, there's no way they'd have been able to dig anything more than a crawl space. We're too close to the water table, which is why it gets so damp down there."

"Then the trapdoor must be on this floor."

He shook his head. "I've already ruled out a trapdoor on this floor. It would have been found years ago."

It wasn't what he said as much as that damn pompous businessman's tone that pricked at Claudia's temper. "In other words, since you've already ruled it out, then it doesn't exist." On the heels of her anger came a terrible wave of hurt. Last night he'd made love with her, become one with her, and he still didn't believe in her. When she felt the sting of tears, she let her anger take over. "Well, I really hate to break this to you, Jonathon, but you aren't infallible."

He arched a cool brow. "I may not be infallible, but at least I'm functioning on logic."

"What's that supposed to mean?"

"Look, Claudia, I don't want to offend you, but I'm not going to stop my methodical search to look for a visionary trapdoor."

"Oh, I see," she declared, affronted. "We aren't talking about finding the secret room. We're talking about following your master plan, which of course, is based on logic. Well, you go right ahead and conduct your methodical search. When you come up empty and decide to look for my 'visionary' trapdoor, let me know. I'll be at home doing something productive, like watching twenty-year-old reruns on television!"

"Damn it, Claudia!" he growled, catching her arm when she swung away from him. He tugged on it until she turned back around to face him. When she did, he cursed succinctly. There were tears brimming in her eyes.

"Come here," he ordered gruffly, instinctively pulling her into his arms. He closed his eyes and fought against the energy that was zapping through him, but it was a losing battle. He'd been convinced it was just an anomaly of physical attraction, something that would cease to have power over him once he'd had her, but he'd made love with her, so why the hell was it still tormenting him? "I don't want to fight with you."

"Then why are you being so stubborn?" she asked as she rested her forehead against his chest and blinked against a new wave of tears. Unbidden, heat washed over her as images of entangled limbs and melting caresses unfolded before her mind's eye. Heaven help her, the erotic visions were back, and they were even more vivid than before. Biting back a moan, she swallowed. She wasn't going to make love with Jonathon again. *She wasn't!* She'd promised herself one night, and that one night was over.

"Damned if I know," he said heavily. "Let's compromise. Today we'll search this floor for a trapdoor. If we don't find it, then we'll go back to my master plan tomorrow."

"That sounds reasonable," Claudia responded slowly, reluctantly stepping away from him. Suddenly she didn't want to leave the shelter of his arms, but it wasn't because of any lingering need for his touch. It was because she'd just been struck with a premonition. Something was about to happen, and she suspected that it wasn't going to be anything pleasant.

As Jonathon moved furniture back into place, Claudia stood in the center of the sitting room and surveyed it in frustration.

After exploring the first floor, she'd agreed with Jonathon that a trapdoor in the grand room and the library was highly unlikely, so they'd concentrated their search on the remaining rooms, which were the kitchen, the dining room and the sitting room. Since both the kitchen and dining room had come up empty, she'd been positive that the entrance to the secret room was in here. All they'd uncovered, however, was an earring that Adelaide had been looking for for days.

"Well, what now?" Jonathon asked, plopping down onto the sofa.

"Aren't you going to say, 'I told you so'?" Claudia inquired dryly.

He gave her a sympathetic smile. "We all make mistakes, Claudia."

She shook her head. "I'm not mistaken, Jonathon. The trapdoor is up here somewhere. I just can't figure out where it is."

"Why don't we have lunch and talk about it? I'm starving."

Claudia nodded her agreement, and they went back to the kitchen. After they were seated at the table, she asked, "Do you know if the floor plan is the same as it was during the Civil War?"

"I'm sure it is," he answered. "The family has always been concerned about maintaining the integrity of the original architecture. That's why Gran left the fireplace intact when she remodeled the kitchen, even though she never uses it."

Claudia shifted in her chair so she could see the fireplace. There was one in every room, but as she regarded this one, she realized that there was something different about it. She got up and walked over to examine it more closely.

"We've already inspected the fireplace," Jonathon reminded.

"I know," she said as she swung around to face him, "but look at it closely. What's different about this fireplace compared to all the others in the house?"

Jonathon studied the fireplace, but he couldn't see what she was driving at. It had the same brick interior, was framed by the same black marble mantelpiece, and had the same raised marble hearth.

"It looks the same to me," he told her.

"The hearth is much larger, Jonathon."

"That's not surprising. It's in the kitchen, which means they used the fireplace for cooking. They probably made it larger to protect the floor from shooting sparks."

"But they didn't cook in the house in pre-Civil War days," she reminded. "They did their cooking in a separate building to protect against fire. This was the sitting room, wasn't it? The women most likely spent the majority of their time in here. That would have allowed them easy access to the secret room during the day. There's also a back staircase that leads into this room, so they would have had quick access to it at night, as well. Don't you see? This was the ideal location for the entrance, and we're looking for a trapdoor. This hearth is large enough for that."

"I don't think so, Claudia. Remember, the secret room was built to protect the women, and they wore hoop skirts in the 1860s. As big as that hearth is, it isn't large enough to accommodate a hoop skirt."

"They would have just taken the hoops off," Claudia explained.

"They could have been under instant attack. Could they have gotten out of them that quickly?"

"Sure. Hoops were tied around their waists. All they had to do was hike up their skirts, untie, and they'd collapse at their feet."

"It can't be that simple, can it?" he asked, excitement vibrating in his voice.

He joined Claudia at the fireplace. As he studied the hearth, he realized that it was nearly a shade lighter than the mantelpiece. He supposed that could be accounted for by age, but gut instinct said it was because it was a different piece of marble altogether. The slab of stone was roughly five feet wide by four feet deep and about four inches thick. It would be too heavy to lift. He dropped to his knees and ran his fingers around the edges. There was an almost indistinguishable crack between it and the floor, and he felt a rush of excitement. Bracing himself against one end, he pushed. The hearth didn't budge.

He sat back on his heels and glanced up at Claudia. "If you're right, it's too heavy for them to have moved it. There would have to be some kind of mechanism beneath to make it slide, but where's the trigger? When we examined the fireplace, we didn't find anything unusual."

Claudia regarded the fireplace critically. "A trigger mechanism would have had to be fairly easy to get to, since they couldn't actually be standing on the hearth when it opened. They'd also have to worry about being burned if there was a fire going, so it couldn't be inside the fireplace itself."

"That's not exactly true," he corrected speculatively, thinking out loud. "You adjust the flue in all these old fireplaces by reaching up into the chimney with a poker. They could have installed a trigger device that worked the same way by drilling a hole in the bottom of the firebox and running some chain beneath it to a trigger."

"I don't understand what you're saying," Claudia said in confusion.

Jonathon reached into the fireplace and lifted out the grate that supported a half dozen fake logs, then he pointed to a built-in grate in the floor.

"All the fireplaces on the main floor open into ash pits. You scrape the ashes through the grate and you retrieve them from outside."

"But wouldn't someone have found a chain when they were emptying the pit?"

"Not if it had been concealed by a layer of bricks."

"I get it. They'd make a hollow box of bricks to conceal it," Claudia said, a nervous, foreboding excitement stirring within her.

A part of her was thrilled at the possibility of proving her vision as correct, but it was quickly being overshadowed by the reminder that the secret room presented danger to someone, and the someone could very possibly be Jonathon. One look at his ecstatic expression assured her, however, that he wasn't in the mood for predictions of doom.

"But if they had to drill a hole in the floor, wouldn't we be able to see that?" she asked, determining that it was best to keep her concerns to herself for the moment.

"Not if they ran a layer of bricks on the inside, too."

"That's ingenious!" Claudia exclaimed.

"It's also pure conjecture."

"But it makes perfect sense." She knelt on the hearth, leaned into the fireplace and looked up into the chimney. "Heavens, I can't see anything. It's as black as night in here."

"That's because we've capped the chimney to conserve energy. Let me get a flashlight."

When he returned, he extended the flashlight. "I'll let you have the honors. You're the one who figured this out."

"Oh, no," she demurred. "You do it."

He shook his head. "You're smaller than I am, so you can get into the fireplace better. If you do find something, however, don't pull it. I don't want you tumbling into the basement."

"Are you sure?" she asked as she searched his face. This was his secret room, and she didn't want to take away any of his pleasure at finding it, particularly since it might well be the only pleasure he would derive from it.

"I'm sure. See what you can find."

Convinced of his sincerity, she took the flashlight and shined it up inside. The bricks were blackened from years of wood smoke, and it took her a moment, but she eventually identified a slight projection on the sides of the chimney. She didn't see a chain, so she ran her hand along the right ledge, finding nothing. She tried the left ledge, and when she encountered what felt like a piece of metal, she let out a whoop.

"What is it?" Jonathon asked, his voice tight with repressed excitement.

"It feels like a piece of chain," Claudia answered quickly as she backed out cautiously.

She thrust the flashlight at him, grinning. "There's a ledge about a foot and a half up on the left side. See if it feels like a piece of chain to you."

She scooted out of his way, and he leaned into the chimney. A minute later, he backed out, his grin broad. He tucked the flashlight into his back pocket, tossed his arms around Claudia and gave her a hug. "I think we've found it!"

He released her from the hug and stood. "It's definitely a chain, but some of the links must have broken off. It's too close to the wall to use the poker, so I'll see if I can find some heavy twine to thread through it."

He went into the pantry, came back with a piece of clothesline and leaned into the chimney. When he backed out this time, he was holding the clothesline in his hand.

He stood and ordered, "Get away from the hearth, Claudia. We don't know where it will go if it moves."

"Not *if* it moves, Jonathon, *when* it moves," Claudia declared as she scrambled to her feet and held her breath. She was filled with a combination of expectancy and anxiety.

"Hot damn, Claudia! You found it!" Jonathon exclaimed with a delighted laugh as he pulled the clothesline and the hearth began to move.

Claudia was only vaguely aware of his words. Her attention was centered on the widening black hole in the floor. For every inch the hearth moved, she became more anxious. As it opened further to reveal a dusty staircase, she was hit by a sudden wave of terror so powerful she couldn't move or speak.

The paralyzing spell was broken when Jonathon announced, "I'm going down."

"No!" Claudia exclaimed harshly as she leaped forward and grabbed his arm. "You can't go down there, Jonathon. If you do, you'll be in terrible danger!"

He laughed at her warning and gently pried her hand loose. "Come on, Claudia. It's just an old room. There's nothing down there that can hurt me."

"You can't go down there!" she repeated urgently, her heart racing with fear. "Please, Jonathon. Just close the hearth and forget the room. *You have to forget about it!*"

Frowning slightly at the edge of panic in her voice, he knew he'd have to go down there regardless. Someone had to show her there were no spooks or dangerous elements. He eluded her hands when she reached for him again, saying, "I'll be back in a few minutes."

Claudia wrapped her arms around herself as she watched him disappear. The terror continued to build inside her, and she closed her eyes tightly and concentrated, willing Jonathon's mind to open up to her so she could keep track of him. When he remained as closed to her as ever, she wanted to sit on the floor and dissolve into tears.

She opened her eyes and stared at the black hole. It seemed as if hours had gone by. What was happening down there? Should she go after him? No sooner had the thought crossed her mind than he hurried to the steps. When she was halfway down, she saw him.

He swung toward her quickly and harshly ordered, "Claudia, get the hell out of here!"

Frozen in horror, she couldn't obey. She'd only had a brief glance of what he'd been looking at, but she'd had anatomy in high school. She knew a human skeleton when she saw one.

"I told you not to come down here," she said in a hollow voice, beginning to tremble. She wrapped her arms around herself again. The significance of her earlier visions, of the bleak, dark pit where the air was so heavy she couldn't breathe was suddenly obvious. It had been a forewarning of death. *"I . . . told . . . you."*

As she burst into tears, Jonathon hurried up the stairs and swept her up against him. He cradled her head against his chest. "It's all right, honey. Just calm down. It's all right."

She buried her face against his shirt and told herself she couldn't fall apart. She had to be strong, because the danger the shadow represented was now crystal clear. She'd been summoned to Magnolia to stop a killer from killing again.

Chapter 9

Claudia sat in the great room waiting for Jonathon, who was in the kitchen with Sheriff Helton. It seemed as if days had gone by since they'd found the secret room, but a glance at the old grandfather clock assured her it had only been a few hours.

She studied her surroundings, noting the high windows that were framed by molded plaster friezes, which also circled the ceiling. Turkish carpets covered the gleaming hardwood floor. The furniture was Victorian, and many of the pieces were as old as the house. Her surroundings were so gracious that it seemed impossible anything as gruesome as a murder could have taken place here. Shuddering inwardly, she wished Jonathon would come and tell her what was going on.

As if thoughts of him were enough to conjure him up, he and Sheriff Helton walked into the room. Impossible though it seemed, Jonathon looked even grimmer than he had earlier.

"What's going on?" she asked, wasting no time on preliminaries.

"We've made a tentative identification of the body," Jonathon answered. "The Sheriff found a ring. It belonged to Billy Joe."

"The caretaker who disappeared?" When Jonathon nodded, she added, "What happened to him?"

"We don't know yet, ma'am," the middle-aged, beefy sheriff answered as he sat down on the chair across from her. "We'll have to wait for the coroner to tell us that. For now, I'd like to take your statement as to what happened today."

When Helton finished taking her statement, he rose and said, "My deputies should be done within the hour. I'd appreciate it if you would stay out of the kitchen until then."

"Why don't we go over to the guest house and have some coffee and maybe something to eat?" Claudia suggested after the sheriff left the room. She was eager to leave the forebodingly heavy atmosphere that had pervaded the house since their discovery.

"You go," Jonathon replied. "I'd better hang around until everyone's gone. I'm also going to have to call Gran and tell her what's happened. The sheriff wants to contact her as soon as possible, and I want the news to come from me."

Claudia frowned in concern, trying vainly to connect with him. If she could just pick up on his emotions, she'd be able to tell if he needed her to stay for moral support.

"Are you all right, Jonathon?"

"I've had better days."

"You know, it's not healthy to keep your feelings locked inside. What happened today was traumatic. You should talk about it," she probed gently, noting how tense his shoulders were.

"I don't have time to talk right now, Claudia," he said, his voice tinged with impatience. "Just go to the guest house. I'll come by after Sheriff Helton's done here."

Reluctantly Claudia left, though she was seriously concerned about Jonathon. When she reached the guest house, she glanced back at the mansion and shivered. A cloud had just passed over the sun, draping Magnolia in shadow.

* * *

Claudia lifted the curtain at the front window. It was growing dark, and she was beginning to fret. The sheriff and his entourage had departed Magnolia nearly an hour ago, and still there was no sign of Jonathon. He'd said that he would come over after everyone was gone, so where was he? She considered calling him, but she was afraid if she did, he might beg off altogether. Unable to bear being alone a moment longer, she decided to go looking for him.

When she reached Magnolia's back door, she hesitated. She wasn't sure she was ready to go back into the kitchen. Maybe she should go around to the front door. She was wavering in indecision when the door opened. With a yelp, she leaped backward.

"Are you all right?" Jonathon asked as he stepped onto the porch.

"Yes," she answered, pressing her hand against her galloping heart. "You startled me."

"Sorry."

"That's okay. I was worried when you didn't come over right away, so I came to check on you."

"I decided to take a shower and shave. I thought it might make me feel human again."

Claudia regarded him worriedly. There was a haunted look in his eyes, and it wrenched her heart. She'd been feeling pretty haunted herself for the past several hours. She wanted to help him, but she didn't know how, so she reached up and caressed his jaw.

"What can I do to help you through this, Jonathon?"

"I don't know," he answered, catching her hand and holding it against his cheek. He closed his eyes, hoping the warmth of her flesh would dissolve the numbing cold that had settled inside him. He'd been so thrilled about finding the secret room, and that momentary happiness—the first true happiness he'd experienced since his wife's death—had been stolen away from him, just as she had been stolen from him. "I feel so empty inside."

"Then let me fill you up," she whispered impulsively, unable to control the need to chase the bleakness from his eyes. Standing on tiptoe, she brushed her lips against his.

He wrapped an arm around her waist and pulled her against him, returning her kiss with a hungry urgency that overloaded Claudia's senses. As he tangled his fingers in her hair and plunged his tongue into her mouth, an all-consuming passion swept through her. Heat exploded in her, scattering her intentions of soothing. When he began to withdraw his tongue, she followed it, determined to ravage him as he'd just ravaged her. She let out a whimper of protest when he jerked away from the kiss before she could carry out her plan.

He pushed her away with a muffled curse and strode to the gallery railing. As he gripped it, he bit out, "Leave, Claudia. Just get the hell away from me."

"I'm not going anywhere, Jonathon. After the way you just kissed me, I don't think you really want me to leave."

He spun around to face her, his expression a tight mask of fury, a man pushed beyond his limit. "Damn it, what do you want from me?"

"How about a little friendship? A little support? We just found the remains of a body today," she answered, her own temper rising. "Maybe you can chalk it up as one of life's little quirks, but it's rattled the hell out of me!"

"And you think it hasn't rattled the hell out of me? All my life Magnolia has been the center of my world. No matter what happened, it never changed. It was here. It was mine, and it was a safe haven.

"Now that safe haven has been violated," he continued, his chest heaving with all the repressed emotions that had been simmering inside since he'd found Billy Joe. Anger and fear came surging to the surface, and he knew it was because of Claudia. She was making him feel again, and he didn't want to feel. He wanted to stay numb and cold, and yet he also wanted to haul her into his arms and love her, let her soothe away his turmoil. She was making him *need* her, and he didn't want—couldn't *afford* to need her. That kind of need hurt too badly when it was taken away.

When she stared at him, looking bewildered and hurt, he steeled himself against the urge to comfort her and gave free reign to his anger, saying, "Someone has desecrated Magnolia, and I can't stand it, Claudia. If you don't get away from me, I'm going to haul you over there to the chaise, toss up your skirt and take all this anger and frustration out on you. Is that why you came over here? Is that why you kissed me? Do you want to be used? Because if that's what you want, just say the word, and I'll be happy to oblige!''

Claudia hugged herself and stared at her feet as his words pummeled her. It wasn't what he was saying that hurt as much as the demeaning, caustic edge to his voice. He sounded as if he despised her. When he was finished, she looked up at him, barely aware of the tears streaming down her cheeks.

''I came here because I was worried about you,'' she said in a soft voice. ''I kissed you because I wanted to give you some comfort, and I thought maybe you'd give me a little comfort in return. I see now that I was wrong. You don't need comfort or support from anyone. All you need is your precious Magnolia, and now that I know that, I won't bother you again.''

She stumbled toward the steps, but before she could reach them, Jonathon stepped in front of her and pulled her into his arms. She struggled against him, but he only held her more tightly until she finally gave up.

''I hate you!'' she cried as she buried her face against his chest with a sob.

''Good,'' he rasped as he lifted her into his arms and carried her toward the guest house, knowing instinctively that Claudia wasn't emotionally ready to go back into the mansion. For that matter, he wasn't up to it either. ''Just keep hating me, honey. That's the best thing you can do for the both of us.''

Jonathon decided that he should be entered into the *Guinness Book of World Records* for callousness as he settled into the porch swing and cradled Claudia on his lap. Though her sobs had subsided, she was still crying.

He couldn't believe he'd verbally attacked her like that. He'd known how upset she was when they found the body, but he'd become so engrossed in his own worries that he'd ignored her needs. Now he realized that he'd had an easy day compared to her. He'd been able to distance himself from the horror by dealing with the sheriff and his people. Claudia had had nothing to do but sit and relive the horror over and over again, and when she'd reached out to him for comfort and support, he'd turned on her.

He heaved an inward sigh. She'd said she hated him, but she couldn't possibly hate him as much as he hated himself. Hadn't he learned anything from Katie's death? Was he condemned to make the same mistakes over and over?

"Feeling better?" he asked as he smoothed her hair away from her tear-drenched cheek. She'd finally stopped crying and was lying quietly in his arms.

"I'm sorry I fell apart," she murmured as she tried to pull away from him.

He tucked her back against his chest. "You had every right to fall apart, Claudia. It's been a tough day. I'm sorry I wasn't more sensitive."

"You're not my keeper, Jonathon. It's up to me to take care of myself."

"As long as you're at Magnolia, you're a part of my responsibility."

"I don't want to be another burden for you to bear."

"I have wide shoulders."

"Maybe. But even Atlas got tired of holding up the sky."

"I'm not holding up the sky. Just my little part of it." When she didn't respond, he said, "Talk to me, Claudia. Tell me what you're thinking. What you're feeling."

"I'm scared," she answered honestly. "Really scared."

"Join the club. I'm not feeling very brave myself right now."

She was silent for a long time before she asked, "How did Adelaide take the news?"

"Better than I thought. She and Aunt Virginia will be here tomorrow."

"You mean Adelaide's coming back without making you grovel? You must be ecstatic."

"Yeah." He hesitated before saying, "Claudia, I want to ask a favor of you, and I hope you'll grant it. When Gran comes home, will you help keep an eye on her? I know Aunt Virginia's going to be here, but I'm afraid my aunt is as flighty as Gran."

"Of course, I'll help, but you're talking as if you're leaving." When he didn't say anything, she leaned her head back and searched his face. His expression was unreadable. "Are you leaving, Jonathon?"

"I hope not," he answered tersely.

"What does that mean?"

"That means that I don't plan on leaving, but if something unforeseen happens, I want to know that someone responsible will be watching out for Gran."

He considered her responsible? As much as Claudia wanted to take his words at face value, she couldn't. Sensing that he was withholding something, she started to question him further, but he silenced her with a kiss that drove all conscious thought from her mind.

When he finally let her come up for air, he said hoarsely, "After the way I've treated you, I know I have no right to ask this... but I can't stand the thought of being alone tonight. Would you please let me stay with you?"

The warning bells were going off inside Claudia's head. He was right. After the way he'd treated her, she should give him an unequivocal no. But she suddenly couldn't stand the thought of being alone, either, and even if she had wanted to be alone, she couldn't have denied his request. Jonathon might be a mystery to her, but she was certain of one thing. He was an extremely proud man, and she didn't need clairvoyance to know how much that question had cost him. Her heart melted. He needed her.

How much is saying yes going to cost you? a nagging voice asked.

She ignored the voice and said, "I suppose I could agree to one more night."

Helping Claudia undress, Jonathon concluded that she had to be the most beautiful woman in the world. It wasn't her physical beauty that had him regarding her in awe. It was the shyness of her smile. The gentleness of her touch as she began to help him undress. She looked so delicate, so fragile, yet he knew that when he finally drew her into his arms, she'd be warm, alive and vital. She would restore the balance in his world, which had been off kilter ever since they'd found that accursed secret room and Billy Joe's skeletal remains.

As the knowledge of just how much he needed her tonight surfaced, every survival instinct he had began blaring at him in warning. When it came to a woman, need was an insidious emotion that sneaked through you when you weren't looking. The next thing you knew, it was wrapped around your heart.

He might have managed to persuade himself to leave if Claudia hadn't chosen that moment to tentatively trail her hand down his chest. Every nerve and muscle in his body quivered in response to her curious touch, and he became so aroused that he groaned. She glanced up, her eyes wide and startled by the sound. When she started to jerk her hand away from his chest, he caught it and held it in place.

"Don't stop touching me, honey. I want you to touch me. Everywhere."

Her tongue nervously flicked across her lips, her eyes growing even wider. "Everywhere?"

"Damn," he muttered hoarsely, his eyes intent on her lips. Not wasting another minute, he swung her up into his arms and placed her on the bed. Then he hurriedly shed the remainder of his clothes and lay down beside her. Pulling her into his arms, he encouraged, "Yes, honey. Everywhere."

Smiling shyly, Claudia resumed her journey down his chest with her hand, and when she began moving lower, Jonathon closed his eyes and swallowed back another groan. Though he was anticipating her touch, the hesitant brush of her fingers over his hardness sent a wave of pleasurable shock coursing through him. When she wrapped her hand around him, he was sure he was going to explode.

"You're so soft," she whispered. "So hard, but so soft."

He opened his eyes, and when he saw the wonder of her words reflected on her face, it touched him so deeply that he felt his throat constrict.

"And you're soft and sweet and sexy," he murmured gruffly as he rolled her beneath him. "It's also *my* turn to do some touching. *Everywhere.*"

* * *

When Claudia opened her eyes and discovered Jonathon propped on an elbow and staring at her, she concluded that she didn't like this morning after any better than the last one.

"Hi," she murmured, blushing as she reached for the sheet at her waist and dragged it to her neck. She knew her show of modesty was ridiculous after the way they'd made love the night before. They'd fulfilled every detail of her erotic visions and more. If she wasn't careful, Jonathon could become an addiction.

"Hi, yourself," he said, smiling in amusement. "How come you're blushing?"

"How come you're staring at me?"

"I was enjoying the view until you covered it up. There's no need to be embarrassed, Claudia. You have a beautiful body, and you should be proud of it."

"Yeah, well, I'm kind of new at this. I haven't quite figured out the proper protocol."

Regarding her somberly, he reached out and brushed her hair away from her face. "You deserve more than this, Claudia. You need to go out and find yourself some wonderful man who will worship the ground you walk on."

"I'd hate that kind of devotion," she replied, her breath catching painfully at the way he was excluding himself from her life. Striving for a casual tone, she determinedly ignored the curious ache in her heart. *No regrets.* "I'd always be trying to live up to someone's image of me, which means I'd be destined to fall flat on my face."

"But that's what's so wonderful about that kind of devotion. When you fell, he'd help you up, dust you off and start worshiping you all over again."

Claudia was bemused by this side of Jonathon's personality. Despite the fact that he was, in effect, pulling away from her, he was most assuredly spouting romanticism. He didn't strike her as a romantic. "Have you ever been that devoted to a woman?"

She regretted the question the moment she asked it, because his expression immediately hardened. She was sure it was pain glittering in his eyes, but there were so many other emotions reflected there, too, that she couldn't be certain.

"You know for someone who claims to be clairvoyant, you sure as hell don't show much ability in that area," he drawled with heavy sarcasm.

Claudia was more startled than hurt by the unexpected attack. As she stared at him, trying to decide how to respond to his goad, it dawned on her that anger was Jonathon's defense mechanism. Whenever he was faced with a situation he couldn't control or an emotion he couldn't handle, he reacted with anger.

"I'm sorry if it seems like I was prying, Jonathon," she stated quietly, determined not to let him prod her into battle. "But if you didn't want me to follow our conversation through to its natural conclusion, you shouldn't have started it in the first place. It's also unfair of you to personally attack me because I did."

Dark color flew into his cheeks at her rebuke, and he rolled out of bed, tugged on his jeans and stalked to the window. As he stood staring out, his hands propped on his hips, he said, "I'm sure Gran's told you that I was married and my wife died from leukemia a few years ago."

"No, she didn't tell me," Claudia answered as she sat up. Clutching the covers to her chest, she leaned against the back of the antique tester bed and studied his stiff posture. She considered offering her condolences over his wife's death, but she suspected he'd consider it a platitude.

He turned to face her with a look of disbelief. "I'm surprised that she didn't tell you the whole story."

"I don't know why you think she would. That's a very personal part of your life, and Adelaide would never invade your privacy by discussing it with a virtual stranger."

"But didn't you . . ."

"Didn't I what?" she encouraged when his voice trailed off.

Jonathon shook his head, unable to complete his question, because he'd been about to ask why she hadn't read his grandmother's mind. He turned back to the window, reeling from the significance of him even entertaining that question.

When had he actually begun to believe in Claudia's clairvoyance? *From that first day when he'd discovered she'd been right about the chocolate pie falling off the back seat.* It had been such a trivial event, which was exactly why her knowledge of it had been so profound. There was no way she could have known about it unless she'd picked up the information from his grandmother's mind.

His mind reeled. The thought that Claudia might be able to read his mind terrified him. There were so many secrets he had to hide—so many doubts and fears that he couldn't face himself. But it was impossible for a person to read another's mind, wasn't it?

"Claudia, tell me about your clairvoyance," he said abruptly, turning to face her. "I want to know what it's like. What you do."

Claudia clutched the covers more tightly to her chest as she regarded him uncertainly. How had he leaped from a discussion about Adelaide revealing his private life to her clairvoyance? She searched his face, looking for some clue as to what he was after. Unfortunately, all she could ascertain was that he was tensely waiting for her answer.

"I don't *do* anything," she replied warily. "I'm a receiver. People are emotional, and they generate very strong vibrations. I pick up on them."

"And from these...vibrations, you determine their future?"

"In a manner of speaking, but it isn't that simple."

She raked her hand through her hair as she tried to figure out how to explain what she really didn't understand herself. "All I can tell you is that I connect with people. Sometimes the link is weak and sometimes it's strong. Sometimes I only receive a sense of their emotional state. Other times I pick up on their thoughts. Then there are times when everything seems to...blend, and I catch glimpses of their future."

"And it's just there? Like some sort of predestination?" he prodded.

She gave an adamant shake of her head. "I don't believe in predestination, Jonathon. At least not in the literal sense of the word. Even when I give my clients predictions for a rocky future, I emphasize that the events aren't fated to happen—that foresight gives them the knowledge and the ability to make positive changes in their lives."

He frowned thoughtfully before saying, "There's only one problem with that theory, Claudia. You said that you have an eighty percent accuracy rate in your predictions. If foresight gives them the ability to change events, it would seem that your rate would be much lower."

She smiled wryly. "First off, not all my predictions are bad. Second, I've found that even with foresight, it's difficult for people to make changes, especially if those changes require a confrontation. Then there's the fact that a person's future is often linked with someone else's. No matter how determined you are to maintain control over your own life, you can't regulate the actions of others. And finally, a prediction can come true without coming true in its entirety.

"A good example of that would be when I saw a client of mine seriously injured in a car accident," she explained. "My client was a smoker, and I saw her lighting a cigarette just before the accident occurred. I couldn't tell her not to drive, because her job requires her to, and that would have endangered her livelihood. I did, however, caution her about smoking in the car. A couple of weeks later, she was involved in a car accident. Because she wasn't lighting a cigarette—her attention was on the traffic—she walked away with a few bruises and scratches instead of ending up in the hospital."

"That could have been a coincidence," Jonathon pointed out. "You just said her job required her to drive. Her odds of being involved in an accident would be higher than normal."

"You certainly have a case for coincidence," she conceded. "And that's why it's so difficult for people to believe in E.S.P. skills. So much of what we do can be attributed to coincidence or chance. What it really comes down to in the end, I guess, is that you either believe or you don't."

"Can you read my mind?"

Claudia blinked at the sudden question. She noted that Jonathon was wearing the same expression of cool impassivity he'd worn yesterday morning when they'd first come face-to-face after having made love. Then, it had been a mask to cover his confusion. Was he feeling confused now? And if he was, what did it mean? That he was beginning to believe?

There was a part of her that desperately needed him to believe in her. Yet there was a part that just as desperately needed him to disbelieve, because at that moment, Claudia realized that Jonathon had the capacity to hurt her deeper than anyone—including her parents—ever had. She was on the verge of falling in love with him, and he'd made it clear that he wasn't interested in a commitment. As long as he disbelieved, she could keep up the walls.

She briefly considered telling him that she could read his mind, but she couldn't bring herself to lie to him. Besides, he was intrinsically linked to whatever was going to happen, and instinctively she knew that if he thought she could read him, he would avoid her. And that could prove to be disastrous.

"No, Jonathon, I can't read your mind," she said with a heavy sigh. "In fact, I can't even pick up on your emotions. You're completely closed to me."

Jonathon drew in a deep breath and released it a rush. *She couldn't read his mind! His secrets were safe!* It was as if some heavy burden had been lifted from his shoulders. Only now did he realize he'd been carrying it around since the moment his grandmother had called him and announced that she'd moved a psychic into the guest house.

He no longer needed to fear Claudia, and as he stared at her, he murmured, "It must be hard."

She stared back at him in wide-eyed confusion. "What must be hard?"

"Living the life you live. You have one group of people who want you to give them all the answers. Then you have the group that doesn't want to believe in you at all. Everything is a high or low for you, isn't it? You don't have any middle ground to retreat to."

Claudia was dumbstruck. No one, not even herself, had ever been able to describe her life in such simplistic terms. The fact that he had, both confounded and amazed her.

"How did you know?" she asked tremulously as he walked toward the bed.

"Intuition," he answered, sitting down on the edge of the bed. He reached out and smoothed her sleep-tousled hair away from her face. "For as long as you're here, Claudia, I can offer you some middle ground to retreat to. Think about it."

With that, he retrieved the rest of his clothes from the floor and walked out without a backward glance.

Claudia continued to sit with the covers clutched to her chest, staring, transfixed, at the empty doorway. What had he been suggesting? That they could have a relationship, or had he merely been offering her an affair?

Her common sense told her it was the latter, but she wanted to believe differently. She needed more than that from him, because when he'd brushed her hair away from her cheek, her mind had been flooded with new erotic visions.

With a groan she closed her eyes and tried to ignore the images, but they were too strong to dismiss. She stopped trying and let herself flow with them.

They were standing in the shower. The water coursed down her back while Jonathon's soapy hands circled her breasts in slow, sensuous strokes. As her nipples grew hard, his hands trailed lower, and she cried out his name as he slipped one between her thighs. He laughed softly, huskily, as he caressed her until she had to cling to his shoulders to keep from falling. When she was sure she couldn't stand one more moment of torture, he cupped her buttocks and lifted her until she was astride him. He entered her swiftly, urgently, sending her into immediate release. But even as she climaxed, her passion began to build again. She peaked a second time, and then a third, at which Jonathon reached his own release. As they shuddered in each other's arms, she whispered, "I love you, Jonathon."

The vision had ended before Jonathon had responded to her avowal, and instinct told Claudia it was because *she'd* fallen in love with him, but he wasn't in love with *her*. Which meant that all he'd ever be able to offer her was an affair.

"I don't believe in affairs," she whispered shakily, "and I'm *not* going to have one with him!"

So why did she have this sinking feeling that even with foresight, nothing she did was going to stop the visions from coming true?

Sitting in the porch swing, Claudia tried to grapple with the emotions that had been tormenting her since Jonathon had walked away from her this morning. It was clear he wanted her, wanted to have an affair, but having an affair just wasn't in her. She believed in love and marriage and commitment. So how had she gotten into this mess?

That was easy. She'd let her emotions sweep her along, and now she was faced with a decision that was as tempting as it was unacceptable.

Her troubled thoughts were interrupted as Sheriff Helton drove around the side of the mansion. Instead of going to Magnolia, however, he parked his car next to the guest house. Why was he coming here instead of going to see Jonathon?

As she watched him approach with a deceptively lazy gait, she nervously pushed her foot against the porch floor and set the swing in motion. Sheriff Helton wasn't an easy man to read, but she'd picked up enough to understand that beneath his slow-moving, good-old-boy act was a quick mind and a tendency to expect the worst of everyone. She supposed it was an occupational necessity, but she couldn't imagine spending every day of your life being suspicious of nearly everyone you met.

"Mornin', ma'am," he said when he reached the porch steps. "It sure is a beautiful day, isn't it?"

"Good morning, Sheriff Helton," she returned. "And you're right. It is a beautiful day."

He reached into his shirt pocket, pulled out a toothpick and eyed it. Finally he slipped it between his teeth and pushed his hat back on his head.

"We identified the body you and Mr. Tanner found yesterday. It sure enough is Billy Joe Jordan," he announced.

"I see," Claudia murmured, not knowing what else to say. "Do you know what happened to him?"

"Yep. I don't suppose you knew Billy Joe?"

"No, Sheriff, I didn't know him," she answered.

He switched the toothpick from one side of his mouth to the other. "You're not from around these parts, are you?"

Claudia regarded him warily. "I told you yesterday that I'm from Jackson."

He nodded. "Billy Joe has a lot of kin over in Jackson. Are you sure you never met him?"

"I'm positive, Sheriff. I have an excellent memory, and I have never met anyone by the name of Billy Joe Jordan."

"I did a little checking this morning, and I was real surprised to discover that you still have an apartment in Jackson. Why is that?"

"I decided to get away from the city for a while." The first time they'd met she'd recognized that he was a doubting Thomas, so telling him the truth would only be a waste of time. "I guess you could say I'm on vacation."

"So you aren't planning on moving here permanently?"

"No."

"I don't suppose you could remember where you were over the Fourth of July weekend two years ago."

"Are you asking me for an alibi, Sheriff Helton?"

"Yep."

Claudia swallowed hard at his blunt answer. If he was asking for an alibi, then he was confirming what she'd surmised yesterday. Billy Joe Jordan had been murdered.

"Two years ago I was participating in a psychic research project at the University of California," she told him. "I was in Los Angeles from the middle of May until the end of August. Dr. Susan Hill was in charge of the project, and I'll be happy to give you her number so you can verify my presence there."

"I'd appreciate that, ma'am. It's not that I don't believe you, you understand. It's just part of my job."

"I understand. Is there anything else?"

He took the toothpick out of his mouth, eyed it again, and then stuck it back into his pocket. "Well, now that you mention it, there are a couple of things I'd like to clear up. You said that you had a vision about that trapdoor, and that's how you and Mr. Tanner found the secret room. Are you sure that Mr. Tanner didn't, well, put ideas into your head about where to look?"

Claudia arched a brow. "Jonathon did not put any ideas into my head, Sheriff. I know you don't believe it, but I am a clairvoyant. I had a vision, and that vision was about the trapdoor."

"I wasn't trying to insult you, ma'am. It just seems to me that even clairvoyants might be susceptible to suggestion. So, as far as you can remember, Mr. Tanner didn't do or say anything to draw your attention to the fireplace?"

"Jonathon did not draw my attention to the fireplace," Claudia replied, though there was a nagging voice inside reminding her that that wasn't exactly true. When she'd asked if he knew if the floor plans were the same, he'd said that the family had always tried to maintain the integrity of the mansion. He'd then gone on to say that was why Adelaide had left the fireplace intact when she'd remodeled. If he hadn't mentioned that, she probably wouldn't have focused her attention on the fireplace and recognized that there was something different about it. *Had* he been directing her attention there?

Suddenly she was assailed with doubts, and she resisted the urge to rake her hand through her hair. She also firmly informed herself that she was letting Helton's projection of suspicion interfere with her common sense. If, as he was implying, Jonathon was the killer, why would he have begun to search for the secret room in the first place?

The slam of a door caused her to glance toward Magnolia, and she saw Jonathon striding toward them. As she watched him approach, she knew with unwavering certainty that Jonathon had not killed Billy Joe Jordan. They couldn't have been as intimate as they'd been without her

perceiving something that heinous. Jonathon might be capable of many things, but she didn't need her clairvoyance
to tell her the truth. Jonathon Jackson Tanner, III, was not
a murderer. The vibrations emanating from the sheriff,
however, told her that he was as sure of Jonathon's guilt as
she was of his innocence. But why? What did he know that
she didn't?

"Sheriff Helton," Jonathon nodded as he joined them.
"Have you been able to identify the body?"

"Yep," the sheriff answered, retrieving his toothpick and
putting it into his mouth. "It's Billy Joe, all right. The
coroner's preliminary report says that the cause of death
was several blows to the back of the head. I don't suppose
you know anything about that?"

"You suppose right," Jonathon answered easily, though
even Claudia could sense his tension. The vibes radiating
from the sheriff told her that he sensed it, too.

"In that case, you won't mind coming down to my office and answering a few questions, right?"

"Right. I'll follow you in my car."

Sheriff Helton nodded and walked away, saying,
"Goodbye, ma'am. You have a nice day."

When he was out of earshot, Claudia scowled at Jonathon and accused, "You knew this was going to happen last
night, didn't you? That's why you asked me to keep an eye
on Adelaide. What's going on? Why does he think you
killed Billy Joe?"

He smiled grimly. "Because when I caught Billy Joe
stealing those antiques, I was so mad I threatened to kill
him, and I did it in front of the entire family. As soon as the
sheriff told me he was going to talk to the family, I knew
Uncle Richard would jump at the chance to tell him, and I
would be Helton's primary suspect, anyway. So I told him
what I'd said on my own."

"You're more than a suspect. The sheriff is convinced
you killed Billy Joe!"

"He's going to need more than conviction to arrest me,
Claudia, and before he can put together a case, I'll have
proved who the real killer is."

A bolt of fear lanced through her at his words. "What are you planning on doing, Jonathon?"

"Nothing for you to worry about," he answered. "Now, I'd better get going before Helton has a change of heart and decides to drag me down to his office in chains. Gran should be home anytime now. Keep an eye on her."

Claudia wanted to kick something as she watched him walk away. There was plenty for her to worry about, particularly if he was going to go hunting for a murderer. What was he trying to do? Get himself killed?

As soon as she asked herself the question, a feeling of impending doom coursed through her. She hugged herself as she watched Jonathon and Sheriff Helton drive away, and then she glanced toward the mansion. The aura of danger emanating from it was so palpable she shuddered.

"You aren't going to win," she whispered harshly. "Do you hear me? *I'm not going to let you win!*"

A sudden gust of wind hit her. As it whistled in her ears, it sounded like demonic laughter.

Jonathon stared out the sheriff's office window while he fought against his rising frustration. He'd spent the past two hours being grilled about a murder he hadn't committed. During the first hour, he'd been almost amused by Sheriff Helton's interrogation. Now, it was just damn irritating.

When Sheriff Helton announced, "I'd like to go through this one more time, son," Jonathon had to draw upon all his reserves to keep from losing his temper.

After he was sure that he had his emotions in check, he turned to face the sheriff. "Sheriff Helton, we've gone through this a dozen times already. I did not kill Billy Joe."

"But you did threaten him."

"It was a figure of speech. I was angry. He was stealing from my grandmother, for Pete's sake. And if I *had* killed him—which I didn't—" he quickly added, "why would I have started a search for the secret room?"

Sheriff Helton leaned back in his chair and propped his feet on his desk. "Well, maybe you wanted something that was in that secret room. Something valuable."

Jonathon raked his hand through his hair, praying for patience. "If there had been something valuable in there that I wanted, why wouldn't I have just waited until the house was empty and gone down there and gotten it?"

"Well, now, you do have a point there," the sheriff drawled as he pulled his toothpick from his pocket, studied it and then put it back into his pocket. "Been trying to quit smoking, and now I feel like a beaver chewing on these danged toothpicks. You ever smoke?"

"I quit a year ago," Jonathon answered as he dropped into the chair in front of the sheriff's desk. "It's a hard habit to break."

"That it is, son. That it is. What brand did you smoke?"

Jonathon started to answer, but then stopped himself. He eyed the sheriff warily. "Why do you want to know?"

Sheriff Helton dropped his feet to the floor and opened his desk drawer. He removed a plastic bag and handed it to Jonathon. "That the brand?"

He accepted the plastic bag and stared at the three obviously old cigarette butts with horrified fascination. The brand name printed across the paper had faded, but it was still readable. His father had always said that smoking those fancy European cigarettes would someday get him into trouble.

"I think," he said as he handed the plastic bag back to Helton, "that I'm not going to answer any more questions without an attorney."

Claudia released an audible sigh of relief when the phone rang and Adelaide was on the other end. Jonathon had been gone for nearly four hours, and since he'd indicated Adelaide would arrive any minute, she'd been worried sick.

"Adelaide, where are you? I thought you were coming home today."

"There's been a change of plans, dear. We're at Steven's. I'm afraid that Ruth collapsed when she heard the news about Billy Joe. She's such a frail little thing, and so emotional. I guess all of this is too much for her. Of course, Steven is frantic, and Virginia and I can't possibly leave them at a time like this. I've been trying to reach Jonathon to tell him that we'll come this weekend with the rest of the family, but he isn't answering. Is he with you?''

''The entire family is coming this weekend?'' Claudia asked in surprise, trying to decide if she should tell Adelaide about her grandson and the sheriff. She didn't want to upset her, but what if the sheriff had arrested him? Shouldn't Adelaide know so she could make sure he got an attorney? Of course, if Jonathon needed an attorney, surely he'd call one himself.

''Why, certainly, dear. Hasn't Sheriff Helton talked to Jonathon? He called me this morning and said he wanted to speak with the entire family this weekend about Billy Joe's death. We were all at Magnolia that Fourth of July weekend when he disappeared, you know. I suppose we were the last people to see him alive.''

''I see,'' Claudia murmured as she nervously twisted the telephone cord around her hand, still unsure whether she should mention Jonathon's whereabouts. ''Adelaide, when you spoke with the sheriff, did he, uh, say anything about Billy Joe's death?''

''I'm not sure what you mean, dear.''

''Well, did he say anything about *how* he died?''

''He said it looked like foul play. It's shocking, isn't it? I mean, as far as I know, there's never been a murder at Magnolia.''

''Yes, it is shocking. Did the sheriff indicate who might have done it?''

''He didn't say, but I'm sure he thinks it's Jonathon. After all, Jonathon did threaten Billy Joe, but, of course, Jonathon would never harm anyone. He's like his father and his grandfather before him. All bark and no bite. But don't you worry, dear. Sheriff Helton will figure that out in no time, and if he doesn't, you'll just use your clairvoyance to find out who did it. As I told Virginia and Steven, that's the nice thing about having a clairvoyant around. Where is my grandson? You never did say.''

''Sheriff Helton asked him to come into his office for questioning,'' Claudia answered, deciding if Adelaide knew of the sheriff's suspicions, it was okay to tell her the rest.

"He's been gone for four hours, Adelaide. Maybe someone should check on him."

Adelaide chuckled. "Don't be ridiculous, Claudia. Jonathon can take care of himself. Tell him we'll be home Friday night and that he should call Mrs. Massey and ask her to stock the kitchen for me. Now, I have to go, dear. Steven is wearing out the carpet with his pacing, and I really should try to calm him down. I'll see you this weekend."

Before Claudia could answer, Adelaide hung up, and she stared at the telephone receiver in dismay. It was obvious that Adelaide had no concept of just how serious this situation was. She also couldn't help wondering if Jonathon really understood its gravity. He'd acted as if being the primary suspect in a murder was nothing more than an irritating glitch in a business contract.

She supposed both Jonathon and his grandmother were functioning on the principle that because he was innocent, he had nothing to worry about. Unfortunately Sheriff Helton functioned on a guilty-until-proven-innocent wavelength. She was also worried about Jonathon's claim that he'd prove who the real killer was before the sheriff could build a case against him. What was he planning to do?

After prowling restlessly through the guest house for another half hour, Claudia stepped out onto the porch. She braced her hands against the railing and stared at Magnolia, wishing she had the ability to receive telepathic communication through objects. There was so much soul to the mansion she was sure that all she'd have to do was touch its walls to discover who had killed Billy Joe.

But she didn't have that ability, and she released a frustrated sigh as she pushed herself away from the railing and headed for the magnolia grove. Perhaps there she could find some momentary peace until Jonathon came home.

When she reached the center of the grove, she settled on the bench cross-legged and forced herself to push her worries about Jonathon out of her mind. What she needed to concentrate on, she firmly informed herself, was the shadow, because intuition told her that this weekend would be the showdown.

Though she'd now come to think of the shadow as a person, she recognized that it was really only a representation of danger. However, it still wasn't clear just who was in danger. It could be Adelaide, Jonathon or another member of the family. But whoever it was, she was sure of one thing, Jonathon was the link. But was he the danger or the catalyst? she wondered in frustration.

There was no doubt in her mind that Jonathon was innocent in Billy Joe Jordan's death. That didn't, however, mean that he was incapable of future violence. Despite Adelaide's claim that he was all bark and no bite, Claudia couldn't dismiss the rage he'd exhibited last night. He considered Billy Joe's murder a desecration of Magnolia, and he'd said that Magnolia had always been the center of his world.

Suddenly Claudia recognized just how significant this statement had been. And what else was it he'd said? Something like *No matter what happened, it never changed. It was here. It was mine, and it was a safe haven. Now that safe haven has been violated.*

With a clarity that could almost have been visionary, she understood an integral part of Jonathon's personality. He wouldn't—*couldn't*—commit himself to a personal relationship, but then, he didn't need to, because he was using Magnolia to fulfill his emotional needs.

A shiver crawled up her spine. Jonathon was a carefully contained and controlled man, and when he felt threatened, he reacted with anger. And what could be more threatening than to have the place you felt emotionally safe defiled?

Later she couldn't say what it was that had made her glance toward the path opposite from the one she had taken, but when she did, she wasn't surprised to see Jonathon standing there. His expression was tense, and he was watching her through a screen of lashes that hid any emotion that might have been reflected in his eyes.

"Adelaide won't be home until this weekend," she announced, sliding her legs from beneath her, and placing her feet on the ground. She regarded him warily. "Ruth collapsed when she found out about Billy Joe, and Adelaide and Virginia are with her and Steven. Adelaide said that Sheriff Helton has asked the entire family to come to Magnolia this weekend for questioning. She would appreciate it if you'd contact Mrs. Massey and ask her to stock the kitchen.''

He didn't respond. He just continued to stand there, staring at her. What was going through his mind? And why couldn't she connect with him? she asked herself in frustration for what seemed like the millionth time. Was it because he was the danger? And if he was, could she stop him?

''You're beautiful,'' he suddenly murmured in a voice that was strangely detached. ''So very beautiful.''

''What happened at the sheriff's office?'' she asked tremulously as he began sauntering toward her with a pantherlike grace that sent a shiver up her spine.

''No, you're not beautiful, you're gorgeous,'' he said, still sounding detached.

''Jonathon, what happened at the sheriff's office?'' she repeated, frantically fighting against the sensual heat that was engulfing her. He looked and sounded so...*predatory*. She shouldn't be sitting here trembling with desire. She should be running for her life!

''I take that back,'' he rasped as he came to a stop in front of her. ''You're beautiful *and* gorgeous. I want to make love with you, Claudia. I want to make love with you now.''

''Jonathon, no!'' she whispered breathlessly when he grabbed her arms and drew her to her feet. ''If we go to bed with each other again, it has to be because you want me. Not because you're upset.''

''I do want you,'' he muttered deeply, lowering his mouth to hers.

Oh, heaven help me, was he right about that! she wailed inwardly as he plunged his tongue into her mouth and grabbed her hip, molding her against him. The strength of his arousal made her knees buckle.

As he swept her up into his arms and headed down the path toward the guest house, she rested her head against his shoulder and blinked against sudden tears. It didn't take clairvoyance to understand that he was using her, but even worse was the realization that she didn't care. With Jonathon, nothing seemed to matter, only that he needed her.

When he strode into the guest house and dropped her to her feet beside the bed, she told herself to stop this before it went any further. But before she could speak, he tangled his fingers in her hair and murmured hoarsely, "*Claudia.* Beautiful, gorgeous, sweet Claudia. I need you so much right now. So much."

There was such desperation in his words that she couldn't pull away from him. He needed her, and for now that was enough. She wrapped her arms around his neck and kissed him with a hungry urgency.

"So sweet!" he muttered feverishly as he wrenched his lips from hers and tumbled her to the bed. "How can you be so damn sweet?"

"Make love with me!" was her gasping reply, and she reached for the hem of his T-shirt and began jerking it up.

He sat back on his knees, pulled the offending garment over his head and tossed it aside. Then he reached for her blouse. They undressed frantically and came together in a frenzy. The passion simmering between them was so hot, Claudia could almost hear the sizzle.

When Jonathon rolled to his back so that she was sitting astride him and whispered in her ear, "Make love to me, honey. I need you to make love to me," desire licked through her veins and settled heavily in her womb.

She lowered her lips to his as she slowly mated with him, and began a primal dance she hadn't even realized she knew.

Chapter 10

He had no idea how much time had passed since Claudia had brought him to the most explosive climax he'd ever experienced. But night had fallen, and Jonathon couldn't summon up the energy to move. Claudia still lay atop him, and he smoothed one hand up her silken back, while stroking one soft hip with the other. Not since his wife's death had he experienced this intimate closeness. He hadn't realized how much he'd missed it.

That alone should have had him jumping out of bed, he supposed, but when Claudia began to shift off him, he caught her thigh, holding her in place. "Don't move. I enjoy holding you like this."

"But I must be getting heavy."

He slid his hand into her hair and massaged his fingers against her scalp. "You're about as heavy as a handful of feathers."

"If you keep giving me wonderful compliments like that, I'll never move."

He chuckled and stroked her hip again. They lay quietly for several more minutes before he said, "I love the night, don't you?"

"No. I hate the dark."

"Why?" he asked, continuing to massage her scalp.

She pressed her cheek against his chest. "When I was little, I had all these crazy pictures running through my head. I was too young to understand that they were visions, and I was afraid that if I saw the pictures in the dark and couldn't see something familiar, I'd get lost and wouldn't be able to find my way back."

She paused for a long, reflective moment before going on. "My parents thought I was overimaginative. They also didn't believe in indulging children in their fantasies, so they wouldn't let me have a night-light. Every night I'd lie in bed, shivering and terrified to go to sleep. Because of that, I developed an intense dislike of the dark, and night, that's always with me."

"Lovely people, your parents," Jonathon said tersely, a muscle twitching in his jaw. How could they have treated a vulnerable little girl's fears that way? If he ever met them, he'd—

"They weren't being purposely cruel," she defended. "They just refused to believe that I was different because they didn't know how to handle it."

She must have felt some subtle, involuntary change in his body, Jonathon realized, because she suddenly reached up and traced the frowning curve of his lips with her fingertips. "It's all right, Jonathon. It doesn't matter that you don't believe in me."

As he tucked her head into the curve of his neck, guilt swamped him. He did believe in her clairvoyance, but he couldn't bring himself to tell her that. It would mean accepting what she was, and that was something he could never do. It was too dangerous. But he was also instinctively aware that offering her belief without acceptance would be more cruel than the way her parents had treated her—and were still treating her from the few things she'd said about them.

He was relieved when she changed the subject by asking, "What happened at the sheriff's office?"

"He was trying to trick me into confessing to Billy Joe's murder."

"You can't confess to something you didn't do," Claudia murmured as she folded her arms on his chest and raised her head so she could see his face. There wasn't enough moonlight for her to make out his expression, but their closeness made her acutely aware of his tension. "What else happened?"

After spending half the day trying to convince Helton that he wasn't guilty and failing miserably, her belief in his innocence caused a warm glow to blossom deep inside. He tenderly brushed her hair off her forehead and released a heavy sigh. "Helton has some evidence I didn't know about. They found three cigarette butts in the secret room."

"Why would that mean anything? You don't smoke."

"I did until a year ago," he stated grimly. "I also smoked a distinctive brand of European cigarettes that a tobacco store special ordered for me. Guess what brand they found?"

"Oh, Jonathon, no!"

"My sentiments exactly." He eased her off him, sat up and turned on the bedside lamp. As he drew up a knee beneath the sheet and draped his arm across it, he frowned at the wall in front of him. "As my attorney told the sheriff, there were other smokers in the house, and any one of them could have grabbed a pack of my cigarettes. I'm afraid Sheriff Helton wasn't impressed. He simply pointed out that I was the only smoker who'd threatened to kill him."

Claudia sat up beside him, saying, "Do you think the killer was trying to frame you?"

Jonathon shook his head. "That's too farfetched, Claudia. The only reason to frame me would be if the killer expected the body to be found, and I'm sure he expected it to remain hidden in the secret room forever. He probably just ran out of cigarettes and grabbed a pack of mine."

"Do you have any idea who might have killed him?" she asked next.

"Uncle Richard, of course. He had everything to lose if Billy Joe implicated him in the thefts. Not only would I have cut off his allowance, but if I'd filed charges against Billy Joe—which I had every intention of doing—he could have been facing criminal charges himself. Believe me,

Uncle Richard would do anything to keep from going to jail.''

"Did you tell the sheriff all of this?"

"Sure, but again, he wasn't impressed. I don't have any proof that Uncle Richard and Billy Joe were working together, just gut instinct."

Claudia gnawed at her bottom lip as she thought about the situation. "Jonathon, just for the sake of argument, was there anyone else at Magnolia that weekend who could have killed Billy Joe? Maybe someone outside the family?"

"Gran's housekeeper, Wilma, was the only other person here, and Wilma was so crippled with arthritis that she could barely get around. That's why she retired this year. It's also highly improbable that someone outside the family knew about the secret room, Claudia. This has to be an inside job."

"Okay. Who else in the family could have done it?"

He leaned back against the headboard and shook his head again. "You've met Aunt Virginia, Steven and Ruth, so you know that there's no way they could have done it. Uncle Richard's wife, Doreen, is also out. She literally faints at the sight of blood. Patrick and Patricia are malicious to the core, but I don't see either of them as killers. Patricia would be too worried about breaking a fingernail, and it would be too much work for Patrick. He doesn't believe in working up a sweat. There's no question that Uncle Richard did this," he stated with conviction. "He's the only one with any real motive. If Billy Joe had confessed to working with him, he'd have lost everything. His only alternative was to kill him."

"I don't know, Jonathon," Claudia murmured thoughtfully. "It seems to me you're so focused on your uncle being guilty that you're closing yourself off to any other alternative. If you're looking for a motive, it would seem that his wife and kids would be high on the list. It's quite possible that one of them did it to protect Richard."

Jonathon released a short, harsh laugh. "Protect him? Believe me, Claudia, once you meet them, you'll see that isn't even a viable alternative. In this family, it's everyone for himself. Uncle Richard did it. Now all I have to do is prove it.''

''You're dealing with a killer, Jonathon. You should leave the investigation up to the sheriff,'' Claudia stated worriedly.

He eyed her askance. ''If I leave it up to Sheriff Helton, I'll end up singing the jailhouse blues. He thinks I'm guilty, so he isn't going to waste his time looking for the truth.''

She wanted to deny his assertion, but she suspected he was right. ''What are you planning to do?''

''I haven't figured that out yet, but I'll come up with something before the weekend.''

''Look, before you start putting any plans into action, give me some time with your family. I know you don't believe in my clairvoyance, but it *is* real. If I try to connect—''

''No!'' Jonathon interrupted forcefully. Pushing away from the headboard, he grabbed her upper arms and gave her a hard shake. ''Stay out of this, Claudia. Uncle Richard has to be feeling desperate. If he thought for one moment that you could read his mind... God, I shudder to even think about it! Leave him alone. I mean it!''

For a moment she considered telling him that his uncle was afraid to touch her, which meant he'd probably already considered that possibility. She stopped herself in time, though. She suspected that Jonathon would insist that she leave. And there was no way she would leave, because from the moment she'd first dreamed of the shadow, she'd understood that she was the only one who could divert disaster.

''I'll leave him alone,'' she said, mentally crossing her fingers.

''You promise?'' he asked distrustfully.

''Good heavens, Jonathon. What do you want me to do? Sign my name in blood?'' she teased.

He frowned. ''No. I want your reassurance that you aren't going to make my uncle think that you're poking around inside his head.''

''Consider yourself reassured.'' She slipped out of bed and reached for her robe, which was lying across the back of the nearby rocking chair. "How about some dinner? I don't know about you, but I'm starving."

When he didn't respond, she glanced over her shoulder at him. He was staring at her with an expression that seemed to be a combination of disbelief and shock. She also noticed that the color was draining from his face.

"What is it?" she asked in concern. "Are you ill?"

He closed his eyes and gave a hard shake of his head. Then he opened his eyes and raked a hand through his hair, mumbling, "No. I'm fine. It was just a trick of the light."

"What was a trick of the light?"

"It's nothing, Claudia. And dinner does sound good. I haven't eaten since breakfast."

Claudia continued to regard him intently. The color was returning to his face, but he wouldn't look at her directly. "Are you sure you're all right, Jonathon?"

"I'm fine!" he declared tersely.

"Okay," she said, holding up her hands in a pacifying gesture. "I'll go start dinner."

Once she was gone, Jonathon berated himself for snapping at her, but he hadn't been able to deal with her tender concern. He'd been too busy controlling the panic that had started spreading in his stomach the moment she'd climbed out of bed.

Slowly he turned his head toward the rocking chair. When Claudia had stepped toward it to get her robe, a shadow hadn't really engulfed her, he told himself firmly. It had been nothing more than a trick of the light.

She was used to being alone. Indeed, because of her inability to deal with crowds, the majority of her life was spent in solitude. It was true that she often felt isolated, but she'd never before felt this terrible ache of loneliness, she decided as she settled onto the sofa in the guest house living room.

When she tried to get herself interested in Steven's manuscript, which she'd received in the mail two days before, and failed, she wanted to blame Steven's writing—it really was atrocious. But she knew she was lying to herself. Jonathon was the problem and had been for the past three days. Somehow, she'd entered into an affair with him, and she still wasn't sure how it had happened. At night he showed up at dinnertime. After eating they either read, or watched a little television, and then they went to bed. Their lovemaking was fabulous, but was strangely tinged with a fevered note of desperation, as if they both feared each time would be their last. And the dark foreboding surrounding them increased daily. Jonathon was always gone when she awakened in the morning, and she didn't see him all day.

It wasn't his excluding her from his daytime activities that bothered her, but the fact he wouldn't tell her what he was doing. She was sure he was working on a plan to catch his uncle, and her instincts were telling her that was dangerous. She just hoped that her clairvoyance worked when his family arrived. Counting Adelaide, she'd be dealing with the emanations of eight people. It had been years since she'd left herself open to that much input at one time, and considering the reason they'd be at Magnolia, their emotions would be running high.

But even if she could handle them, she probably wouldn't be able to use her abilities to identify the killer. If he—or she—was determined to keep their secret, she'd never be able to discover it. It was one of the aspects of her clairvoyance that had always fascinated her, and she'd often wondered if it was related to her general inability to pick up anything from the past. And a secret wouldn't be a secret if it wasn't a part of the past. She would have to concentrate on trying to discover who was in danger, because that would lead to a prediction of the future. She was certain that by identifying that person, she'd be able to figure out who had killed Billy Joe.

Restless, she dropped the manuscript to the table and headed for the porch. The swing wasn't appealing, so she decided to take a walk. Initially she strolled toward the magnolia grove, but then on impulse turned toward the river. As she passed the mansion, she only cast an absent glance toward it. Last night Jonathon had told her he was going to spend today at his office and wouldn't be home until late. Would he come to the guest house when he returned, or would he spend the night in his own bed?

The thought of him not coming to her made her more depressed, and she stopped at the edge of the wide, grassy field that separated Magnolia from the river. An arc of ancient oaks curved around one end of the field, their numbers dwindling as they neared the river. There was a large expanse of space between them and the lone tree she and Jonathon had sat beneath.

The sight of it brought tears to her eyes. It looked as sad and lonely as she felt. And that was when she faced the truth. When she finally left here, she'd be sadder than ever, because, heaven help her, she'd fallen hopelessly in love with Jonathon.

And hopeless was the right term, she decided as she started across the field toward the tree. As she'd confessed to Merlin, she'd always dreamed of becoming romantically involved with a man she couldn't read. Now that wish had been fulfilled, and she realized that she could never spend her life with someone like that. It was too much like being on a wild roller-coaster ride, and she hated roller coasters. She needed the security of knowing how a man felt about her—the certainty of what their future held together. She had to know that what they shared was going to last.

Not that she didn't know exactly what her future was with Jonathon, she reminded herself as she settled beneath the tree and stared morosely at the river. He'd told her right from the beginning that there would be no future. He didn't want a commitment.

So why had she let herself fall in love with him? Her brain argued that it was because she hadn't had the safety net of her clairvoyance, and she'd had to deal with him like an ordinary woman. But her heart said something different. She'd been drawn to Jonathon in ways beyond the normal, and she wasn't just thinking about the visions. No, she was compelled to be with Jonathon. She *needed* him in ways she could never explain. Now she was going to suffer through the pain of an ordinary broken heart. Had becoming intimately involved with Jonathon really been worth it?

Yes, she decided as she leaned back against the tree trunk and released a melancholy sigh. Because once the pain faded, she'd have the memories to help fill the hours of the lonely days that lay ahead.

The thought of those days was more than she could bear. She drew her knees up to her chest, buried her face against them and wept.

It was midafternoon by the time Jonathon finished the paperwork on his desk. Normally he could have accomplished the task in a couple of hours, but he hadn't been able to concentrate. If his thoughts had been centered on his troubles at Magnolia, he wouldn't have minded the preoccupation. To his annoyance, however, they'd been focused on Claudia and the nights of wild lovemaking that they'd shared. He couldn't believe he was wallowing in thoughts of their passion when he should be concentrating on catching his uncle. It was inexcusable and it irritated him to no end. It also had him horny as hell.

When a knock sounded on his door, he brusquely called out permission for entrance. His senior vice president, Allen Gregory, entered. Allen was a tall, robust black man a few years older than Jonathon. He was also one of the most astute businessmen Jonathon had ever met. For years the competition had been trying to woo him away from Tanner Transportation. Allen received a top-notch salary, but the truth was he'd never be able to advance beyond his current position here. When his father had died, Jonathon had fully expected Allen to resign so he could move on to a business with promotion opportunities. But his vice president had surprised him by announcing that Jonathon's father had had his loyalty, and that he'd now give that loyalty to Jonathon. That had been five years ago, and not only was Allen loyal to the company, but he'd become Jonathon's best friend as well.

"What's up?" he asked when Allen settled into the chair in front of his desk.

"Why don't you tell me?" Allen responded. "Rumor has it that you're as bad-tempered as a cottonmouth today."

"I haven't been *that* bad," Jonathon grumbled.

"Don't ask the staff to put that to a vote. There's talk of mutiny at the water cooler."

"Damn," Jonathon muttered, collapsing back into his chair. "I suppose that means I'm going to have to apologize to everyone. But what else is new? For the past few weeks, 'I'm sorry' has been my mantra."

Allen chuckled. "It always is when you've been rescuing Adelaide from one of her messes. How did she handle you evicting her psychic?"

Jonathon shifted uncomfortably in his chair. "I didn't evict her."

Allen gaped at him in shock. "The woman's still at Magnolia?" When his boss nodded, he said, "Why?"

"It's a long story."

"Well, give me the condensed version."

Jonathon wasn't sure he wanted to give any version to his friend. So far he'd managed to keep the news about Billy Joe's murder out of the newspapers. He wanted to keep it that way until after the weekend. Having reporters underfoot would complicate the plan he'd come up with to catch his uncle. With Sheriff Helton breathing down his neck, he didn't need any more complications. There was also the business to consider. Having his name as a potential murder suspect spread across the front pages could cause irreparable damage. That was why he had to resolve this mess this weekend. His gut instinct told him that if he didn't, come Monday morning, Sheriff Helton would be arresting him.

But as he studied his friend's face, he concluded that it would be good to share the events with Allen. He was not only completely trustworthy, he was the most levelheaded person Jonathon knew. Perhaps he could offer new insight into the entire mess.

He gave Allen the long version, excluding his physical relationship with Claudia, of course. When he was done, he said, "So, what do you think?"

Allen gave a dazed shake of his head. "I can't believe it. A murder at Magnolia. Adelaide must have been furious at missing out on finding the body."

Jonathon arched a brow. "Don't tell me you're also psychic. I haven't told anyone that."

"Anyone who knows Adelaide would figure that out," Allen said with a wry grin. "She likes to be in on the action."

"Yeah. And it looks as if there'll be plenty of it this weekend."

Allen nodded his agreement. "You know, of course, that even though you threatened Billy Joe, the sheriff's case against you hinges on those cigarette butts. And even with them, he'll have to prove that you smoked them, and there's every possibility that Billy Joe smoked them."

"No, Allen, that's one scenario that's definitely out. Billy Joe's father was a heavy smoker who died of lung cancer. Billy Joe was an adamant nonsmoker, and he used to lecture me on the evils of smoking every time I lit up around him."

"So, whoever killed him, smoked them," Allen stated.

"No. Uncle Richard smoked them before he killed Billy Joe," Jonathon corrected.

Allen frowned. "I don't know. I can see your uncle engaging in a lot of criminal activities, but murder isn't one of them. I don't think he has the guts."

"He could have been facing prosecution along with Billy Joe," Jonathon reminded, "and I know he doesn't have the guts to handle jail."

"I still can't see him beating someone over the head. It's too . . . personal."

"Come on, Allen," Jonathon said with a scowl. "You know my family. Uncle Richard is the only one who could have possibly done it."

"Jonathon, don't you see what you're doing? You're doing to Richard what Sheriff Helton is doing to you. You're looking at the obvious, and assuming that it's true."

"I hate it when you play devil's advocate," Jonathon muttered as he spun his chair around to stare out the fourth-story window that gave him a clear view of the Mississippi River. For several seconds he watched a barge inch its way up the river, before adding, "Claudia does the same thing."

"Claudia's the psychic, right?"

"Yeah. Do you believe in clairvoyance, Allen?"

"I don't know. Outside of a few episodes of déjà vu, I've never had any psychic experiences myself. From some of the articles I've read, however, it appears to be a fairly accepted phenomenon."

"I think she's for real," Jonathon announced. It was the first time he'd made the admission aloud, and he was surprised at how easy it had been. "But is it really possible to predict the future?"

"Tanner Transportation does it every day. We promise delivery of everything from household goods to medical supplies. We're predicting that we can fulfill those promises."

"Those promises are based on facts," Jonathon pointed out, swinging his chair back around. "Claudia functions on . . . Hell, I don't know what she functions on, but it's eerie. The first time I met her, she told me that Gran had bought a chocolate pie and it was going to fall off the back seat of her car. It was such a stupid prediction, but it came true."

Jonathon picked up his pen and toyed with it. "You said you're undecided about clairvoyance, but you do believe in intuition, right?"

"Of course. You know as well as I do that a lot of the decisions we make around here are based on gut instinct."

Jonathon tossed the pen onto his desk and began to massage the bridge of his nose. "Well, my intuition is telling me that Claudia's in danger. I figure that it's probably from my uncle, and my instincts say I need to send her away from Magnolia so she'll be safe."

"But?" Allen prompted. "I definitely hear a 'but' in there somewhere."

"But what if I'm wrong?" Jonathon answered. "What if the danger is coming from somewhere else? If I send her away, will she be able to cope with it alone? In some ways she's the strongest woman I've ever met, but she's also the most vulnerable, and she doesn't have anyone to protect her."

"And you want to protect her."

"I want her to be safe. She's a good woman."

"Good woman? If I didn't know better, I'd say you're falling in love."

"I am *not* falling in love," Jonathon declared with another scowl. "I like her, and I don't want to see anything bad happen to her. It's nothing more than that."

Allen regarded him doubtfully. "Katie's been gone three years, Jonathon. The time for mourning is over, it's okay to fall in love again."

"Damn it, Allen! Why is everyone so quick to dismiss Katie? I loved her, and I let her down!"

Allen rolled his eyes at the argument they'd been having since Katie's death. "Come on, Jonathon. How many times do we have to go through this? I know how much you pride yourself on being in control of every aspect of your life, but there are certain things outside of your control. Katie's illness was one of them, and as I've told you a hundred times, it's ridiculous for you to blame yourself. It's also ridiculous for you to fight against falling in love again."

"I am not—repeat *not*—falling in love," Jonathon declared, slashing his hand through the air. "I *like* Claudia, Allen. Do I need to show you the definition of 'like' in the dictionary?"

"A man 'in like' is not a man who resorts to the dictionary," Allen answered blithely. "And if you want to deny your feelings, that's okay by me. As for this intuitive danger you sense surrounding her, my advice is to keep her close at hand. If you don't and something *does* happen to her, you'll never forgive yourself. You don't need to saddle yourself with another irrational guilt trip.

"Now, I have to go," Allen continued, glancing at his watch. "I have an employee interview in just a few minutes. Keep me posted on what's happening at Magnolia, and give Adelaide my love."

After he was gone, Jonathon spun back around to face the window. He wasn't falling in love. He was too smart for that. If he was anything, he was in lust. And in like. He only had to think about Claudia to want her, but she also filled all those lonely, empty crevices in his life. Was that so wrong?

Even as he asked himself the question, he knew the answer. It was not only wrong, it was totally unacceptable. He was using Claudia, and she deserved more than that. Instead of wasting her time on him, she should be out looking for some knight in shining armor who'd sweep her off her feet and carry her away to live happily ever after. And to make sure she did exactly that, he was going to end their relationship, such as it was. Since the family would arrive tomorrow and he'd be too busy to devote any time to her, tonight would be as good a time as any to tell her it was over.

He dismissed the sharp little pain in his chest as heartburn. As he was only 'in like' with Claudia, it couldn't be anything else.

Claudia had always been a disciple of a good cry. She recognized that it didn't solve her troubles, but it did relieve the stress and allowed her to look at things more objectively.

As she dried her tears, she was able to view her situation with Jonathon from a new perspective. She perceived herself as being in love with him, but it was more likely an upheaval of hormones that had been dormant for too long. When this crazy relationship they had was over, it would hurt, but it wouldn't be any worse than a parting from Merlin. It would be that poignancy of saying goodbye—that acknowledgment that for a time Jonathon had made her life a little brighter and a little happier. And he had made her happy. He'd made her feel like a woman instead of a freak. For that, she'd always be grateful.

Her spirits bolstered, she rose to her feet. It was then that she felt a spattering of raindrops, and she grumbled a curse. She'd known it was going to rain, for pity's sake. She shouldn't have wandered so far away from the house. Unless she hurried, she was going to get drenched.

She ran across the field and was panting by the time she reached the path at the back of the mansion, but the rain was starting to get heavier, so she didn't dare slow down. She rounded the corner of the mansion blindly and let out a scream when she collided with a large, solid body.

"Damn it, Claudia, you scared the daylights out of me!" Jonathon yelled as he circled his arm around her waist to steady her.

She tilted her head back and glared up at him. "*I* scared *you?* You just took ten years off my life sneaking up on me like that!"

"I wasn't sneaking up on you," he snapped irritably. "I was looking for you. It's raining, for Pete's sake, and when you weren't at the guest house, I thought something had happened to you."

Claudia regarded him in bemusement. He really did look as if he'd been worried about her, and she couldn't remember the last time someone had truly cared enough to do so. With the exception of Merlin, of course, but then, he didn't count. He was her best friend, and best friends always worried about each other.

"Well, as you can see, I'm all right. Shall we get out of the rain? I'm wash and wear, but I bet the label inside your designer suit says Dry Clean Only."

She didn't wait for his response, but slipped out of his arms and resumed her dash toward the guest house. When she reached the front door, he was right beside her.

Once they'd entered the house, she asked, "Why are you home so early? I thought you were going to work late."

"Yeah, well, I decided that we needed to have a talk," he answered as he tossed back the tails of his suit coat and shoved his hands into his pants' pockets. He jingled the change before saying, "I did some thinking about us today, Claudia, and I realized that I'm being unfair with you."

"I see," Claudia murmured as she regarded him warily. "Why don't you sit down and tell me about it?"

He shook his head. "This is something I should say standing up." He drew in a deep breath and announced, "Claudia, I've decided that we should stop seeing each other."

"I see," she said again as she walked over to the sofa and sat down on the edge. It was the only way she could stop her shaking knees from giving out. Just a short while ago, she'd told herself that when the time came for her and Jonathon to part, it wouldn't hurt that bad. Boy, had she been kidding herself! "May I ask what brought about this sudden decision?"

He gave an uncomfortable shrug. "I just got to thinking about us, and I like you, Claudia. I like you a lot, but you deserve more than this. Since I'm going to be busy with the family this weekend and won't be able to spend any time with you, I figured that now was as good a time as any to end everything."

"I guess ending a relationship like ours is like quitting smoking. You make up your mind to stop, and then you just go cold turkey," she mused, half to herself.

He regarded her in concern. "Claudia, if I've hurt your feelings, I'm sorry. But believe me, this is for the best."

"You haven't hurt my feelings," she denied, deciding that it wasn't a lie. The pain that was building inside her could in no way be described by such a simple word as hurt. But she had her pride, and there was no way she'd let him know that. "You told me in the beginning that you weren't looking for a relationship, and I accepted that. If you think it's time to end this relationship, then I guess it's time to end it."

She flashed him her best smile as she lifted Steven's manuscript off the table. "Now, if you don't mind, I'd appreciate it if you'd go so I can finish reading Steven's manuscript. I'm sure he'll want my opinion on his clairvoyant when he arrives tomorrow, and it would be rude of me not to have one for him."

He frowned at her, as though confused by her reaction. "Well . . . I'm glad there are no hard feelings."

"There are no hard feelings. Good night, Jonathon."

He nodded and let himself out the door. The moment he closed it, Claudia drew in several deep breaths, feverishly telling herself that he had been right. This was for the best. Even if she had wanted to try to build a permanent relationship with him, he'd just proved that it would never work. She needed a man she could read, and this was exactly the reason why. A man she could connect with would never have been able to emotionally ambush her like this.

She'd have seen the bad news coming and been prepared for it.

When she felt the sting of tears, she blinked them back impatiently. *She wasn't going to cry*. What she *was* going to do was read Steven's manuscript, and then she was going to get a good night's sleep. Tomorrow Adelaide would be back, with the entire Tanner clan in tow. With any luck, Claudia would finally figure out who she was supposed to help here. Once she'd ascertained that, she could do whatever she had to do, and with a little more luck, she'd be on her way home before the weekend was over.

Chapter 11

Jonathon glanced toward the clock on the dashboard and cursed as he noted the hour. He couldn't believe that today of all days there'd been an emergency at the office that no one but he could handle. It was particularly irritating since he'd just been in the office yesterday. By now the entire family would be at Magnolia, and the big announcement he'd planned on making when they arrived would have to be delivered at dinner. He'd wanted his uncle to have a few hours to stew over the matter before the meal so he could set him up immediately afterward. He couldn't believe that his plans had already gone awry.

When he arrived at Magnolia, his disposition worsened. There were enough cars parked at the end of the drive to qualify it for a parking lot. He never had figured out why everyone had to bring their own cars when most of them lived within two miles of each other.

By the time he managed to squeeze his car between his grandmother's Cadillac sedan and his cousin Patricia's sporty red racer, he was muttering a litany of four-letter epithets. As usual Patricia had taken up enough space to accommodate one and a half cars and, also as usual, her front tires were parked on the grass. He squeezed out of his car, slammed the door and tramped toward the house.

He scowled when he reached the gallery steps and saw Patricia draped against one of the Ionic columns in her best blonde-bombshell pose. As his eyes flicked over the black silk sheath that showed her model-slender figure to perfection, he had to concede that she was one of the most beautiful women he'd ever seen. Unfortunately she was also the personification of the saying that beauty is only skin deep. She was greedy, selfish and determined to see how many men she could marry in one lifetime. She'd just divorced husband number six—a thirty-third birthday present to herself—and according to his grandmother, already had her sights set on number seven.

"Patricia, I'm not going to tell you this again," he groused. "The next time you park on the grass, I'm slashing your tires and having your damn car towed away. Got that?"

"Why, cousin Johnny, hello to you, too," she simpered. "It's so nice to see that you're as obnoxious as ever."

He shook his head in disgust and started up the steps. He'd just reached the gallery when he heard a bright, musical laugh behind him. Frowning, he turned around, and his mood turned downright foul. Patrick was walking across the grounds with Claudia on his arm. The sight of his cousin's bright blond head bent close to her dark one was bad enough. But the fact that he'd made Claudia laugh—something *he* had never heard her do before—set his blood to boiling. Why was she laughing with Patrick when she'd never laughed with him? He'd been her lover, for Pete's sake!

"So that's our little fortune teller," Patricia drawled. "I suppose she's a cute little thing, if you like cute."

"Your claws are showing, Patricia, and I'm warning you. Leave Claudia alone. If you don't, you'll answer to me."

"Well, well, well. It sounds like cousin Johnny is feeling territorial. Just what games have you two little mice been playing while Grandmother's been away?"

Jonathon glared at her. "You can get your mind out of the gutter, too. I mean it, Patricia. If you insult Claudia you can kiss that little business proposition you want me to finance goodbye."

Pique warred with excitement on her mobile face. Finally the excitement won. "Are you really going to finance my health spa?"

"Let's just say that if you remain on your best behavior this weekend, I might be open to negotiation."

It was obvious that she wasn't pleased with his answer, but Jonathon knew he'd hit her at her most acquisitive spot. For the past two years she'd been wanting to open her own health spa. He might not like Patricia, but he was convinced that she had the shrewdness, intelligence and know-how to be a fabulous success in the business. It was her marital merry-go-round that made him reluctant to finance her. If she married some jet-set playboy and ran off to Tahiti, he'd be stuck with the spa, and he didn't want to be in the health spa business.

As Claudia and Patrick drew closer and Claudia laughed again, he jammed his fists into his pockets. It was the only way he was going to keep from punching Patrick in the nose. What could the dimwit possibly be saying that she'd find so funny?

Unlike his sister Jonathon didn't consider Patrick shrewd. He was supposedly a real estate developer, but as far as Jonathon could tell, the only thing Patrick had managed to develop was an intimate acquaintance with bankruptcy court. Jonathon hadn't been able to decide if Patrick's problems stemmed from overzealousness or simple stupidity. Of course, his overactive libido might be part of the problem. He was so busy maintaining his playboy reputation that he couldn't have much time to devote to business. Right now he was turning all that practiced charm on Claudia, and there wasn't a damn thing Jonathon could do about it. Why in hell hadn't he waited to break off their relationship until after the weekend? If Patrick so much as breathed on her heavily, he'd wring his neck!

"Patrick, cousin Johnny's here. Hurry along so you can say hi to him before he goes to change for dinner!" Patricia trilled.

Jonathon shot her a dark look, and she gave him a conspiratorial smile. "Just trying to help out."

"I don't need any help," he muttered tersely.

"Don't underestimate the competition, cuz. Better men than you have made that mistake and lived to regret it."

"Claudia and I are just friends, Patricia."

"Why sure, Johnny. Whatever you say," she murmured agreeably just as Patrick and Claudia reached them.

"Hello, Jonathon," Patrick said.

"Patrick," Jonathon acknowledged with a curt nod, unable to tear his eyes away from Claudia. She looked positively ravishing! One side of her long, black hair was pulled back, and she'd pinned a magnolia blossom over her ear. Her dress was made out of white-eyelet lace, and the puffed sleeves were pushed off her slender shoulders, exposing them to the air's caress. The bodice fitted her like a second skin, and the full-circle skirt draped seductively over her hips and fell to mid-calf. She looked so feminine and sexy that he had to clear his throat to speak.

"Hello, Claudia. You look lovely tonight. Are you joining us for dinner?"

She gave a shy duck of her head. "Thank you, Jonathon, and, yes, I am."

"Since you have these two gentlemen so dazzled they've forgotten their manners, I guess I'll have to introduce myself," Patricia announced. "I'm Patricia, and you, of course, are Claudia. I may call you Claudia?"

"Of course," Claudia murmured as Patrick led her up the stairs. "It's very nice to meet you Patricia."

"Oh, believe me, the pleasure's all mine," Patricia said airily as she looped her arm through Patrick's free one. "Now, if you don't mind, I'm going to steal my brother for a few minutes. He and I have some urgent business to discuss. Jonathon will keep you company, won't you, Jonathon?"

"Patricia, can't this wait?" Patrick asked impatiently. "Claudia and I were just talking about—"

"No, it can't wait," Patricia interrupted as she began dragging him toward the kitchen door.

Jonathon couldn't decide if he was irritated or pleased by *atricia's obvious ploy to give him some time alone with Claudia. He did decide, however, to take advantage of the pportunity to warn Claudia about his infamous cousin.

"You and Patrick seemed to be hitting it off," he said.

"He's very interesting," she replied, leaning against the olumn Patricia had vacated and gazing toward the mag-olia grove. She'd told herself that she was prepared to face onathon, but she'd been kidding herself again. Just the ight of him had caused an ache inside that made her want o throw herself into his arms and kick him in the shin at the ame time.

"Patrick made you laugh," Jonathon commented stiffly.

"He's very funny."

"What did he say that was so funny?"

"He told me a joke."

"He must have told you two jokes, because you laughed wice."

Claudia glanced toward him in confusion. "So, he told ne two jokes. Is something wrong with that?"

"There could be," he said solemnly. "Patrick isn't the ype of man you want to get involved with, Claudia. He's oo...well, experienced for you."

She gaped at him in angry disbelief. My word, he was varning her off Patrick, and after he'd just dumped her last ight! Talk about unmitigated gall!

"Well, Jonathon, I can't think of any better qualifica-ion for a man to have than experience, and if I want to get nvolved with Patrick, I will."

"Damn it, Claudia, he's left a string of broken hearts rom Memphis to New Orleans!" Jonathon railed. "He sn't interested in a commitment. All he wants to do is core!"

She regarded him cooly. "It sounds as if he's doing a reat job of carrying on the family tradition."

"What's that supposed to mean?" he bellowed.

"What in the world is going on out here?" Adelaide sked as she rushed out the door.

"Not a thing, Adelaide," Claudia replied, turning her ack on Jonathon. "Do you know where Patrick has dis-

appeared to? He and I were having an interesting conve
sation, and I'd like to continue it.''

"Claudia, I am not finished speaking with you," Jon
thon stated in a low voice that fairly vibrated with anger.

She tossed him a disdainful glance. "If you recall, Jo
athon, you finished speaking with me last night. See you
dinner.''

He couldn't remember ever being so furious as
watched Claudia flounce into Magnolia with his gran
mother. She'd not only lumped him in the same category
Patrick, she'd implied that the only reason he'd slept wi
her was to score! She may have thought they were finishe
speaking, but he had plenty more to say, and before t
night was over, he *would* say it.

Claudia was hit by two impressions when the family f
nally gathered in the dining room. The first was that she'
never seen so many handsome people in one room. T
second was that she'd never sensed so much hostility in h
life. It came at her in waves and was so intense that sh
recognized she'd never make it through dinner without t
psychic barrier in place. She closed her eyes and focuse
inwardly until she'd consciously shut out at least the ove
powering vibrations. She'd been practicing the techniqu
for years, so she was able to erect the barrier in a matter
seconds.

As everyone gathered around the table Adelaide insiste
that since Claudia was a guest, she had to sit next to Jon
thon, who, of course, occupied the seat at the head of t
table. Adelaide was on her right, and across from her we
Patrick and Patricia, who were sniping at each other li
two grade-school children.

Claudia studied them thoughtfully. She'd already spe
enough time with Patrick to doubt that he had killed Bil
Joe. He was calculating, and envisioned himself a lady
man, but his only worry appeared to be about a real esta
project that he was working on. From what little she'
picked up from Patricia when they'd met, she also doubte
that she'd committed the crime. Patricia's only emotio
seemed to have been an irritation with Jonathon.

But, she reminded herself, her purpose here was not to catch a killer, but to stop him from bringing harm to someone else. She needed to concentrate on finding that person. Since she'd picked up no hint of impending danger in their futures, she ruled out Patrick and Patricia for the moment and let her gaze stray down the table to Virginia. They'd only exchanged a few words before coming into dinner, and she'd again picked up on Virginia's animosity and an underlying fear, but no sense of peril. Next to Virginia was Richard's wife, Doreen. Although they'd also only spoken briefly, Doreen was as easy to read as a large-print book. Claudia was ninety-nine percent convinced that Doreen was incapable of violence, though she would like to strangle her husband, whom she suspected of having an affair. She'd also seemed free from peril.

Claudia moved on to Richard, who sat at the other end of the table from Jonathon. She hadn't had an opportunity to talk with him nor had she received any impressions from him. He'd shown up only moments before they'd come into the dining room, and he'd ignored her completely. She didn't need her clairvoyance, however, to understand that a good portion of the hostility in the room was being generated by him. If looks could kill, the ones he was shooting down the table at Jonathon would have blown him apart. An involuntary shiver slithered through her. She could see why Jonathon was so convinced Richard had killed Billy Joe. His creepy eyes alone made him look like a psychopath. She couldn't help wondering how he could possibly be Adelaide's son. Surely he was a changeling.

She couldn't clearly see Steven and Ruth, who sat on the other side of Adelaide, but she could easily recall what they'd looked like before dinner. Ruth was so pale she looked ghostly, and she'd huddled in a corner chain-smoking, not speaking to anyone or even looking up. Steven had had the pinched look of a man who'd reached his wit's end as he'd hovered over her in concern.

Though Claudia hadn't been able to pick up anything but worry from Steven, Ruth was terrified. Which brought to mind the fact that Ruth had collapsed when she'd heard about Billy Joe. Did she know something about his death, and if so, was she in danger because of it? There was only one way to find out, and that was to spend time with her. The trouble was, when she'd tried to approach Ruth before dinner, the woman had started generating vibrations that verged on hysteria. Claudia had quietly backed off, the last thing she wanted to do at this point was create a scene.

She was pulled away from her musings when Virginia said, "Tell us exactly how you found the secret room, Jonathon."

While he explained how they'd found the room, Claudia dropped the psychic barrier long enough to see if she could pick up on any implicating thoughts. Again, there was too much hostility for her to focus on anything, and she quickly put the barrier back in place.

When Jonathon was done, Patricia leaned back in her chair and said, "Well, as interesting as your little tale is, I want to know why the sheriff has dragged us up here. He can't really think one of us killed Billy Joe."

Claudia was startled by her comment. As she noted the anticipatory looks on the rest of the family's faces, she realized that none of them knew the sheriff was convinced that Jonathon was guilty.

"That's exactly what he thinks," Jonathon said blandly.

"That's crazy!" Patrick gasped.

"Do you think it's crazy, Uncle Richard?" Jonathon asked.

Richard, who'd just taken a sip of wine, choked on it. When he caught his breath, he glared at his nephew. "Just what are you insinuating?"

"I'm not insinuating anything. I'm merely asking for your opinion," Jonathon answered smoothly.

"Ha! You never ask for anyone's opinion. You're a petty dictator just like your father, and your grandfather before him."

"Now, Richard, you shouldn't speak ill of father or our brother," Virginia chided. "They were both good to you, and so is Jonathon, for that matter. Your problem is that you want the world to be handed to you on a platter. Well, it doesn't work that way. If you want the good life, then you have to go out and earn it."

"Just like you did?" he sneered. "Hell, you only married Thomas Gage because he was filthy rich and had one foot in the grave."

"I'll have you know that I loved Thomas," Virginia huffed. "I'd have married him if he'd been a pauper."

"Now, that's a hoot!" Patricia crowed. "Come on, Aunt Ginny. You can tell us the truth. You married old Thomas and kept a lover on the side, right? Why, I'd bet that Steven—"

"That's enough, Patricia," Jonathon interrupted in a low, firm voice.

She jerked her head toward him, and opened her mouth as if to speak, but evidently thought better of it. She clamped it closed and glared at him instead.

"Thank you, Jonathon, but you didn't have to defend me," Steven said, leaning forward and giving him a bemused smile. "Even if I was illegitimate, it wouldn't matter. Compared to the vastness of the universe, we are nothing more than a microscopic piece of dust forever destined to ride the wind."

"What in hell does that mean?" Jonathon muttered.

"It means that it's time for dessert," Adelaide remarked brightly as she rose from her chair. "I'll go tell Mrs. Massey that we're ready, and while I'm gone, do try to behave. We have a guest tonight, remember?"

When everyone's eyes suddenly turned on her, Claudia wished she was one of Steven's microscopic pieces of dust.

"Yes, Claudia, you must tell us what it's like to be a psychic," Doreen said.

"I prefer the term clairvoyant," she replied.

"What's the difference?" Patrick asked.

"Psychic is a very broad term that covers all forms of extrasensory perception. I'm a clairvoyant, which means I generally see into the future."

"Can you tell me who my next husband's going to be?" Patricia inquired as she perched her elbows on the table.

Claudia shook her head. "Sorry, but I usually can't be that specific."

"Well, that's no fun," she said with a pretty pout.

"Claudia, you say you generally see into the future. Do you ever see into the past?" Virginia asked.

"I haven't yet," she answered.

"But it's possible that you could?" Doreen questioned.

"I've learned to never say never, but it's doubtful."

"Could you... touch something of Billy Joe's and find out who killed him?" Ruth ventured shyly.

Claudia, who now had a clear view of Ruth since Adelaide was gone, blinked at her in surprise. Despite the psychic barrier, she was starting to pick something up from Ruth. It was faint, but she was sure it was significant, and she immediately dropped the barrier.

But before she could home in on whatever Ruth was projecting, it suddenly became scrambled. The only way Claudia could describe the sensation was to compare it to the sudden interference sometimes received on a television set. She frowned in confusion. She'd never had anything like that happen before!

"No, Ruth, I don't have telepathic communication through objects, so I couldn't tell you anything if I touched something of Billy Joe's."

"What if we had a séance?" Virginia asked. "Could you contact Billy Joe and find out what happened to him?"

"No," she replied with an amused smile. "You're talking about a medium, who is generally a spiritualist. I don't communicate with spirits."

"Who would ever have believed that meeting a psychic could be so complicated?" Patricia said.

"Patricia, getting up in the morning is complicated for you," Patrick gibed.

"Stuff it, Patrick," she sniped.

"That's your specialty," he sniped back.

"Both of you put a lid on it," Jonathon ordered irritably, though his ire wasn't directed toward them. It revolved around the conversation regarding Claudia's clairvoyance. She hadn't said anything that could be considered threatening, but he'd sensed that she was trying to use her powers. That made him furious with her, because she'd promised him she wouldn't. He was going to remind her of that promise at the earliest opportunity.

"Here's dessert!" Adelaide announced as she returned with Mrs. Massey. "Fresh apple pie, and for those of you with a sweet tooth, you can have it à la mode."

As soon as Mrs. Massey left the room, Jonathon decided that now was the time to put his plan into action, and he announced, "I thought all of you should know that there's been a new development in Billy Joe's murder. This morning I received a call from a man who claims he has a letter from Billy Joe that will reveal his killer."

There was a collective gasp at the table, and then Richard demanded, "Well, who did it?"

"The man refused to tell me over the telephone," Jonathon answered. "He said he'd call me back and set up a meeting, at which time he'll give me the letter."

"Have you told the sheriff?" Virginia asked anxiously.

"It might be a crank call, Aunt Virginia, so I'm going to wait until I hear from him again. Now, if you all will excuse us," he continued as he stood, "Claudia and I have some business to discuss, so I'm going to walk her home."

Claudia's jaw dropped. She wasn't ready to go home, and she certainly didn't want him walking her there! Jonathon's determined expression, however, prodded her out of her chair. She had the distinct feeling that if she didn't do as he said, he'd bodily haul her out of the room.

The moment they stepped onto the gallery and he closed the door, she asked, "What was that story in there about a letter from Billy Joe? What are you up to, Jonathon?"

"I think that's obvious, Claudia. It's my plan to catch the killer."

"Then it's all a scam? No one called you?" When he shook his head, she yelped, "Are you trying to get yourself killed? Damn it, Jonathon, every time the phone rings or you leave the house, the killer will think you're going to meet with your mythical informant!"

"That's exactly what I want him to think. It's the quickest way to get him to play his hand."

"You're crazy," she charged. "Absolutely bats-in-the-belfry nuts!"

"What I am, is determined to get this damn mess over with before my name gets dragged through the mud. And speaking of names being dragged through the mud, just what in hell did you mean by that crack about Patrick carrying on the family tradition?'' he demanded as he glowered at her.

"To quote you, 'I think that's obvious,' '' she snapped, and whirled away from him, stomping down the stairs and starting across the grounds. "Don't bother walking me home. I'm quite capable of getting there on my own power."

"Don't you dare walk away from me!'' he raged as he followed her. "I am not through talking with you."

"Well, I'm through talking with you."

He grabbed her arm and spun her around to face him. "The hell you are. You don't accuse me of sleeping with you to score and then walk away from me. We had more going on between us than that, and you know it!"

She jerked her arm out of his grip, perched her hands on her hips and glared at him. "I thought we had more going on than that, too, but that was before you so cavalierly showed up yesterday and said, 'Hey, it's been fun, but now it's time to move on.' That isn't something *more,* Jonathon. That's a brush-off, and what really infuriates me, is I didn't do anything to deserve it. I treated you like a friend, and you dumped me with as much ease as you'd use to throw out the garbage!"

"I explained I was doing it for you, Claudia," he reminded gruffly. "You need to get on with your life, and you won't do that if you're seeing me."

"If that's the case, then why were you hassling me about Patrick?"

"Because he's not the type of man you want or need," he stated flatly.

"And how do you know what type of man I want or need?" she yelled, out of control. "You don't know what I think. You don't know how I feel. You don't know anything about me, Jonathon Jackson Tanner the Third, because you never bothered to take the time to find out! So don't you dare stand there and tell me that you dumped me for my own good. You dumped me because our relationship was getting to the point where you'd have to take the time to get to know me, and you couldn't deal with that.

"You're worse than Patrick could ever be," she continued, her chest heaving and her eyes brilliant with tears, "because you've convinced yourself that when you treat a woman like dirt, you're not a cad. You're just being noble!"

With that, she spun on her heel and raced toward the guest house. Jonathon was so stunned by her diatribe that she'd already reached her door before her departure registered. As she disappeared inside, he told himself that her accusations were untrue. He had gotten to know her!

If that's true, then why didn't you ever hear her laugh?

Because he'd been afraid she'd get too close. Because he'd been afraid he'd begin to care. He'd been so busy protecting himself that he hadn't given a thought to her feelings. She was right. He was worse than Patrick.

He wanted to go to her and explain, but what was he supposed to say? "Hey, I'm sorry, but you have to understand that I can't get close to you, because I might dream about your death and jinx you?" Or how about, "If you get too close you might worm your way into my mind and find out that I have this quirk. I dream about the deaths of the people I love. Instead of taking them as warnings and doing something about them, I dismiss them as nightmares and let the people they involve die?"

And that's what it really amounted to, he admitted. With his grandfather and his father, he'd had very little warning. Their heart attacks had followed within hours of the dreams. But with Katie, he'd had the dream two months before her illness had been diagnosed. Instead of insisting she go to the doctor, he'd dismissed it as a nightmare, because he didn't want to believe she could die. Maybe if he had made her go to the doctor, she would have responded to treatment. Maybe she'd still be alive today. It was those guilt-ridden maybes that wouldn't allow him to fall in love again, which was the paramount reason he'd had to keep his distance from Claudia. It would be too easy to fall in love with her.

He supposed he owed Claudia an apology for his treatment of her, but he wasn't going to give her one. She might forgive him, and then it would be too easy for him to push away the guilt and give in to the temptation to grab hold of her and never let go.

He turned back toward Magnolia. He hadn't taken two steps when he heard the scream. It had come from the guest house.

Jonathon reached the guest house just as the door flew open and Claudia raced out. He bounded up the stairs and caught her in his arms. "Claudia, what's wrong?"

She was shaking so badly that her teeth were chattering, and she buried her face against his chest and burst into sobs. He clutched her to him tightly, eyeing the open door behind her. Nothing within his line of vision seemed amiss. What had happened to upset her like this?

He caught her chin and raised her pale face to his. "Tell me what happened, honey."

Shuddering violently, she stammered. "Th-the... b-bedroom. It's...s-so...*awful!*"

She again buried her face against his chest, and Jonathon stroked her hair soothingly. "I have to go inside, Claudia. You sit in the swing until I get back."

"No!" she exclaimed frantically as she leaned her head back and clutched the lapels of his sport coat. She knew she sounded hysterical, but she couldn't help herself. The wash of hatred that had permeated her bedroom was one of the most frightening experiences of her life. "Don't leave me alone! Please, Jonathon," she begged.

"I'm not going to leave you alone," he said calmly, leading her to the swing and urging her into it. "I'm just going inside for a minute. I'll be right back, okay?"

She shook her head mutely and buried her face in her hands. He was torn about leaving her, but he had to find out what had happened. "I'll be right back," he reassured as he stroked her bowed head.

Without waiting for a response, he hurried inside. When he reached the doorway to the bedroom, the sight that met his eyes caused bile to rise to his throat. The covers had been stripped from her bed, and in the center of the snowy sheet that covered the mattress was what appeared to be a mangled bird lying in a pool of blood.

He turned swiftly away from the door and walked to the telephone, where he placed a call to Sheriff Helton. Then he joined Claudia. She'd stopped crying and was staring vacantly into space. He sat down beside her and pulled her close to his side.

"Sheriff Helton's on his way," he told her. "As soon as he's gone, we're packing your bags and getting you away from here."

"No!" she gasped, pulling away from him. She turned to face him, her face pale and her eyes wide. "I have to stay!"

He scowled at her. "Damn it, Claudia, don't you understand what that is in there? It's a warning. I'm not letting you stay, and that's final!"

She rose and began to pace. "You can't make me leave. My rent is paid. You have no legal right to make me leave."

Jonathon stared at her in open-mouthed shock. She had a dead bird in the middle of her bed, and she was talking about legal rights? And she'd had the audacity to say *he* was bats-in-the-belfry nuts?

"Claudia, you aren't being rational. That damn bird in there is a warning," he repeated. "If you stay here, you'll be in danger!"

"I *can't* leave!" she declared passionately. "I'm *needed* here!"

Her words thrust Jonathon's mind back to the first day they'd met. She'd made that same impassioned speech and had had the same fervent look in her eyes. He regarded her narrowly. "Exactly why are you needed here, Claudia?"

"Because someone is going to die without my help," she mumbled as she raked both hands through her hair in agitation.

"What makes you think someone is going to die?" he fired at her.

"I had a vision," she answered as she wrapped her arms around herself and stared toward the magnolia grove. "I was in a magnolia grove . . . and there was this terrible, malevolent shadow. It was stalking someone, and I knew that if this person was to survive, he or she had to have my help.'' She swung around to face him, unconsciously challenging him. ''I was summoned to Magnolia, Jonathon. Someone here is in terrible danger, and I'm the only one who can avert disaster. So, you see, you can't send me away.''

A tight ball of fear had formed in his stomach at her reference to a shadow, and he had to swallow hard to find his voice. ''You said this shadow was stalking someone. Who's it stalking?''

''I don't know,'' she said forlornly.

''Could it be stalking you?''

She blinked at him in surprise. ''No.''

''What makes you so sure about that?''

''Because it's a vision of the future, and I rarely have insight into my own future.''

''But you do have insight into it on occasion?''

She heaved a frustrated sigh and said, ''I can't fill both hands with the number of times I've had visions of my own future. This involves someone else's future, and as long as I'm here, the danger will focus on me,'' she finished on a sudden flash of insight.

Jonathon bounded out of the swing, crossed to her and gripped her arms. He gave her a shake as he stated determinedly, ''If you think I'm going to let you stay here and place yourself in danger, you're crazy. You're leaving tonight.''

''I'm not leaving,'' she responded stubbornly.

''Claudia—'' he began, but stopped as the sheriff's car pulled up at the guest house. He released her and stepped back. ''We'll finish this discussion later.''

She didn't respond, but walked to the swing, sat down and set it into motion.

''The bird isn't real?'' Claudia questioned as she stared at Sheriff Helton in astonishment.

''It's a stuffed bird, and it looks like the blood is that fake stuff you can buy in those Halloween specialty shops.

Do you know why someone would do this to you, Ms. Peppermill?''

"I think that's fairly obvious," Jonathon muttered, causing Claudia to glance toward him. He had a hip propped against the porch railing and his arms folded over his chest. He'd been standing in the same position since the sheriff had arrived. "Someone was giving her a warning."

Sheriff Helton slowly swiveled his head toward him. "And why would someone want to do that?"

"That's also obvious. It has to be Billy Joe's killer. He's afraid Claudia will use her clairvoyance to identify him. This was his way of telling her to leave or else."

"It sounds as if you have it all figured out, Mr. Tanner."

"It doesn't take a genius to figure it out," he snapped. "That's why I'm getting Claudia out of here as soon as you're gone."

"I'm not going anywhere," Claudia stated.

"Oh yes, you are."

"Well, now, I think it's best if Ms. Peppermill hangs around for a few days," Sheriff Helton announced.

"You're joking!" Jonathon exploded in disbelief.

"I don't joke, son," the sheriff responded. "I'd also like a few minutes alone with Ms. Peppermill. Why don't you go tell your family that I'd like to talk to them when I'm done here?"

Jonathon opened his mouth as if to object, but evidently thought better of it. He nodded curtly and headed down the stairs. Sheriff Helton waited until he'd reached the mansion before switching his attention back to Claudia.

"Do you know why someone would do this to you, ma'am?" he asked.

She sighed. "I'm afraid Jonathon's probably right, Sheriff Helton. Whoever did it is worried that I'm going to identify him."

"Can you identify him?"

She shook her head. "Not outright. He'd have to want me to know, or if he means to bring harm to someone else,

I may be able to identify him by connecting with that person."

Sheriff Helton nodded as he sat down next to her, pushed his hat back on his head and retrieved his toothpick from his pocket. After he'd tucked it into the corner of his mouth, he said, "You've spent a lot of time around Mr. Tanner. Have you done this psychic stuff with him?"

She gave him a wry smile. "Why, Sheriff Helton, if I didn't know better, I'd think you're beginning to believe in my clairvoyance."

He switched the toothpick from one side of his mouth to the other. "I've been doing a little reading on the subject. I can't say that I'm a believer, but then again, I'd hate to ignore something that may be important just because it doesn't make sense to me. But back to my question. Have you done whatever you do with Mr. Tanner?"

Claudia was picking up enough to know that he was still convinced of Jonathon's guilt. She hedged, "I've spent enough time with Jonathon to know that he didn't kill Billy Joe."

Sheriff Helton studied her pensively. "Well, now, ma'am, that wasn't really an answer to my question, was it?"

"No, I guess it wasn't," she stated in resignation. She'd already determined that Sheriff Helton had a quick mind. It had been silly to think she could trick him. "And, no, I haven't connected with Jonathon, but I do know that he didn't kill Billy Joe. It would be out of character for him."

"Well, I'd hate to think murder was in character for anyone, ma'am." Before she could respond, he said, "You said everything was fine here when you went to the main house for dinner. Do you know if Mr. Tanner could have sneaked over here between the time you left and the time you returned?"

"Sheriff, just about anyone in the house could have sneaked over here."

"I'm sure that's true, ma'am, but you said you locked the place up before you left. Now, Mr. Tanner said that as far as he knows, the only other people to have a key are him and his grandmother. I just can't see Mrs. Tanner doing this, can you?''

"Of course not," Claudia said impatiently, "but what possible reason could Jonathon have for doing it? It doesn't make sense, Sheriff."

"Well, there could be a couple of good reasons for him to do it, but if you don't mind, I'll keep them to myself for now."

He took the toothpick out of his mouth, tucked it into his pocket and pushed himself to his feet. "I'm going to mosey on over to the big house and have a talk with everyone to see just where they were tonight. As for you, you be careful, Ms. Peppermill. In fact, you may want to take Mr. Tanner's advice and leave."

"You said you wanted me to hang around for a few days," Claudia reminded.

He shrugged nonchalantly. "I'm kind of contrary that way, ma'am. When someone starts insisting that someone else should do something they don't want to, I tend to stand up for them. But this is the second time I've been called out here and discovered that something's happened to you. You might want to think about that.

"My deputy will be finished cleaning up in there shortly," he continued. "He'll also be patrolling around here tonight, so if you need any help, you just call 9-1-1, and he'll be here in a jiffy. Good night, ma'am."

As Claudia watched him amble toward Magnolia, she nibbled fretfully at her lower lip. While the sheriff had been talking, she'd been hit with a very clear vision of the future. It had been of the sheriff putting handcuffs on Jonathon!

Chapter 12

Claudia couldn't remember being more exhausted as she stepped onto the porch the next morning. She sat in the swing and sipped at her coffee while watching a mockingbird forage in the grass. Just the sight of the bird was enough to make her shudder. Even though the surprise in her bed last night had proved to be a fake, it didn't alleviate the gruesomeness of the sight. Whoever had come up with the idea had to be sick.

She frowned as her mind began to worry over the same problems it had grappled with all night. An arrest was in Jonathon's immediate future unless she came up with a way to prove who the real killer was. Jonathon, of course, had already instituted a plan, but it was too dangerous for him to carry out alone. Somehow she had to persuade him to let her help, but it wasn't going to be an easy chore. In the first place, he wanted her to leave Magnolia. Even worse, she'd accused him of being just like Patrick. He might accept her staying, but his ego would never forgive her for telling him he was a cad. Why had she let her temper get the best of her?

Because she loved him, she admitted morosely, and the fact that he didn't return her feelings hurt like hell. And there was no question that he didn't return them, because if he did, he'd have checked on her after the sheriff had left last night. But the only communication she'd had from the mansion was a call from Adelaide.

Her thoughts were interrupted by a sudden reception of vibrations. Someone was watching her, and she glanced toward the mansion. No one was there, so she switched her attention to the magnolia grove just as Richard stepped out of it and walked toward her.

Warily she watched him approach, pushing her foot against the floor to set the swing in motion. Even from a distance, his hostility was palpable.

"Good morning," he said when he reached the porch. He gave her what could only be described as a sneer. "You're up early."

"I'm an early riser," she responded.

He climbed the steps, leaned against the post and stared at her.

"Is something on your mind?" she asked when he didn't speak. His opaque eyes were giving her the creeps, and all she was receiving from him was that staggering hostility.

"You don't know what I'm thinking?" he asked mockingly.

"No."

"If you don't know what I'm thinking then how do you, uh, predict things?"

Claudia recognized he was playing a game with her. She just hadn't figured out what it was. "It happens in a lot of different ways, but usually people tell me what they want to know. It sort of opens up a channel that lets me focus on that specific point."

"So if I wanted you to predict something, I'd just ask you about it?" When she nodded, he studied the fingernails on his right hand before glancing up and saying, "All right, Claudia. How much is it going to cost me?"

"I don't have a set fee for a reading," she replied. "People pay me what they think my predictions are worth. In your case, however, I wouldn't expect any remuneration."

"Oh no, I couldn't do that," he said, his lips curving into another sneer. He pushed away from the post and retrieved his wallet from his back pocket. "After all, that's what it's all about, isn't it, Claudia? I give you what you want, and you give me what I want. I'm just surprised it took you this long to ask for it."

She regarded him in bewilderment. "I don't know what you're talking about, Richard."

"Oh, come now, Claudia. It's just you and me. You can drop the act," he said as he withdrew a handful of bills and waved them at her. "I know you'll want more than this, but since I wasn't prepared for your scam, you'll have to accept this as a down payment."

"Richard, I don't want your money," she stated as he stepped forward and dropped the bills into her lap.

Those weird eyes flashed at her malevolently as he said, "If you expect Jonathon to pay you more, forget it. My sanctimonious nephew will promise you the moon, but as soon as you hand it over to him, he'll turn you over to the cops.

"I can probably scrape together ten grand, but it'll take me a few days to do it," he continued as Claudia gaped at him incredulously. "All you have to do is sit tight until then, and don't even think about crossing me, Claudia. I can guarantee that you'll be sorry."

Automatically recoiling from the threat, she gulped as she met his eyes. The hostility radiating from him now was downright menacing. As she continued to stare at him, she realized that the only way she was going to figure out what he was talking about was to connect with his mind.

As he put his wallet back into his pocket, she closed her eyes and concentrated on linking with him. Just as she started to connect, however, everything became scrambled. It was the same type of interference she'd had with Ruth at the dinner table last night! She opened her eyes and frowned. What was going on?

"What's going on here?" Jonathon drawled, causing both Claudia and Richard to jump.

Claudia's gaze flew to him. He was leaning against the edge of the house, his arms crossed over his chest. Though his expression was neutral, his body language was communicating extreme displeasure.

Richard regarded him with a cool haughtiness that didn't match the panic that was suddenly emanating from him. "Claudia was giving me a prediction, and I'm paying her."

"I see," Jonathon said, shifting his gaze to Claudia. "What was the prediction?"

"That's privileged information," Richard answered before Claudia could speak. "Thank you, Claudia. And remember what I said about the moon."

When he was gone, Jonathon slowly climbed the porch steps, demanding, "What was that all about? Were you trying to use your clairvoyance on Uncle Richard?"

"What if I was?" she questioned, her temper sparking, though she knew it wasn't Jonathon that had her so upset. It was that strange meeting with Richard and his threat.

"You promised me you wouldn't use your clairvoyance on him, and by damn, you're not going to use it!" Jonathon bit out coldly.

She automatically bristled at his dictatorial order. "Well, this may come as a big shock to you, but I don't have to obey your orders. And if you'll recall, I made that promise to you when we were...still friends. Since that relationship no longer exists, then any promise I made to you is null and void."

He glared at her, frustrated, and she glared right back. He couldn't believe she was being so damned stubborn! Didn't she realize that the more she poked and prodded, the more danger she was placing herself in? Hadn't last night's incident proved to her that his uncle already considered her a threat? She didn't have to put up a neon sign that said Come and Get Me.

"Claudia, I'm going to say this once and only once. You will *not* use your clairvoyance on my uncle, or anyone else in this family, for that matter. If you do, you leave Magnolia, and I don't give a damn what Sheriff Helton says about it!"

How dare he gave her an ultimatum! she fumed. Just who did he think he was?

That was obvious. He was the lord and master of Magnolia, but if he thought he could stand there and order *her* around, he had one heck of a surprise in store for him!

"If you even try to throw me out," she raged as she unconsciously scooped Richard's money from her lap, jumped to her feet and propped her hands on her hips, "I'll have you hit with so many legal writs that it will take you a week to dig your way out! And the way Sheriff Helton is feeling about you at the moment, I'm sure he'll be more than happy to serve you with every one of them. Now, if you will excuse me, I have things to do!"

She whirled away from him and stalked into the house. When he followed her in, she wanted to scream. Instead she tossed the money onto the fireplace mantel, walked over to the overstuffed chair and sat down. She glared at him as he sat down on the sofa across from her.

"I've never seen this afghan before," he said, fingering the lightweight afghan lying across the arm of the sofa. "Where did you find it?"

His tone was so pleasant, Claudia eyed him suspiciously. "I made it."

"You made it?" he repeated in amazement. When she nodded, he said, "You've very talented. It's beautiful. Do you do a lot of this kind of stuff?"

She nodded again, and he regarded her intently. Uncomfortable beneath his scrutiny, she crossed her legs and adjusted the hem of her sundress over her knee. The silence was driving her crazy, but she wasn't about to be the first to break it.

Finally he said, "Did you pick up anything from Uncle Richard?"

She arched a cool brow. "Don't patronize me, Jonathon."

"I'm not patronizing you."

"Of course, you are. You don't believe in my clairvoyance, remember?"

"You're wrong," he announced leaning back against the cushions and spreading his arms across the back of the sofa. "I do believe in your clairvoyance."

Claudia blinked at him, sure that she'd misunderstood him. But his sober expression assured her that her hearing hadn't failed her.

"Since when?" she demanded distrustfully.

He hesitated, not sure how to answer, or even why he'd told her in the first place. As he'd determined before, giving her belief without acceptance would be cruel. But they'd been closer then, and now they were... He didn't know what they were, and that disturbed him.

"Do you remember the first day we met and you predicted that the chocolate pie would fall off the seat in Gran's car?"

"Vaguely," she answered.

"Well, it did fall off, and I couldn't think of one plausible way you could have known that was going to happen. I kept telling myself that there had to be some reasonable explanation, but I've come to realize I was only kidding myself. There was only one way you could have known, and that was through clairvoyance."

"I see," she said, stunned by his announcement. *He believed in her!* Just two days ago, she'd have been shouting with joy over the news. Now it only made the ache in her heart worse. "In that case I guess you'll believe me when I tell you that while I was talking with Sheriff Helton last night, I had a vision of him putting handcuffs on you."

He bolted upright. "When is this going to happen?"

"I don't know, but it had a feeling of immediacy to it."

He muttered a curse as he sprang to his feet and began to pace. Eventually he stopped and eyed her consideringly. "Claudia, when you spoke with Uncle Richard, did you pick up anything from him? Something that might help me prove that he killed Billy Joe?"

"No," she answered ruefully. "I was on the verge of connecting with him when I got this strange interference."

"Interference?"

"I don't know how to explain it. It was sort of like the interference you get on a television set sometimes. It was weird, because the same thing happened when I tried to connect with Ruth at dinner last night."

"Why in the world were you trying to connect with Ruth?"

"She's terrified. I think she knows something about Billy Joe's death."

He shook his head dubiously. "I doubt Ruth spoke ten words to Billy Joe. How would she know something about his death?"

"Lord, I'm beginning to sound like a broken record, but I don't know. But don't you think it's strange that she collapsed when she found out about Billy Joe?"

"Knowing Ruth, I don't find it strange at all. She's afraid of her own shadow, Claudia. Just the thought of having been in the same house as a dead man would be enough to give her the heebie-jeebies."

"You may be right," Claudia murmured uncertainly. "By the way, I said I didn't pick up anything from your uncle, but we did have the strangest conversation. When he first arrived, I thought he wanted a reading, but then he told me he knew it was just a scam. He insisted on giving me money, and said it would have to serve as a down payment. When I told him I didn't want his money, he said something like, 'If you expect Jonathon to pay more, forget it. My sanctimonious nephew will promise you the moon, but as soon as you hand it over to him, he'll turn you over to the cops.' Then he said he could probably scrape together another ten grand, but that it would take him a few days to do it.

"I had absolutely no idea what he was talking about," she continued with a puzzled frown, "and that's when I tried to connect with him and got that strange interference. About that same time, you showed up."

"He was taking the bait!" Jonathon exclaimed with a triumphant laugh. When she stared at him in bewilderment, he explained, "Uncle Richard thinks you're my informant, Claudia, and he wants you to give him the letter from Billy Joe."

She gaped at him. "He thinks I'm your mythical informant? That's crazy!"

"Not if you think like Uncle Richard." He frowned suddenly. "Damn. It also means he'll consider you a threat, particularly since I'm here with you. You're going to have to leave Magnolia until this is over, Claudia.''

She shook her head firmly. "I'm not leaving. I told you last night that someone here needs me.''

"Don't be stubborn about this!'' he said impatiently.

"I'm *not* leaving,'' she repeated quietly but firmly.

He resumed his pacing. "Claudia, be reasonable. I have Uncle Richard on the run now, and I can't handle him and keep an eye on you at the same time. It's too dangerous for you to remain here.''

"And if I leave it will be dangerous for someone else,'' she argued. "That someone might even be you, Jonathon.''

"I can take care of myself.''

"I wasn't implying that you couldn't, but whoever left that little surprise in my bed last night has a serious mental problem. People like that are unpredictable, and you don't have the time to deal with unpredictability. Let me help you, so you can get this resolved before that vision of you being put into handcuffs can come true.''

When he still looked as if he was going to refuse, she leaned forward in her chair and said, "If you let me help you, you'll also be able to keep an eye on me. That means you won't have to worry anymore than necessary, and can focus all your attention on catching your uncle.''

"That's emotional blackmail, Claudia,'' he grumbled.

She gave an unrepentant shrug, leaning back. "It's not emotional blackmail when it's the truth.''

Jonathon raked a hand through his hair and walked to the window. She'd presented a persuasive case for him to accept her help, so why were his instincts telling him it was all wrong?

Because he couldn't forget the two times he'd seen a shadow engulf her. Everything inside him shouted that it was a warning. He'd ignored the warning with Katie and look what had happened. But he'd seen Katie's death in a dream, and he hadn't been dreaming when he'd seen Claudia cloaked in shadow. *Damn!* He didn't know what to do!

"Jonathon?'' Claudia murmured as she came up beside him and placed her hand on his shoulder.

He closed his eyes and swallowed a groan as the energy zapped through him. *Not now.* He wasn't going to touch her. He *couldn't* touch her. It was over between them! But his body refused to believe it.

When he opened his eyes and slowly turned his head toward her, the desire swirling in the depths of her beautiful, gray-blue eyes caused a tremor to pass through him.

"How do you do it?" he asked gruffly, tangling his hands in her glorious hair and tilting her face up to his.

"Do what?" Claudia whispered breathlessly as she gazed up at him in a daze. The visions of lovemaking flowing through her mind were so vivid and so erotic that she thought she might die from the exquisite pleasure of them.

She could feel the heat of his breath against her lips; the brush of his skin against her skin; and the exquisite wonder of his pulsing manhood as he entered her, making them a whole.

"The energy!" he rasped feverishly as he levered her against the wall and leaned into her. He rocked his hips against her in a mimicry of the arousing vision that had her shooting toward completion. "How do you create the energy?"

"I don't know what you're talking about!" she gasped, unable to stand it any longer and grabbing his hips to pull him even closer. "All I know is that whenever you touch me, I see visions of us making love, and what you're doing to me in them right now is driving me crazy. Make love to me, Jonathon. Please, make love to me now!"

With a hoarse cry, he pulled her away from the wall and lowered her to the Turkish carpet. Even as he lifted her skirt, pulled off her panties, and reached for his own zipper, he was telling himself he couldn't do this. He'd ended their relationship. It was over. He had to let her go!

But even as he made the declaration, he was entering her, and he was struck by the rightness of being with her like this. It was so damn right, because, heaven help him, he'd fallen in love with her.

As she reached her climax and shuddered in his arms, he followed her with a deep cry that was as much a result of grief as it was pleasure.

"I can't believe I've treated you like this," he stated roughly.

"And how have you treated me?" she asked as she lazily opened her eyes and smiled up at him.

He glowered. "For Pete's sake, Claudia, I just made love to you on the floor!"

"Do you hear me complaining?"

"You should be complaining," he snapped as he eased off her and sat up. "You deserve to be treated with respect."

She sat up beside him. "I thought you were very respectful."

With a muttered imprecation, he shot to his feet and turned his back on her. As he adjusted his clothing, he said, "You're too damned innocent for your own good."

Deciding that the better part of valor was to ignore his comment, Claudia went about setting herself to rights. When she was done, she went back to the chair and sat down. Jonathon had returned to the window and was staring out.

She regarded him for a long moment before she said, "Tell me about the energy, Jonathon."

He stuffed his hands into his back pockets and continued to stare out the window. "There isn't much to tell. Sometimes when I touch you, I get zapped by this strange energy. It's like putting my finger in an electrical socket."

Instinctively she knew that there was more to it than that. "Does the energy turn you on?"

He swung around to face her, his brows drawn together in an ominous frown. "Why do you want to know?"

"Because I think that while you're getting zapped by your strange energy, I'm having visions of us making love."

She eyed him speculatively and on impulse tried connecting with his mind. Nothing. But if the theory she was putting together in her head was correct, they were not only capable of linking, but the link they shared was powerful. She would also lay odds that if Jonathon tried to link with

her, she'd be able to identify Billy Joe's killer as well as who
was in danger.

"Jonathon, there's a foolproof way for you to catch Billy
Joe's killer," she announced, excitement in her voice. "All
you have to do is help me connect with your mind."

He was appalled by her suggestion. The only way he'd
been able to come to grips with her clairvoyance at all was
to know that his secrets were safe from her. There was no
way he'd let her into his mind. "Absolutely not!"

"Why not?" she demanded. "It's painless, and it's almost guaranteed to give you the identity of the killer."

"I'm not going to let you invade my mind, particularly
when I already know who the killer is. It's Uncle Richard."

"It wouldn't be an invasion if you invite me in," she
pointed out. When he shook his head adamantly, she
asked, "What are you afraid of? That once I get inside
your head, I'll be able to control you? I could never control you, Jonathon. You'd be awake and aware of everything that was happening."

"I said no, Claudia, so drop the subject."

"I'm not going to drop it. This is the perfect solution,"
she said, forcing herself to speak calmly when what she really wanted to do was rail at him. "We'll know who the
killer is, and we can tell the sheriff. You won't have to carry
out any crazy plans. You won't be arrested, and we'll be
safe. Isn't that what you want? For everyone to be safe?"

"Of course that's what I want," he declared angrily,
"which is exactly why I set this trap to catch Uncle Richard. You don't have to go running around inside my head
to prove what I already know!"

She raked a hand through her hair in frustration. This
was ridiculous! She was offering him the perfect solution,
and he wouldn't even consider it. Why was he being so
stubborn? Then it came to her. The answer was so obvious
she didn't know how she'd overlooked it.

"If you're afraid I'll discover some deep, dark secret,
you don't have to worry. There's a quirk in my ability that
doesn't allow me to pick up on anything people don't want
me to know."

"And I keep telling you that since we know Uncle Richard is the killer, we don't need to play mind games!"

"I agree that the evidence points toward your uncle, Jonathon, but you still don't have proof that he's the killer," she snapped, jumping to her feet as her temper erupted. "If you go after him and it turns out that he's innocent, you could be putting yourself or someone else in danger. But since you're too insecure to put your trust in me, you go right ahead and put your stupid plan into action. In the meantime, I'm going to do what I do best. Use my clairvoyance to find Billy Joe's killer!"

"You stay away from my family, Claudia. I mean it!" he roared as he took a threatening step toward her.

She gave a defiant toss of her head. "What are you going to do if I don't, Jonathon? I don't work for you, so you can't fire me. I'm not in your family, so you can't disown me or cut off my allowance. My rent is paid up, so you can't throw me out. I suppose you could seduce me, but eventually you'd have to crawl out of bed to go play your little entrapment games with your uncle. So, you see, Jonathon, I don't have to take orders from you. You have absolutely no control over me."

She pointed a shaking finger toward the door. "Now, get out. This is my home, and you're here uninvited."

He stood there staring at her, his expression so livid there were white lines around his mouth. When Claudia noted that he was clenching and unclenching his fists at his sides, she experienced a frisson of fear. Had she pushed him too far? Was he capable of physically harming her?

But even as the thought presented itself, she rejected it. Jonathon was a complex man who was carrying around a lot of anger, but she knew in her heart he would never physically harm her or anyone else. Verbally, though, was another matter entirely. She knew he could rip her to emotional shreds, should he so choose.

She raised her chin, prepared for just such an assault, but he surprised her by turning away abruptly and stalking to the door. The windows rattled as he slammed it behind him, and she collapsed in the chair in a trembling heap. She hated being in love. It was too hard on the nerves!

* * *

He was furious. Pacing in his bedroom, he could only think that Claudia was at risk, and she wasn't going to listen to him. His first impulse was to get her away from Magnolia, even if he had to haul her off kicking and screaming. But he suspected that Claudia would do something foolish, like sneak back to Magnolia, and if he didn't know where she was he couldn't keep an eye on her. Of course, if he didn't make up with her now, he wasn't going to be able to do that, either.

He threw himself down on his bed and tossed an arm over his eyes. His mind immediately conjured up the image of her railing at him, her eyes flashing and her hair fairly bristling. At first he'd been stunned by her temerity. No one spoke to him that way and got away with it. But as she'd continued to rant, he'd started getting angry, and his temper had reached epic proportions by the time she was finished. He'd wanted to rage at her—to proclaim that he was in love with her, and that that gave him every right to tell her what to do and demand that she obey him.

He might have even done so if he hadn't seen a sudden flash of fear in her eyes as she'd glanced down at his clenched fists. The fact she could even think that he might harm her had hurt so badly that he'd almost doubled over from the pain.

But he was also grateful for that fear, because it had kept him from making that accursed avowal of love. Even if he could come to grips with his part in his wife's death, there was no way he could build a life with Claudia. She'd implied that the energy was a link between their minds, and instinct told him that if he ever accepted that link, he'd be opening another Pandora's box. And he'd already learned his lesson about Pandora's boxes with the secret room.

He heaved himself off the bed. The sheriff would be here soon, and he wanted to straighten things out with Claudia before he arrived. He'd even grovel if he had to.

Lord, he was in worse shape than he'd thought!

Chapter 13

Claudia nervously glanced around her as she walked to the mansion. Someone was watching her again, and she shuddered as she recalled her meeting with weird Richard. Was he out there somewhere, spying on her?

The feeling intensified as she neared the mansion, and she warily approached the gallery when she saw Steven sitting in one of the redwood chaises. It wasn't Richard spying on her after all.

"Hello, Steven," she greeted as she climbed the steps and went to join him.

"Hi, Claudia," he returned with a wan smile.

"Is everything all right?" she asked. She sat down beside him, regarding him in concern. She could sense his depression.

He shrugged. "I'm just worried about Ruth."

Claudia nodded understandingly. "Adelaide said she took the news about Billy Joe badly."

"I've never seen her like this," he said with a heavy sigh. "She won't even talk to me. I keep telling her that if she won't talk to me, I can't help her, but she just starts crying."

"I'm sure it's only the stress," she soothed.

"I hope so, because I feel like she doesn't love me any-more."

He sounded so pitiful that her heart went out to him. "She still loves you, Steven. You just need to give her some time to work things out for herself."

"Are you sure?" he asked, glancing at her hopefully.

"Pretty sure," Claudia hedged, picking up on serious upheaval in Steven's future. However, she had yet to determine if it had to do with his marriage.

Before she could pursue the connection she'd made with him further, he asked, "Did you get a chance to read my manuscript?"

"Yes, I did," she answered. "Your portrayal of clair-voyance was excellent. My only criticism would be that we don't usually meet someone and know instantly what their future holds, but since you're writing science fiction I don't see any harm in you stretching that point."

"What did you think about the rest of the book?" he asked.

It was the question Claudia had dreaded, but thank-fully, she'd prepared a tactful answer. "I don't read much science fiction, Steven, so all I can really say is that it's very different."

He smiled ruefully. "That's just a polite way of saying you didn't like it." When she opened her mouth to object, he raised his hand. "It's okay, Claudia. To tell you the truth, I'm not too enamored with it myself. I've been thinking about switching to another genre, or giving up writing all together. I just haven't figured out a way to tell Mother yet."

"You haven't figured out a way to tell me what?" Virginia asked, startling them as she walked up.

"How much I love you, of course," Steven answered quickly.

"Oh, that's so sweet, Steven, but you don't have to tell me that," Virginia chirped as she bent down and presented her cheek to him, for a kiss. "I already know how much you love me. What are you doing out here with Claudia? You should be inside with Ruth. She's positively frantic about meeting with the sheriff, and nothing I say will calm her down. Now, run along and take care of her like a good husband should."

"I'll see you later, Claudia," Steven mumbled as he rose to his feet.

"Of course, Steven. It was nice talking with you," she said, watching him thoughtfully as he hurried away. The moment Virginia had arrived, there had been a distinct change in Steven's emotional state. She'd sensed frustration and terrible resentment. It made her wonder about their relationship, particularly why Virginia was so obsessed with her son.

"What were you talking to him about?" Virginia questioned.

Claudia arched a brow as she switched her attention to the woman. The animosity radiating from Virginia was close to hatred. She was also picking up on the underlying fear she'd sensed before. Again the question nagged at her. Why was Virginia afraid of her, and why did she dislike her so terribly? Was it guilt? Could she have killed Billy Joe, or could she know who had and was protecting them? Could Steven have done it?

"I was giving him my opinion on the clairvoyant in his book," Claudia answered.

"And that's all you talked about?"

"We discussed Ruth."

"What did he say about Ruth?"

Virginia's tone was decidedly sharp, and Claudia arched her brow again. Obviously Virginia was starting to panic, but was she concerned about Steven, or Ruth? Things were definitely getting curiouser and curiouser. "Only that he's worried about her."

"There's nothing for him to be worried about," Virginia snapped. "Ruth's just fragile, and as soon as all this mess with Billy Joe is resolved, she'll be fine."

"I'm sure she will," Claudia agreed as she leaned back in the chaise and observed Virginia. The moment they'd started talking about Ruth, Virginia's emanations of fear had increased dramatically. She decided to focus on the fear and see where it took her, but just as she started to connect with Virginia, the woman's attention was diverted. Claudia wanted to curse at the untimely interruption.

"Oh, hello, Jonathon!" Virginia warbled cheerfully as she glanced away from Claudia and toward the door. "Why don't you come join Claudia and me? We were just having a chat about this terrible mess with Billy Joe. Have you heard from that man who has the letter? I still think you should tell the sheriff about it. After all, it could be some terrible trap. Why, for all you know, he could be the one who killed Billy Joe!"

As Virginia chattered away, Claudia watched Jonathon saunter toward them. When they'd parted a short time ago, he'd been so mad he'd rattled her windows, and she narrowed her eyes suspiciously when he gave her a wide smile.

"I haven't heard a thing, Aunt Virginia," he said as he stretched out on the chaise beside Claudia's. "But don't worry. I'm sure he'll call soon. What's the matter with Ruth? I passed her in the hallway a few seconds ago, and she took one look at me and burst into tears."

"Oh, dear," Virginia murmured fretfully. "I'd better go check on her. We'll talk again soon, Claudia."

Claudia frowned in frustration as Virginia left. Something was going on here. She'd been—

"I'm sorry, Claudia," Jonathon said suddenly, interrupting her troubled thoughts. "I had no right to give you orders, and I promise you that I won't do it again."

She eyed him skeptically. He certainly *sounded* sincere, but she didn't trust him. "Your apology is accepted."

"You mean I'm forgiven that easily?"

"I didn't say you were forgiven," she responded coolly. "I said I accepted your apology."

He nodded solemnly. "I guess that means your offer to help me catch Uncle Richard isn't still open."

If she'd been skeptical a moment ago, she was downright leery now. "What are you up to, Jonathon?"

He widened his eyes, the picture of innocence. "I'm not up to anything. I thought about what you said, and I agree that Uncle Richard is too dangerous to handle alone. I could use the backup."

"And if I believe that, you have a couple of acres of swampland you want to sell me, right?"

"Cynicism doesn't suit you, Claudia," he chided.

"Well I'm afraid that you bring out the cynic in me, Jonathon, so I'm sure you'll understand if I decline your gracious offer."

"What do you mean, you decline?" he demanded, sitting upright. "You can't turn me down!"

"I not only can, I have."

"But—"

"Jonathon, telephone!" Adelaide hailed from the doorway.

He muttered a rude and very imaginative curse as he rose to his feet. He scowled down at Claudia. "You wait right here. We're not finished with this discussion."

"Oh yes, we are," she murmured as she rose and followed him, though, coward that she was, she said it beneath her breath.

"Good morning, Claudia," Adelaide said when Claudia and Jonathon reached her. "How are you this morning?"

"Fine, Adelaide. And you?" Claudia asked distractedly, stopping at the doorway and watching Jonathon until he disappeared.

Adelaide gave a frustrated shake of her head. "The sheriff is due soon, and I'm trying to gather the family in the great room. It's not an easy task."

"I'm sure it's not. Do you think you'd have a minute to speak with me after you've gotten them assembled?"

"Sure." Adelaide glanced at her watch. "Why don't we meet in an hour? The sheriff should be through with me by then, and I'll be able to give you all the time you need."

"That sounds great. Would you mind if I waited in the library?" Claudia asked. She knew that Jonathon would come looking for her as soon as he got off the phone so they could continue their "discussion." The last place he'd think to look was the library.

"Of course, dear."

"Thanks," Claudia said, following Adelaide inside. "And, Adelaide, if Jonathon asks where I am, don't tell him, okay?"

Adelaide grinned. "Is that boy giving you a hard time again?"

"Let's just say we're having a battle of wills, and I'm going to win."

Adelaide chuckled. "Good for you. You go on to the library, and I'll meet you there as soon as I can. And don't you worry. I won't tell a soul where you are."

Jonathon wasn't surprised when he returned to the gallery and found Claudia gone. She'd made it clear that she was going to be difficult, and it was probably just as well that Allen had chosen that moment to call with an update on yesterday's problem. Otherwise he'd probably have spoiled everything by yelling at her again. With an irritable sigh, he headed for the guest house, telling himself that if he was going to persuade her to cooperate with him, he couldn't lose his temper. Unfortunately, when it came to Claudia, he didn't seem to have control over any of his emotions.

When he reached the guest house and found Claudia gone, his first reaction was fear. But before he could panic, his common sense surfaced. It was crazy to think his uncle would try something when the sheriff was due to arrive within the hour. Claudia had just gone for a walk.

Since he knew she often walked by the river, he headed in that direction. When he got there and still didn't see any sign of her, he began to worry. But he again reassured himself that with Sheriff Helton on his way, nothing would happen to her. She was probably in the magnolia grove. He should have checked there first.

He started back across the field and stopped when he heard someone call him. The voice was faint, but he was sure it was Claudia's. Everyone else was gathering in the great room back at the house.

He shielded his eyes with his hand as he searched for her. When his gaze landed on the old, dilapidated barn at the other end of the field, he saw her. She was standing inside the doorway and was no more than a shadow. A frisson of fear shot through him. That old barn was a deathtrap. He had to get her out of there!

He began to run toward the barn, yelling at her to move away. He cursed when she just waved again and then disappeared inside. When he got his hands on her he'd shake her until her teeth rattled! This damn refusal of hers to obey orders was getting out of hand!

When he reached the barn, he stopped at the door and said, "Claudia, get the hell out of there! This old barn isn't safe. It could fall down at any minute."

He frowned in annoyance and stepped inside when she didn't answer. "Come on, Claudia. I know you're in here. Don't play games. I'm serious. This barn is a deathtrap."

When she still didn't answer, he became concerned. Had something happened to her? He jerked his head toward the hayloft when he heard a noise. Dear God, she wouldn't climb into the hayloft... Nearly every board up there was rotted!

"Damn it, Claudia, say something!" he demanded as he strode toward the hayloft. When he reached the rickety ladder leading up to it, he heard another noise. He turned toward it quickly.

He thought he saw her in one of the shadowed corners, but as he started to take a step toward her, a terrible shattering noise overhead made him pause. He glanced up just in time to see the hayloft coming down on him.

"Claudia, get out of here!" he bellowed, and then everything went black.

"Oh, excuse me, Ms. Peppermill. I didn't realize anyone was in here. Is it all right if I put these books away?" Mrs. Massey asked as she stood hesitantly in the library doorway.

Claudia smiled at the housekeeper. "Good morning, Mrs. Massey, and please, do come in. I'm just waiting for Adelaide."

The woman nodded and entered. As she started sliding books into empty spaces on the shelves, Claudia asked, "Where did all those books come from?"

"Mostly from Miss Virginia's room. She's writing a book, you know. It's all about the history of Magnolia and the surrounding area. She says that a lot of these old books can't be found anywhere else, so whenever she visits she does as much research as she can."

"Mrs. Massey, did you know Billy Joe Jordan?" Claudia asked on a sudden impulse. She knew the housekeeper was aware of Billy Joe's death because Adelaide had confided that she hadn't felt comfortable asking the woman to work over the weekend without telling her why she'd be needed.

"Everyone in these parts knew Billy Joe."

"Can you think of anyone who might have wanted to kill him?"

"Half the women between Natchez and Vicksburg, not to mention their fathers, husbands, brothers and boyfriends," she answered as she continued to put books on the shelves. "I know a person shouldn't speak ill of the dead, but Billy Joe was a womanizer. He didn't care what they looked like or how old they were. It was a game to him, and the more inaccessible the woman, the more he wanted her. He broke up a lot of marriages, and I suspect that a good number of the illegitimate children around here are his."

"He doesn't sound like a very nice man," Claudia remarked.

"That's the funny part about Billy Joe. You couldn't help but like him. He was a charmer. Now, if you'll excuse me. I need to get back to work."

Adelaide swept into the library, just as Mrs. Massey was leaving. Claudia grinned at her. "You look flustered."

"What I am is mad," Adelaide grumbled, plopping into the chair next to Claudia's. "First everyone complained about having to be questioned. Then they complained about having to wait in the great room until the sheriff arrived. Then as soon as Sheriff Helton arrived and said he was ready to start the questioning, they started fighting, because they all wanted to go last.

"Virginia suggested that they go in alphabetical order," Adelaide went on. "Richard threw a fit, because that meant she'd get to go last, so she suggested they go in reverse alphabetical order. That made Richard mad, because that meant the first three to be questioned would be Virginia, Steven and Ruth. He said it wasn't fair that her family would get done first and his had to sit around twiddling their thumbs all day.''

"So how did you resolve it?" Claudia asked in amazement, unable to believe that grown people could behave so childishly.

"I made them draw straws. Do you have any idea how embarrassing it was to have to resort to something so juvenile in front of Sheriff Helton? Thank heavens, Jonathon wasn't there. He'd probably have punched Richard in the nose, and Richard would have made the sheriff arrest him for assault."

"Why wasn't Jonathon there?" Claudia asked, suddenly alert. She couldn't see him not being on hand to get the family ready for the sheriff's questioning. He would have anticipated a problem and never left Adelaide to cope with it alone.

"I don't know," Adelaide answered with a perturbed frown. "The last time I saw him was when I called him to the telephone."

Claudia's inner alarms started blaring. "Did Richard know he got a phone call?"

Adelaide gave a confused shrug. "I don't know, why?"

"Who was on the phone?"

"That nice Allen Gregory from Jonathon's office."

"Did you tell anyone who was calling? Think Adelaide. This is very important!"

"I didn't tell anyone. Why?"

"Oh, God! Something's happened to Jonathon!" Claudia exclaimed as she jumped to her feet.

Before Adelaide could respond, she raced out of the room. When she barreled out the back door, she skidded to a halt, because she didn't know where to go. Adelaide said that she hadn't seen Jonathon since he'd taken the telephone call, but Claudia'd bet that he'd come looking for her so they could finish their burgeoning argument. When he hadn't found her at the guest house, he'd have started looking for her elsewhere. But where?

The river! some inner instinct exclaimed.

As she ran toward the river, her mind conjured up visions of him lying in the water drowned. Her stomach clenched into a hard knot of fear, and her eyes blurred with tears. Why had she fought with him? Why hadn't she glued herself to his side? If anything had happened to him...

Claudia wouldn't let herself finish the thought. As long as she believed he was all right, then he'd be all right. But when she reached the river, there was no sign of him.

She ran up and down the bank, screaming his name, but there was no answer. She wanted to dissolve into tears, but she forced herself to calm down. The river didn't flow fast enough through here to have swept him away this quickly. She was sure, however, that this was the first place he'd look for her, and she searched the bank for any sign of his footprints. Because of her frantic dash up and down the bank, it took her several minutes to locate one. When she did, she was flooded with relief. It was headed back to Magnolia.

She scrutinized the area in front of her. Jonathon had been going back to Magnolia, but he hadn't gotten there. So where had he gone? Claudia almost missed the old tumble-down barn nestled in the oak grove at the other end of the field. She'd been down to the river at least two dozen times and never noticed it. Its weathered wood blended right into its surroundings, rendering it virtually invisible. She also knew in her heart that that was where Jonathon was.

She started running toward it, chanting, "Be okay. Please, be okay."

"Jonathon?" she called out when she stepped inside the door. The building was making ominous creaking noises that made her shiver. "Jonathon? Are you in here?"

When there was no answer, she stepped further inside. "Jonathon, I know you're in here. Please, talk to me."

There was still nothing. Should she search for him, or should she go back to the mansion for help? She was still wavering in indecision when she heard a groan. It was so faint that she wondered if she'd imagined it, but then she heard another one. It, too, was faint, but it was like a beacon to her. It was so dark inside the barn that she couldn't see anything more than shadowed lumps, and she moved gingerly in the direction the groan had come from.

She let out a startled yelp when Jonathon suddenly grabbed her ankle and asked weakly, "Claudia? Are you all right?"

"Yes. But what about you? What happened?" she asked, dropping to her knees beside him.

He groaned and sat up, holding his head in his hands. "The damn hayloft fell on me. What in hell were you doing in here, anyway? Couldn't you tell this place is a deathtrap? I knew I should have ignored Gran and torn it down. I don't care if her and Gramps did romp in here when they were first married. Safety has to come before sentimentality!"

Claudia had no idea what he was talking about, but she was relieved by his grumpiness. He couldn't be too hurt if he was complaining.

"Can you stand?" she asked as she stood and took hold of his arm to help him up.

"I think so," he muttered as he managed to climb shakily to his feet. He swayed and groaned. "God, my head is killing me."

"Let's get you home so we can take a look at it." She wrapped her arm around his waist, looped his around her shoulders, and led him to the door. When they stepped outside, she glanced up at him and cried, "You're bleeding!"

He raised his hand to the gash in his forehead and grimaced. "It's just a scratch."

"That's not a scratch, Jonathon. You need stitches. You were also unconscious, which means you probably have a concussion. We have to get you to the hospital!"

"Don't be ridiculous, Claudia," he snapped. "I'm fine."

She opened her mouth to argue with him, but decided that her first priority was to get him home. They'd just started walking across the field when Claudia saw Patrick jogging up from the river. She released a sigh of relief. Jonathon was leaning against her heavily, and she didn't know if she could continue to support him without help.

"Gran said something was wrong and sent everyone out to search for you. What happened?" Patrick panted when he reached them.

"Claudia decided I wasn't virile enough and needed a rakish scar," Jonathon groused.

"You hit him?" Patrick gasped at her.

"Of course not," Claudia said impatiently. "The hayloft fell on him."

"What in the world were you doing in that old barn?" Patrick inquired as he got on Jonathon's other side. "The place is a damn deathtrap."

"Tell that to Claudia. She's the one who lured me in there."

"I didn't lure you in there, Jonathon," she informed him. "I was waiting for Adelaide in the library. When she joined me and said she didn't know where you were, I came looking for you."

He frowned at her and immediately winced at the discomfort the act caused. "That's impossible, Claudia. You called to me, and I saw you."

"No, Jonathon. I was in the library."

"Well, if it wasn't you, then who?"

She didn't have to answer, because she saw realization dawn in his eyes.

Jonathon was cranky, and he decided that he had every right to feel that way. Claudia and his grandmother had made such a fuss about him going to the hospital that the sheriff had told him he either went or he'd arrest him. Certain the sheriff hadn't been joking, he'd been forced to comply. Now, he'd just had ten stitches put in his forehead and gone through enough poking and prodding to swear him off doctors for the rest of his life.

When the doctor announced that he wanted to admit him for overnight observation, Jonathon adamantly refused. There was no way he was going to leave Claudia alone at Magnolia. If his uncle had been desperate enough to drop a hayloft on his head, Jonathon could only imagine what he had in store for her.

Sheriff Helton wandered into the examining room and regarded him for a long moment before saying, "You look as if you'll live."

"Yeah," Jonathon muttered. Then he said to a passing nurse, "Where are my clothes?"

The woman gave him a vacuous smile and kept on walking.

Jonathon uttered a few choice epithets under his breath before asking the sheriff, "Did you find any sign of foul play at the barn?"

"Nope." He hitched his pant leg and rested a hip on the end of the examining table. "That barn is a deathtrap."

Jonathon rolled his eyes toward the ceiling. "I'm aware of that, Sheriff Helton. I've been trying to persuade my grandmother to let me tear it down for the past five years. Unfortunately she has sentimental feelings for it."

The sheriff pulled his toothpick out of his pocket and stuck it into his mouth. "Why'd you go down to that barn, son?"

"I told you, I was looking for Claudia. Someone called to me from the barn, and I thought it was her. Everyone else was supposed to be up at the house waiting for you."

"How long's it been since you've been down there?" the sheriff asked next.

Jonathon shrugged. "A couple of years."

"A couple of years, huh? Maybe around the time that Billy Joe disappeared?"

"Maybe," Jonathon answered warily. Now that he thought about it, that was the last time he'd been down there. When Billy Joe had disappeared, he'd considered that he might be hiding out in the barn, and he'd gone down there to check it out. "Why do you ask?"

Sheriff Helton shrugged as he removed the toothpick from his mouth and tucked it back into his pocket. "We found something down there that might be the murder weapon."

"You're joking!" Jonathon gasped.

"I told you before, son. I don't joke. Since half the day's gone, I'm not going back to Magnolia. I'll be there in the morning to finish my questioning. Ask your family not to leave until I've talked to them.''

When the sheriff was gone, Jonathon sat on the edge of the examining table and scowled at the curtain in front of him. He would have sworn it was Claudia at the barn, but now he knew it had to have been his uncle. The voice had been so faint that it could have been a man's, and he'd been so concerned about getting Claudia out of the barn that he hadn't paid any attention to the size of the shadowy person standing inside the doorway.

He shuddered as he recalled the sheriff's announcement of a possible murder weapon. If whatever they'd found in the barn had been there for two years, would they be able to tell for sure if it had been used to kill Billy Joe? Was it possible that it still had fingerprints on it? If so, that would surely clear him.

But even as he considered the thought, his stomach began to churn with doubt. His first instinct had been that his uncle had lured him into the barn to kill him. It would have been a simple task. All the support beams were termite-ridden. A halfway decent kick to any of them would have brought the hayloft down. What if, however, the purpose hadn't been to kill him, but to get his fingerprints on the murder weapon? With that kind of evidence, Sheriff Helton would toss him into jail and throw away the key!

He raked a hand through his hair and fought against the rising panic. He still had his ace in the hole, and that was the mythical letter from Billy Joe. His uncle had already taken the bait, and all he had to do was reel him in. He was, however, going to have to do it within the next twenty-four hours if he didn't want Claudia's vision of him being placed into handcuffs coming true.

A nurse finally brought him his clothing, and he quickly dressed. When he stepped into the waiting room, his grandmother cried his name and launched herself into his arms. He gave her a reassuring hug and glanced over her head at Claudia. She was standing beside his Aunt Virginia, who'd driven them to the hospital. Claudia was pale and her eyes were filled with worry.

He held out his hand to her, but instead of taking it, she propped her hands on her hips and railed, "Damn you, Jonathon Tanner! I told you that make-believe letter from Billy Joe was going to get you into trouble!"

"Make-believe letter?" Adelaide and Virginia gasped at the same time.

"Yes, make-believe letter," Claudia confirmed before Jonathon could stop her. "Adelaide, I don't want you to take this personally, but your grandson is crazy, and he's going to get himself killed if he doesn't stop playing cops and robbers. Since he won't listen to me, maybe you can talk some sense into him!"

"Jonathon, what is Claudia talking about?" Adelaide demanded as she pulled away from him and mimicked Claudia by propping her hands on her hips.

"I'd like to know the answer to that one myself," Virginia piped in.

Jonathon glowered at the three of them. "If you'll recall, I've just had ten stitches put in my head. Do you think we could go home where I can lie down and put my feet up while I'm being interrogated?"

To his chagrin, his aunt was the only one who registered concern at the reminder of his wound, and she rushed forward and took his arm. "Jonathon's right, Mother. He should get home and off his feet."

"I don't know," Adelaide muttered. "This may be one of those times when he's better off close to the hospital, because I have a feeling that when I hear his story, I'm going to brain him."

"I have a baseball bat I'd be happy to loan you," Claudia offered.

When Jonathon glared at her, she gave him her best smirk, and then took Adelaide's arm and led her toward the emergency room exit. Only when she was sure that Jonathon was a safe distance behind her did she let her relieved tears surface, though she didn't know why she was feeling weepy. After all, Jonathon was safe, and she'd just put a stop to his stupid plan. So why did she have this horrible feeling that his accident had just been the beginning of the nightmare?

Chapter 14

Jonathon suspected that his grandmother's interrogation wouldn't wait until they returned to Magnolia, and he was right. The moment the car was on the road, she began harassing him for the details of his make-believe letter.

He wasn't in the mood for her badgering. His head hurt, and he was still trying to come to grips with the sheriff's announcement about the murder weapon. After casting a dour glance at Claudia, who was sitting in the back seat with him and staring out her window, he released a resigned sigh and told his grandmother about his plan to catch Richard.

When he was finished, she gave a disbelieving shake of her head. "You can't really believe that Richard killed Billy Joe! He isn't capable of murder, Jonathon!"

"Come on, Gran, if he didn't do it, who did? Patrick? Patricia? Steven? Ruth? Or better, yet, how about Aunt Virginia?"

"I'm telling you, it wasn't Richard!" Adelaide exclaimed tearfully.

Jonathon raked a hand through his hair. He hated to upset her like this, and he shot another dour glance in Claudia's direction. "I know you don't want to believe me,

Gran, but I just told you that he tried to bribe Claudia for the letter.''

"Claudia, is that true?" Adelaide questioned uncertainly.

"Yes, Adelaide, I'm afraid it is," Claudia answered regretfully.

"I still don't believe it," Adelaide murmured. "I know that Richard has problems, but murder? Virginia, you don't believe it, do you?"

"Well, Mother, as Jonathon said, if Richard didn't do it, who did? No one else in the family would have had a reason to kill him."

"Well, it's not true!" Adelaide stated adamantly as they reached the driveway leading to the plantation. "And I'm going to prove it. I'll just ask Richard if he did it."

"You aren't going to do any such thing!" Jonathon yelled. "You're going to stay out of this and let me handle it!"

"If you think I'm going to stand by and let you railraod my son into prison just because you don't like him, you're as crazy as Claudia says you are!" Adelaide yelled right back.

Virginia brought the car to a stop at the bottom of the gallery steps, and Adelaide leaped out. Jonathon leaped out right behind her.

He caught her arm and brought her to a stop. "Just give me twenty-four hours, Gran. Let's see what happens with Richard."

"No!" she exclaimed as she jerked her arm from his grasp and glared up at him through tear-filled eyes. "I've stood by and watched you and your father pick on Richard for years, and I'm not going to stand for it anymore! If you want to accuse him, then you accuse him to his face instead of sneaking around behind his back!"

With that she raced up the stairs and into the mansion. Virginia walked up to Jonathon and gave his arm a comforting squeeze as she passed into the house. "Everything's going to be fine, Jonathon."

He was so angry, he couldn't respond, and he closed his eyes against the uncontrollable rage building inside him.

He'd been so close to catching his uncle, and now all his plans were blown to hell because of Claudia, who chose that moment to touch his arm. As the energy surged through him, Jonathon grabbed onto it and used it to feed his fury instead of his libido.

Claudia was unprepared for the feeling of fury that hit her when she touched Jonathon's arm. It was so intense that she let out an involuntary cry of fear as she immediately jerked her hand away from him and took several hasty steps backward.

When he opened his eyes and looked at her, she gulped. Never had she seen anyone in such a rage, and she recognized that Jonathon had lost that careful control he maintained over his emotions. If he was capable of violence, he was at the point where he was apt to commit it.

"You couldn't mind your own business, could you, Claudia?" he drawled so softly that the air around her seemed to vibrate with menace. "You had to interfere where you weren't wanted and you didn't belong."

"I was only trying to help," she defended, wrapping her arms around herself protectively. "I didn't want anything to happen to you."

"You didn't want anything to happen to me?" he mocked with a humorless laugh that was positively chilling. "Well, you just guaranteed me a one-way ticket to jail!"

"Jonathon, I'm sure you're overreacting, and—"

"*I am not overreacting!*" he bellowed. She'd just blown any chance of his tricking his Uncle Richard into confessing, which meant that he was going to remain Helton's primary suspect. If he was arrested, he wouldn't be here to protect her. Couldn't she see the danger she'd placed herself in?

He forced himself to lower his voice as he continued, "The sheriff thinks he found the murder weapon in the barn today. Do you know what that means, Claudia? It means that my uncle wasn't trying to kill me at the barn. He was trying to frame me with the murder weapon! That fake letter from Billy Joe was the only chance I had of catching him and proving that he killed him. Now, because of you,

I don't have that, and because I don't, there's a good possibility that I'll end up in prison for a crime I didn't commit!"

Claudia wanted to deny his assertion, but she kept seeing that vision of Sheriff Helton putting handcuffs on him. Dear God, was he right? Had she just guaranteed his arrest by doing what she'd thought was best for him?

"Jonathon, I'll get you out of this, and—"

"The only thing you're going to do for me is leave Magnolia," he interrupted in a voice carefully devoid of emotion. He recognized that what he was about to say next was cruel, but he had to get her away from here for her own safety. There was only one way to guarantee she'd leave, and that was to make her think he hated her.

He steeled himself against the tears brimming in her eyes and said, "I want you gone from here by noon tomorrow, and don't you ever come near Magnolia or my family again, because I promise you that if you do, you'll live to regret it."

As he turned on his heel and stalked up the stairs and into the mansion, Claudia stood rooted in place. She loved him, and because she did, she'd been trying to protect him. Now it looked as if she'd ruined his life, and there was nothing she could do to help him, because he hated her and would never accept her help. She'd never felt more helpless or miserable in her life.

She was so focused on her own internal pain that she was unaware of Ruth until she stepped out of the shadows along the gallery and frantically asked, "Is it true, Claudia? Is that letter from Billy Joe a fake?"

Claudia had to swallow hard to find her voice, and she still sounded hoarse as she replied, "Yes, Ruth, it's a fake."

"Oh no!" Ruth wailed. "I wanted it to be a fake, but now that I know it is, I want it to be real! I have to tell, but I can't! What am I going do?"

"Why don't you talk to me about it?" Claudia encouraged as she started up the steps toward the young woman, hope stirring inside her. She was convinced Ruth knew something that would help Jonathon. "What is it you have to tell but can't?"

The vibes emanating from Ruth were such a powerful combination of terror and grief that it effectively blocked Claudia from receiving anything else from her. She mumbled a frustrated curse. Why, when she needed it the most, did her clairvoyance seem to be constantly out of whack?

"Ruth, talk to me," she coaxed as she reached her and touched her arm. "I can help you. I know I can."

Ruth gave a distraught shake of her head. "No one can help!"

"That's not true," Claudia rebutted. "I can help you if you'll talk to me."

"Not now," Ruth whispered, staring in wide-eyed fear past Claudia. "I can't talk now!"

"Ruth, wait!" Claudia exclaimed as the woman whirled around and raced down the gallery. "You don't have to be afraid of me!"

"I don't think it's you she's afraid of," a voice announced coldly, and with a yelp, Claudia spun around to find herself face-to-face with Richard.

If she'd thought his strange eyes were creepy before, she found them positively macabre as he stared at her now. They weren't just opaque; they were eerily luminous.

"She's afraid of you, isn't she?" Claudia charged.

Richard gave her one of his sneers. "Ruth's afraid of everyone. I want my money back, and I want it back now."

"It's at the guest house."

"Fine. Let's go get it."

Claudia didn't want to go anywhere with Richard, but she couldn't see a way to get around him accompanying her to the guest house. She sagged in relief when the kitchen door opened and Adelaide and Virginia stepped out.

"Richard, what are you doing out here?" Adelaide questioned. "I told you that we needed to talk."

"I'll be there in a minute, Mother," he replied shooting an impatient glance over his shoulder at her.

"You'll come in the house right this second," Adelaide stated imperiously. "We're going to get this mess settled once and for all."

"Mother—"

"*Now*, Richard!"

He glared at Claudia before heading for the door.

"Was he hassling you?" Virginia asked solicitously when Adelaide and Richard disappeared.

"He wants his money back. I guess Adelaide told him that there is no letter from Billy Joe."

Virginia nodded. "Why don't I walk you back to the guest house, and you can give me the money? That way, Richard won't be bothering you."

"Thanks, Virginia. I really would appreciate it."

As they walked toward the guest house, Claudia said, "Virginia, I think that Ruth knows something about Billy Joe's death. I think she may even be able to prove that Richard killed him."

"Ruth?" Virginia exclaimed in disbelief. "That's ridiculous! What would make you even think such a thing?"

Claudia raked a hand through her hair. "Because Ruth overheard Jonathon and I talking about the letter being a fake, and she became overwrought. She said that now she knew the letter was a fake, she had to tell something. I had just about convinced her to tell me what she was talking about when Richard showed up. She was terrified of him, Virginia, and she ran away."

"Ruth's always been skittish around Richard, Claudia. To tell you the truth, he makes me skittish. I'm sure it's nothing more than that."

"I'm sure she knows something," Claudia insisted, "and if I'm right, she could be in danger." They'd just reached the guest house, and she stopped and gazed at Virginia imploringly. "At least talk to her about it. If she won't talk to you, see if she'll talk to me. If nothing else, I may be able to psychically connect with her and figure out what's wrong."

Virginia looked as if she'd refuse, but then she nodded. "I'm sure you're imagining things, Claudia, but if it will make you feel any better, I'll talk to her."

It was only after Virginia had gone that Claudia realized she hadn't picked up any animosity or fear from the woman. Indeed, the only emotion Virginia had been radiating was serenity. Apparently she was one of those rare people who grew calm during times of crises.

Claudia would have gladly traded all of her worldly possessions for just a semblance of calm at this point in time. Jonathon had ordered her to be gone by noon tomorrow. That left her less than twenty hours to try to fix the damage she'd done.

Claudia had just persuaded herself that she had to start packing when she heard the knock on her door. When she opened it and found Virginia on the other side, she stepped away from the door and gestured for her to enter.

Virginia, however, remained standing on the porch. She glanced around her covertly before saying, "You were right, Claudia. I talked to Ruth and she does know something, but she won't talk about it at Magnolia. She told Mother that she'd go to the grocery store for her, and she wants you and me to meet her there. She said this is bigger than we'd ever believe."

"Bigger than we'd ever believe?" Claudia repeated in confusion. "What does that mean?"

"I don't know, and we won't find out if we don't get going. There's Ruth now."

She glanced toward Magnolia and waved. Claudia leaned through the door in time to see Ruth waving back as she climbed into her car.

"Why do we have to meet her there? Why can't we just ride with her?"

"She says she's afraid to be seen with you. I told her that was ridiculous, but Ruth is such a nervous soul."

Claudia nodded, agreeing. "Did you tell Adelaide what we're doing?"

"I don't want to upset her any more than she already is, Claudia. If Ruth tells us something significant, then we'll tell Mother. Now, hurry. I don't want to keep Ruth waiting. She might panic and change her mind about talking to us."

She hurried across the porch and down the steps. Claudia grabbed her purse and hurried out to Virginia's car. There was a distant rumble of thunder, and she glanced up at the sky. A storm was moving in, and from the looks of the lightning flashes, it appeared it was going to be a downpour.

When she climbed inside, Virginia said, "I hope the storm holds off until we get back. I hate thunderstorms. Thank heavens they installed storm drains along the highway last year. It used to be that the road flooded every time it rained. You couldn't even get into Magnolia. There would be a big pond at the end of the drive. When Jonathon was little, he used to pray for rain so he could go down and swim in it. He was an adorable child, and he's turned out to be a very fine man."

"Yes, he has," Claudia agreed. "Were you and Jonathon's father close?"

"There were five years between Jack—that's what we called my brother—and me, so I can't say we were inseparable. We were very good friends, though. I really miss him."

"Did he and Richard get along as children?"

"When Richard was little, Jack adored him and took him everywhere with him. But there was eight years between them, and when Jack reached his teens, he no longer wanted his baby brother hanging around all the time. That's when Richard began to change. He became mean and spiteful, and all he could talk about was how he wanted Magnolia. Did Jonathon or Mother tell you that when Jack died, Richard hired a lawyer to see if the in-perpetuity clause could be broken?"

"No," Claudia said in surprise.

"Well, he did. It was awful. It took two years for the courts to uphold great-great-grandfather Tanner's will. My nephew went through hell, and he no more than got the lawsuit out of the way than Katie got sick. Now, this mess with Billy Joe has come up. Hopefully, all his bad luck is over and he can start enjoying life again."

"What's that noise?" Claudia asked as a strange noise caught her attention.

"I don't hear anything," Virginia said.

"It's a bumping sound. Are you sure you don't hear it?"

"I think it's just the pavement, Claudia."

"I don't think so, Virginia. It sounds like a flat tire."

"A flat tire?" Virginia repeated in horror. "I don't know how to change a tire, and there's a thunderstorm coming! We can't walk back to Magnolia in the rain!"

"Don't worry, Virginia. I can change a tire. Why don't you pull over and let me check?" Claudia suggested.

Once they were parked on the side of the road, Claudia got out. Sure enough, the rear tire on the driver's side was nearly flat.

"I don't understand," Virginia said in confusion. "I had the tires checked before I left Natchez, and the man at the service station said they were just fine."

"You probably ran over a nail or a piece of glass. As long as your spare is full, we'll be okay. Get the keys so we can open the trunk."

"You don't think Richard did this do you?" Virginia inquired nervously when she returned with the keys.

"I don't think so, Virginia," Claudia answered as she opened the trunk and checked the spare. Thankfully, it was fully inflated, and she pulled it out. She reached for the jack. "What reason would he have for giving you a flat tire?"

"I don't know. He knows I think he killed Billy Joe. Maybe he wanted me to have an accident or something. Oh, my God!" she gasped.

"What?" Claudia questioned as she jerked her head up.

Virginia's eyes were huge as she stared at Claudia in alarm. "What if Ruth killed Billy Joe? Maybe that's why she's so upset, and maybe that's why she wouldn't let us ride with her. Maybe she's getting us away from the house so she can kill us, too!"

Claudia wanted to tell Virginia that her supposition was ridiculous, but she found herself glancing nervously up and down the road. She had to admit that it made more sense than she liked. Ruth was terrified, and she had collapsed when she'd heard that Billy Joe's body had been found. That could be attributed to a guilty conscience. She also suddenly remembered watching Ruth chain smoke before dinner the other evening, and a chain smoker was likely to run out of cigarettes, which could explain why it was Jonathon's cigarette butts that had been found in the secret room. There was also Mrs. Massey's comment that Billy Joe was a womanizer. She'd said that pursuing women was almost a game for him, and the more inaccessible the woman, the more he'd wanted her. Steven adored his wife, and from all accounts, Ruth adored Steven. What could be more inaccessible than a woman in love with her husband? If Billy Joe had threatened to tell Steven about their affair, Ruth could have been frightened enough to kill him....

"Virginia, we're going to get this tire changed and go back to Magnolia," Claudia stated as she rolled the wheel toward the front of the car. "Get the lug wrench out for me."

"What's a lug wrench?" Virginia asked in bewilderment.

"It's the only wrench in the trunk. It should be somewhere in the wheel well—that's the hole where the tire was," she explained, just in case Virginia didn't know what that was either. "And hurry! We don't have a minute to lose."

She'd just reached the front of the car when the vibrations hit her with a viciousness that made her stagger backward. The killer was here!

"Virginia, get in the car!" she screamed, spinning around.

As she saw the jack handle swing through the air, her jaw dropped and her eyes widened in horror. She tried to ward off the blow, but she was too late. As it hit her head, she heard Virginia say, "I'm sorry it had to be this way, Claudia."

The pain inside Claudia's head was so intense that when she opened her eyes she couldn't see. She closed them and told herself that she was going to count to ten. When she opened her eyes again, she'd be able to see. But when she opened them, it was still dark. Oh, God! She was blind!

"Are you awake yet, Claudia?" Virginia asked.

The voice was coming from somewhere above her, and she tried to turn over. It was then that she realized she wasn't blind. She was laying face-down in some kind of dark tunnel. She braced a hand on either side of her, confirming that there was barely enough room for her to move. Carefully she eased herself to her back. When she did, she found Virginia staring down at her through a heavy grill.

"Where am I?" she asked, unable to keep the quaver of fear from her voice.

"In the storm drain that handles the runoff from the road during a rainstorm," Virginia answered brightly. "It empties the water into the river. Don't you remember me telling you about them putting the drains in?"

Claudia gulped. Virginia's cheerful countenance convinced her that the woman was insane. "Yes, but why am I here?"

"It was the only way I could think of to dispose of your body so you wouldn't be found. There's a severe thunderstorm due anytime now. The roads will flood and the conduit will fill up with water. But don't worry, Claudia. They say that drowning is relatively painless, and I really don't want you to suffer."

"If you don't want me to suffer, then why are you doing this to me?"

"Because everyone is convinced that Richard killed Billy Joe, and I can't let you ruin everything with your clairvoyance," Virginia answered with a heavy sigh. "After all, you told me yourself that the more you're around a person, the more you learn about them, and you just might have picked up on my little secret. I really am sorry it had to turn out this way, Claudia. I think I would have liked you. Now, I must go. I have a lot to do."

"Wait, Virginia!" Claudia exclaimed when the woman began to leave. She had to stall her! With a little luck, someone would come upon them and stop to see what was wrong. "Since I'm going to die, anyway, won't you tell me what happened to Billy Joe?"

"I really don't have time, Claudia. As I said, I have a lot to do."

"That's not fair, Virginia. If I'm going to die because of him, I should know why."

Virginia frowned in consternation. "I suppose you're right. But it will have to be quick, so don't interrupt me with any questions. If you do, I'll leave immediately. Do you understand?''

"I understand," Claudia stated quickly.

"It all started when I found Evelina's journals. They're in an old trunk in the attic." She paused and frowned pensively. "I still don't know how the one ended up in the library. I must have dropped it when I was visiting last time, and Mrs. Massey must have put it away.

"Anyway, Billy Joe and I had an affair before I got married. I think he really loved me, but when I got pregnant with Steven, I knew I couldn't marry him. He was just too crude to be married to a Tanner."

"Billy Joe was Steven's father?" Claudia gasped.

"Oh, yes, dear, but of course Steven doesn't know that and he never will. Thomas adored me, and I did so love him, so when I explained my troubles, he married me instantly."

She stopped speaking and stared vacantly into space for several minutes before continuing, "I didn't see Billy Joe for years, but then he came to me and told me he was down on his luck. He said he knew about the caretaker's position at Magnolia and asked if I'd help him get it for old time's sake. The moment I saw him, it was as if I was a girl again, and he told me he felt the same way. We wanted to resume our affair, but I certainly couldn't let him come to my room when I was visiting. It's right next to Mother's, and I knew if I went to his house, someone would eventually see me. When I found out about the secret room, it was the perfect solution.

"Everything was fine until I overheard Billy Joe and Ruth talking. It turned out that he was also having an affair with Ruth, and they planned to run away together. You can imagine how furious I was. My word, Billy Joe was stealing his own son's wife! And dear Steven adores Ruth. If she'd left him for Billy Joe, it would have devastated him!"

"So you killed Billy Joe," Claudia said.

"I'm afraid he didn't give me any choice," Virginia said with a sad shake of her head. "When Jonathon caught him stealing the antiques, I knew he was in a vulnerable position. I arranged to meet him in the secret room, and I offered him money to leave without Ruth. I was afraid that he might say no. After all, Ruth is very rich, and if she'd gone with him, he could have lived like a king for the rest of his life. That's why I took the fireplace poker down with me. When he laughed at me and said that he and Ruth would be running away together that night, I killed him. Poor Ruth thought he'd taken off without her. Then, when Billy Joe's body was found, she came to me and said that she thought Steven had found out about the affair and killed him in a jealous rage. I knew I had to clear Steven, or she might try to leave him again.''

"So you started framing Jonathon,'' Claudia noted. "You stole the journal..."

"Oh no, dear. I didn't steal the journal. That was Richard. I found it in his room just this morning. And as for framing Jonathon, I'm afraid that was just bad luck. But thanks to you and that dear boy, I now see that Richard is the perfect patsy, and I have every intention of framing him. That will teach him to be greedy, because I really do have a letter from Billy Joe that says he was stealing the antiques for Richard.

"So, you see, Claudia, it's all going to work out for the best. Jonathon will be cleared. Steven and Ruth will be happy, and Richard will finally get what he deserves. Well, now, I must run,'' she finished cheerfully.

"Just one more thing before you go!'' Claudia said when Virginia again started to leave. "How are you going to explain my disappearance?''

"Oh, that's easy. There's a phone just a few miles down the road. As soon as the storm hits, I'll call Richard, disguise my voice and lure him out of the house. Then I'll drive the car into the river. They'll find me on the bank, and I'll claim he forced us off the road. I'll have managed to swim to shore, but because of the storm you must have been caught in the current and swept away. Now, I really do have to go. Good bye, Claudia.''

Claudia tried to think of something else to stall her, but her mind was a blank. Virginia disappeared, and several moments later Claudia heard what must have been the trunk of the car close, before it was started and then driven away.

Panic began to set in when she realized that she was out in the middle of nowhere and the chances of her being found were slim. She forced herself to stay calm. There had to be a way to get out of here.

She pushed her hands against the grill, but it was too heavy to move. The conduit wasn't large enough for her to get into a crouch to try to lift it with her shoulders. The only option she could see was to somehow crawl to where it emptied into the river and try to get out that way.

She couldn't turn around, so she rolled to her stomach and began to scoot backward. The bottom of the conduit was filled with debris that immediately abraded her hands and arms. The deeper she got into the conduit, the darker it got. The darker it got, the harder it became to control the panic. This time, she was really lost in the dark, and it didn't look as if she'd be able to find her way back.

But despite the terror beginning to build inside her, she resolutely kept pushing her way to the other end of the conduit. By the time she finally reached the end, her hands and arms were raw and bloody, but she was barely aware of the pain. All she could think about was that she'd finally found light again. Unfortunately the opening at this end also had a grill.

She collapsed against the bottom of the conduit and took a moment to catch her breath. Then she rolled to her back and kicked at the grill with her feet. It didn't move, and she finally accepted the inevitable. It was bolted into place.

When Claudia realized that she could wait here and possibly drown when the storm arrived, or she could crawl back through the dark to the other end and try to call for help, tears welled into her eyes. The chances of her being heard were slim. The road wasn't heavily traveled, and because of the approaching storm, the weather was sweltering. People would have their windows up and their air-conditioning on.

But no matter how slim the chances were of her being heard at the other end, staying here meant certain death. She maneuvered onto her stomach and began to crawl, retracing her earlier route. When she once again found herself lost in the dark, she stemmed the certain tide of panic by chanting, "I love you, Jonathon. I love you, and somehow, I'm going to get out of here so I can tell you."

Chapter 15

Jonathon bolted upright on the sofa, where he'd fallen asleep. His heart was pounding so hard that it felt as if it would burst right out of his chest. He was drenched in sweat, yet he'd never felt so cold in his life. He'd just had a nightmare about Claudia.

He'd been standing out in a rainstorm and he'd heard her calling for him. He'd turned around and around, trying to figure out where her voice was coming from, but the voice had just gotten fainter and fainter until it had faded away completely. Then suddenly, a shadow had appeared in front of him. It had beckoned him, urging him to come to it, but he'd backed away, because he knew something terrible had happened to Claudia. And if he didn't look then it wouldn't come true. He'd started running away from the shadow, but it had chased him. Every time he'd looked over his shoulder, it had been closer than before. Just as it was about to overcome him, he'd awakened.

He buried his face in his hands. *He was doing it again! He was dreaming about death!* And he knew that was what the shadow had been trying to show him. His subconscious had been trying to foresee Claudia's death. He had to get her away from Magnolia!

He grabbed the telephone receiver and dialed the number for the guest house. By the fourth ring he knew she wasn't there, but he refused to accept it. She had to be there! Except he'd ordered her to leave Magnolia and never come back. If he'd sent her away, and something had happened to her....

The tenth ring resounded in his ear at the same time that lightning struck outside the window and was immediately followed by a boom of thunder. Jonathon could feel the color draining from his face as he stared at the downpour. He'd been standing in the rain in his dream, and it was raining.

"Gran!" he bellowed as he jumped to his feet and raced toward the kitchen.

"Good heavens, Jonathon, what's wrong!" Adelaide exclaimed. She'd been running toward the doorway, and he'd nearly collided with her.

He grabbed her arms to steady her, demanding, "Where's Claudia?"

"She went into town with Virginia."

"When?"

"About an hour ago."

"Where's Uncle Richard?"

"He's upstairs."

"You're sure?"

"Of course I'm sure," she said impatiently. "Now, what in the world is wrong with you?"

He raked his hand through his hair. "I guess I just had a nightmare."

"Well, it's no wonder. You've just had ten stitches to your head. Why don't you sit down at the table? I'll fix you a cup of tea."

He automatically did as she instructed, telling himself that the reason he'd had the dream was because of the storm. Claudia was all right. She was with his aunt, and his uncle was upstairs. There was no way she could be in danger. So why did he have this awful feeling that she was?

"Where did Aunt Virginia and Claudia go?" he asked.

"I told you. Into town."

"But *where* in town?"

"I don't know," Adelaide said, exasperated. "Stop worrying, Jonathon. She's fine."

The storm was increasing in intensity, and Jonathon drummed his fingers against the table. In the dream it had been raining. Outside it was raining. It was a coincidence. He knew it was a coincidence. Claudia was with his aunt. His uncle was upstairs. *Everything was all right!*

His grandmother brought him the tea, and he lifted the cup to his lips at the same time that the telephone rang. He started at the unexpected sound, and then cursed when the hot liquid sloshed onto his hand. But any pain he was experiencing was overridden by his grandmother's conversation when she answered the phone.

"Ruth, where are you? Oh, I understand, dear. No, you stay right there and and wait out the storm. Have you seen Claudia and Virginia? I see. Well, if you see them, tell them to stay put, too. Good bye, dear."

"What was that all about?" Jonathon demanded the instant she hung up.

Adelaide gave him an annoyed look. "It was Ruth. She went to the grocer's for me. She says it's raining so hard that she can't see to drive. She hasn't seen Claudia and Virginia, but if she does, she'll tell them to wait out the storm, too. Now, is there anything else you'd like to know?"

"Yes, is anyone else gone from the house besides Ruth and Aunt Virginia?"

"No. Now, drink your tea. I'm going to go tell Steven where Ruth is."

When she'd gone, Jonathon rose and crossed to the kitchen window, where he stared out at the rain. Claudia was all right. She had to be all right, because he loved her so much it would kill him if anything happened to her.

Why had he yelled at her as he had? Why had he ordered her to leave Magnolia? Why hadn't he told her he loved her? Because he'd been afraid of going to jail. Because he'd been furious with her for interfering with his plans, when all she'd really been trying to do was protect him. And, finally, because he was afraid that if he loved her, irrational as it seemed, he'd dream about her death and ignore the warnings as he had with Katie. But he'd never ignore the warnings with her. Never!

I love you, Jonathon.

Claudia's voice was so clear and so strong that he nearly fell as he spun around. His gaze flew around the room, but she wasn't there. It was impossible for him to have heard her. She was with his aunt. But he had heard her. Was she trying to reach him? Was she calling for help?

Jonathon closed his eyes and willed Claudia to tell him she was all right. Desperately he clung to the fact that he'd willed her to the river that first night they'd made love, and she'd come. She could answer him now if he just concentrated on making her answer him.

I love you, Jonathon.

His eyes flew open and he knew he'd connected with her. She loved him, but where was she? Was she okay?

Suddenly he was hit with a strange, free-floating sensation, and the room seemed to waver in front of him. He closed his eyes, and in his mind's eye he was standing outside in the rain. He could hear Claudia's voice, but it was growing fainter and fainter, and he knew that if he didn't find her quickly, she was going to die.

But he wasn't going to let her die! he vowed as his eyes flew open. He loved her, and he'd move heaven and earth and the whole damned universe if that's what it took to save her! He threw open the door and raced for his car.

His heart was pounding by the time he climbed inside, and he forced himself to take a moment to relax. He had to concentrate on Claudia. As long as he concentrated on her, then he'd find her. He formed a picture of her in his mind, started the ignition and headed for town.

The farther down the road he drove, the stronger the image of her became. He was getting close to her, and he knew it. Then the image started fading. He was losing her...damn it he couldn't lose her! All he had to do was concentrate, and she'd tell him where she was.

He pulled over to the side of the road, closed his eyes and fiercely willed her to tell him where she was.

* * *

Claudia was clinging to the grate above her head. The water was pouring in on her, and she was trying to keep from being swept down the conduit. She knew that once she hit the other end, there'd be no chance for rescue.

As if there's a chance now! a voice inside her mocked.

She refused to listen to its predictions of doom. Instead she closed her eyes and kept chanting, "I love you, Jonathon. I love you." Somehow she knew that if she kept saying the words, she'd find the strength to hold on. She had to—she had to tell Jonathon she loved him!

But the strain of holding on was becoming too difficult, and she knew that it was only a matter of minutes—maybe only seconds—before her cramping fingers gave way.

Just when she was sure she couldn't hold on a moment longer, a strange sensation coursed through her. It was as if someone had invaded her mind, and yet a sudden calm filled her. Her heart told her it was Jonathon, her heart rejoicing, began to pour her love out to him, "I love you, Jonathon."

Though it seemed a dark eternity later, it was probably only scant seconds after she'd sensed him that Jonathon was kneeling above the grate, yelling, "Hold on, Claudia! Keep holding on!"

He grabbed hold of the grate and pulled, but the combined force of the water rushing down the drain and Claudia's weight made it impossible for him to move it. He sat back on his heels and wiped the rain from his face as he tried to figure out what to do. If he could just lever it up enough to grab onto her hand, then she could release her hold on the the grate. Without the additional weight, he'd be able to get rid of it and pull her out.

"I'll be right back!" he yelled. "Keep holding on!"

He ran toward his car. The only possible thing he could think of to use as a lever was a jack handle. When he reached the car, he dropped his keys, and he let out a violent curse. The rain was coming down so hard he couldn't see his hand in front of his face. How in hell was he going to find his keys?

He dropped to his knees in the mud and moved his hands out in ever-widening circles. *How could this be happening?* Claudia was fighting for her life, and he couldn't find his damn keys!

Just when he was beginning to really panic, his hand hit metal. He grabbed the key chain and leaped to his feet. A moment later, he had the jack handle out of the trunk and was racing back to the grate.

He knelt beside it and put his mouth close to the opening, yelling, "I'm going to lever up the grate, Claudia. When I do, grab my hand and let go of the grate. I can't lift it off completely if you're holding onto it. Do you understand me?"

Jonathon had no idea if she'd even heard him, let alone answered. The wind was howling in his ears. Thunder was reverberating every few seconds. He couldn't remember the last time he'd seen a storm this violent.

Fearing that she might not have heard his instructions, he started thinking them, willing them into her mind as he inserted the jack handle into the grate, put his knee on it and pushed.

For a moment, he didn't think it was going to work. He could feel the tension of her weight on the grate fighting against his weight on the jack handle. Then the grate began to lift.

The moment it had risen high enough for him to get his hand beneath it, he slid his hand inside, grabbed her wrist and yelled, "Let go, honey! Let go!"

She did as he instructed, and Jonathon's heart leaped into his throat as he felt her hand slipping through his.

Fear gave him the strength to heave the grate away. He grabbed her wrist with his other hand and hauled her up through the opening and into his arms. She collapsed against him, and he swept her up into his arms, carrying her to the car.

When he put her inside, she grabbed his arm. "The killer's Virginia, Jonathon. It's not Richard. It's Virginia!"

"I know, honey," he soothed as he tenderly brushed her soaked hair away from her face. "Just sit back and relax.

We're going to get you to the hospital, and everything's going to be okay.''

"I love you, Jonathon," she said, bursting into tears. "I was so afraid I wouldn't get to tell you, but I love you!"

"Oh, honey, I love you, too," he said hoarsely as he hauled her back into his arms. As she sobbed against the front of his shirt, he buried his face in her wet hair and wept tears of joy and relief.

"How is she?" Adelaide whispered as she slipped into Claudia's hospital room and came to Jonathon's side.

"Asleep," he whispered back, looping his arm around her waist and giving it a squeeze. He regarded her in concern. "How are you?"

She gave a weary shrug. "I'm fine. I know this will sound crazy, but it's almost a relief to know it was Virginia rather than Richard. I've always felt that I failed him in some way."

"You didn't fail him, Gran. He failed himself."

"Well, I think that we're going to see some positive changes in him. He was shocked to discover that we even thought he was capable of murder."

"I think this experience is going to make us all do some reevaluating," Jonathon predicted grimly. "It's time we stop going for each other's throats and learn the meaning of family. Thank God, we've got you around to give us a swift kick in the behind if you see us slipping back into old habits."

"I guess I'm still good for something in my twilight years."

"Hey, you may be old, but you're not in decline!"

She gave him a watery smile. "Well, I'd better get back downstairs and check on Virginia. Give Claudia my love when she wakes up."

When she was gone, he scooted his chair closer to Claudia's bed. He wanted to hold her hand, but he feared he'd disturb her bandaged arm. Instead, he rested his fingers against the silken strands of hair spread across her pillow.

It was several hours later before Claudia groggily said, "Jonathon?"

He leaned forward so she could see him, and smiled at her. "Hi. How are you feeling?"

"Like I've been hit in the head and thrown into a storm drain."

"Hey, look at it this way. We get to compare bandages."

She lifted an arm and grimaced. "Mine are bigger than yours."

"I can't argue with that."

She frowned worriedly. "Did they find Virginia?"

He stroked the frown lines away. "Yeah. Her car had slid off the road just a few miles from where I found you. When the sheriff told her I'd rescued you, she broke down and confessed to everything. Steven's already arranged to have her transferred to a psychiatric hospital for evaluation."

"How's Adelaide holding up?" Claudia asked in concern. "I know she and Virginia are close."

"She's fine. She was in here earlier and said to give you her love when you woke up."

She regarded him for a long moment before she asked, "How did you find me, Jonathon?"

"That's a tough question to answer," he said carefully. "How do you think I found you?"

"You opened up your mind and let me inside. You have psychic abilities, don't you, Jonathon?"

He leaned back in his chair and raked his hand through his hair, regarding her in puzzlement. "If I am psychic, I never realized it, and I'm certainly not like you. But before tonight, I'd had three... for lack of a better word, clairvoyant, experiences. I dreamed of my father's death, my grandfather's death, and my wife's. My...grandfather and father had their heart attacks within hours of the dreams. But Katie..."

"What happened with Katie?" she prodded gently when he fell silent.

He looked away from her, then back again, his entire body rigid. "I had the dream two months before she was diagnosed with leukemia, and I dismissed it as a nightmare instead of making her go to the doctor. By the time she did go, it was too late."

"And you blamed yourself?" Claudia asked, though it was obvious that he had.

"Yeah. There's a part of me that keeps saying that if I hadn't ignored the warning, she might have responded to treatment . . . and maybe she'd be alive today."

Claudia swallowed thickly, her heart going out to him at his admission. "Most clairvoyants go through the same trauma, Jonathon. You see something bad happen, and when it comes true, you feel as if it's your fault. I think the hardest thing I had to come to grips with was the fact that I don't have Godlike powers. But if you let me, I can help you learn to deal with your gift."

He shook his head, denial still uppermost in his shadowed eyes. "I don't consider it a gift, Claudia, and quite frankly, your abilities scare me to death. Whenever I saw you with a member of my family this past weekend and I knew you were trying to use your clairvoyance to see if they'd killed Billy Joe, I went into a panic. I kept telling myself that I had to stop you, but I didn't know how."

"That's where the interference was coming from!" Claudia burst in disbelief.

"Interference?" he repeated, bewildered.

"Remember me telling you about the interference I was getting every time I started to connect with someone in the family?" When he nodded, she said, "It was coming from you, Jonathon. It had to be, because now that I think about it, you were always close by. . . You were projecting your fears into my mind and scrambling my reception!"

He arched a brow and eyed her askance. "Come on, Claudia. For me to do something like that, I'd have to have some kind of super psychic powers, and I just told you that my experiences have been very limited."

She smiled and held out her hand. "Take my hand, Jonathon." When he did, she asked, "What's happening to you?"

"I feel that . . . energy," he said hoarsely.

"And I'm having very vivid visions of making love," she said just as hoarsely. She slipped her hand from his and gave him a wavering smile. "So you see, when your power links with mine, we create a sort of 'super power.' It's pretty simple when you think about it. You were worried about me, so you interfered with my clairvoyance. When I needed you tonight, I was able to bring you to me.

"The only thing I can't figure out is why I can't connect with you otherwise," she continued. "It's as if you have a psychic barrier in place, and yet it's got to be subconscious, because it would take too much energy for you to consciously maintain it twenty-four hours a day, seven days a week."

He looked at her, a sudden light beginning to dawn in his eyes. "Maybe I do have a subconscious barrier in place. After Katie died, I told myself I'd never have those kinds of dreams again . . . and until I had that dream about you tonight, I haven't."

"You dreamed about me?"

He nodded. "I dreamed I was standing in the rain and you were calling for me, but I couldn't find you. Then your voice disappeared and a shadow appeared. As soon as I saw it, I knew you were in desperate trouble."

"You dreamed about the shadow?" she gasped in amazement.

He rolled his eyes. "It gets more bizarre. The first day we met, I saw this shadow engulf you. It happened again the night I returned from the sheriff's office and we . . . made love. When you told me that you'd come to Magnolia because you'd had a vision about a shadow stalking someone . . . Well, let's just say, it gave me pause."

"*That's* why you wanted to know if it was a vision of my own future," she declared suddenly understanding. "And in a way, maybe it was, because I think it was you that brought me to Magnolia in the first place, and my future was intrinsically linked with yours."

"Well, I hope it *stays* intrinsically linked with mine," he rasped, sitting on the edge of the bed and carefully lifting her hand into his. "I love you, Claudia, and after tonight, I know I can't live without you. Will you marry me?"

At the sweet words, Claudia gazed up into his face, and realized that she still couldn't connect with him, that there was a chance she never would. Suddenly, though, it didn't matter. Life with Jonathon would be a roller-coaster ride, but now she understood that part of the mystique of being in love in the first place were the surprises they'd discover together, and she realized that she wanted those surprises with a fierce need beyond anything she'd ever known. She knew, in her heart, that even if she might not connect with Jonathon on a daily basis, if she ever needed him, he'd be there for her.

"Of course I'll marry you," she told him with a delighted laugh as she threw herself into his arms.

"You laughed!" he exclaimed gazing down at her in disbelief. "You actually laughed!"

Now it was her turn to gaze at him in bewilderment. "And just why is that so significant?"

"Because, until now, the only time I'd heard you laugh was when you were with Patrick," he answered somewhat sheepishly. "I wanted to punch him in the nose for making you laugh the other day when you'd never laughed with me."

"Well, I think that would have been a bit of an overreaction, but if it's laughter you want, I'm sure we're going to have plenty of it. No one could be as happy as I am and not laugh all the time."

"God, I love you, and I promise that I'm going to make you so happy that the rest of our days will all be filled with laughter," Jonathon murmured fiercely, grasping her face in his hands and kissing her tenderly.

When their lips met, Claudia smiled inwardly. She had a crystal-clear vision of a very *passionate* immediate future, and she couldn't wait for every one of those erotic images to come true....

* * * * *

For all those readers who've been looking for something a little bit different, a little bit spooky, let Silhouette Books take you on a journey to the dark side of love with

SILHOUETTE Shadows™

If you like your romance mixed with a hint of danger, a taste of something eerie and wild, you'll love Shadows. This new line will send a shiver down your spine and make your heart beat faster. It's full of romance and more—and some of your favorite authors will be featured right from the start. Look for our four launch titles wherever books are sold, because you won't want to miss a single one.

THE LAST CAVALIER—Heather Graham Pozzessere
WHO IS DEBORAH?—Elise Title
STRANGER IN THE MIST—Lee Karr
SWAMP SECRETS—Carla Cassidy

After that, look for two books every month, and prepare to tremble with fear—and passion.

SILHOUETTE SHADOWS, coming your way in March.

 Silhouette®

SHAD1

AMERICAN HERO

It seems readers can't get enough of these men—and we don't blame them! When Silhouette Intimate Moments' best authors go all-out to create irresistible men, it's no wonder women everywhere are falling in love. And look what—and who!—we have in store for you early in 1993.

January brings NO RETREAT (IM #469), by Marilyn Pappano. Here's a military man who brings a whole new meaning to macho!

In February, look for IN A STRANGER'S EYES (IM #475), by Doreen Roberts. Who is he—and why does she feel she knows him?

In March, it's FIREBRAND (IM #481), by Paula Detmer Riggs. The flames of passion have never burned this hot before!

And in April, look for COLD, COLD HEART (IM #487), by Ann Williams. It takes a mother in distress and a missing child to thaw this guy, but once he melts...!

AMERICAN HEROES. YOU WON'T WANT TO MISS A SINGLE ONE—ONLY FROM

IMHERO3R

**Silhouette Books
is proud to present
our best authors,
their best books...
and the best in
your reading pleasure!**

Throughout 1993, look for exciting books
by these top names in contemporary
romance:

CATHERINE COULTER—
Aftershocks in February

FERN MICHAELS—
Whisper My Name in March

DIANA PALMER—
Heather's Song in March

ELIZABETH LOWELL—
Love Song for a Raven in April

SANDRA BROWN
(previously published under
the pseudonym Erin St. Claire)—
Led Astray in April

LINDA HOWARD—
All That Glitters in May

When it comes to passion,
we wrote the book.

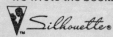

BOBT1R

Take 4 bestselling love stories FREE
Plus get a FREE surprise gift!

**Silhouette Intimate Moments
is proud to present
Mary Anne Wilson's
SISTER, SISTER duet—
Two halves of a whole,
two parts of a soul**

In the mirror, Alicia and Alison Sullivan both had brilliant red hair and green eyes—but in personality and life-style, these identical twins were as different as night and day. Alison needed control, order and stability. Alicia, on the other hand, hated constraints, and the idea of settling down bored her.

Despite their differences, they had one thing in common—a need to be loved and cherished by a special man. And to fulfill their goals, these two sisters would do anything for each other—including switching places in a life-threatening situation.

Look for Alison and Jack's adventure in TWO FOR THE ROAD (IM #472, January 1993), and Alicia and Steven's story in TWO AGAINST THE WORLD (IM #489, April 1993)—and *enjoy!*

SISTERR